"ZACH, IT'S TAKEN ME SUCH A LONG TIME."

Leigh spoke slowly, unable to meet his piercing gaze. "Since I was a kid, I've dreamed of being a director. Now I've got the chance, and I don't want to blow it."

Zach gathered her in his arms and pressed her against his chest. His fingers twined in her hair as he kissed her over and over, brushing his lips against her forehead, her eyelids, the curve of her cheek. Then his lips moved to the pulse beating madly at the base of her throat. When at last he lifted his head, it was to look into the dreamy depths of her eyes.

"Oh, my love," he said softly. "I know you're scared, but we'll work it out...I promise."

And Leigh already knew Zach was a man who kept his promises.

ABOUT THE AUTHOR

Dianne King is a writing team from Fresno, California. Elnora King teaches creative writing, critiques manuscripts, edits and ghostwrites. Pamela Wallace is a much published romance author as well as a screenwriter. Her latest credits include the movie *Witness,* which she wrote with her husband. Elnora's and Pam's experience, combined with their talent, makes them one of the most accomplished writing teams in romance today.

Books by Dianne King

HARLEQUIN SUPERROMANCE
101—WHEN DREAMS COME TRUE
182—BELIEVE IN MAGIC

HARLEQUIN TEMPTATION
10—FRIEND OF THE HEART
68—ESSENCE OF SUMMER

These books may be available at your local bookseller.

Don't miss any of our special offers. Write to us at the following address for information on our newest releases.

Harlequin Reader Service
P.O. Box 52040, Phoenix, AZ 85072-2040
Canadian address: P.O. Box 2800, Postal Station A,
5170 Yonge St,, Willowdale, Ont. M2N 6J3

Dianne King

BELIEVE IN MAGIC

Harlequin Books

TORONTO • NEW YORK • LONDON
AMSTERDAM • PARIS • SYDNEY • HAMBURG
STOCKHOLM • ATHENS • TOKYO • MILAN

Published October 1985

First printing August 1985

ISBN 0-373-70182-9

Printed in Canada

A Far And Silver Star

Close to the heaven's edge
a night wind rustles
the needled green of tall pines
poised on granite balconies
above crystal lakes and alpine meadows.

Here on the rim of the world
lovers and seekers
chart their course
by a brightly shining
far and silver star.

PROLOGUE

THE WHITE-HAIRED MAN, dressed in tattered black tie and tails, tapped once, twice, three times on the faded black silk top hat. Then, winking at the little girl who sat mesmerized, he reached into the hat and with a flourish pulled out a red silk scarf that hadn't been there a moment before.

"*Voilà!*"

The little girl clapped her hands. "More, grandpa, more!" she cried gleefully.

Breathing hard, the old man sat down beside her and wiped his sweaty brow with the bright scarf. Sleight of hand demanded iron control. It was a long moment before he could speak. "No encores tonight, Leigh. I'm tired. Must be getting old."

"You're not old, grandpa. I don't want you to get old. Ever."

For a moment as he smiled down into her eager face, he felt young again—and strong. As strong as he'd been when he'd headlined the Midwest vaudeville circuit right after World War I.

"Teach me that trick, Grandpa."

The fleeting illusion of strength deserted him. Still, he struggled to his feet and performed the trick, step by step. She followed his every move, her tiny hands more dexterous though less sure than his.

When they'd finished, she tried the trick on her own. As she whipped out the red silk from the hat, he applauded and reached out to hug her.

She burrowed under his arm and begged, as she had a hundred times before, "Tell me about show business."

Marvelling at her inexhaustible curiosity about something that had died long before she was born, he told her about vaudeville. "We made people laugh. And sometimes we made them cry. But only happy tears. They paid a quarter to see our show and we gave them a little magic."

Holding her close in his loving embrace, he finished, "Everybody needs a little fantasy in his life."

"Daddy calls it foolishness."

"It's not foolishness. It's—" the old man hesitated, then softly continued—"it's enchantment. Surprise. And all those things that take us away from the ordinary...if only for a little while."

The youngest Adams leaned back to look into the face of the oldest. "I want to do that, too." Her voice was as sober as the expression in her wide-set gray eyes.

"I believe you will."

She frowned slightly. "Rodney Blankenship says girls can't be magicians."

He met her look without a trace of doubt or condescension. "You tell Rodney there are all kinds of magicians."

She leaned her small cheek against his chest. He knew she was comforted by the familiar sensations of his smooth cotton shirt and the smell of tobacco from the pouch in his pocket. Familiar things. The ordinary.

Then he heard her soft whisper, "How can you tell I'll make magic?"

Dropping a light kiss on the tip of her nose, he whispered back, "Because you believe. And to be a magician—you must believe in magic."

CHAPTER ONE

SUNLIGHT DANCED OFF the polished chrome of the white VW as it zipped in and out of traffic. The top was down and Leigh Adam's long, wavy hair tossed in the wind. Her best feature, it was neither carrot-red nor auburn, but a deep burnished bronze. As silken tendrils brushed her cheek, she absentmind-edly pushed them back.

It was early Friday afternoon, and already the Los Angeles Freeway was crowded. But the warm sun on her face and the light wind ruffling her hair helped to make the drive a pleasurable one, despite the traffic.

Santa Monica Freeway was coming up fast. Glancing quickly over her shoulder, Leigh changed lanes. The transition was perfectly smooth as she merged into the flow of traffic headed toward downtown Los Angeles. Today, because the air was smog free, Leigh could see the downtown skyline— the top of city hall and the shimmering cylinders of the Bonaventure Hotel. Even the peaks of the San Gabriel Mountains to the east were visible on this clear, late-April afternoon.

Beside the freeway, she caught fleeting glimpses of jacarandas with purple blooms nestled in old neigh-borhoods. And palm trees. Always, and every-where, palm trees.

She threaded her way past a chauffeur-driven limousine, long and black and sleek, a station wagon loaded with children and a motorcycle driven by a clean-cut young man. As she passed the motorcyclist, he shot a quick, admiring glance at her immaculate convertible, grinned engagingly at her and shouted, "Way to go, Red!"

Leigh laughed, then, thanking heaven for freeways, exited onto Melrose. If her luck held, she'd be on time.

A few minutes later, she braked hard at the front gate of American Film Studios. As she gave her name to the uniformed guard in the cubicle, she willed him to be quick. She checked her watch, then drummed her fingers impatiently on the steering wheel.

Oblivious to the fact that Leigh was obviously in a hurry, the guard glanced perfunctorily at her, then at the list of names of people approved to enter the lot.

"Okay." The word was a bored mumble as he pushed the button that raised the bar blocking the entrance.

Leigh caught the faintly dismissive tone in his voice and smiled dryly to herself. Obviously a young woman in an ancient Volkswagen Beetle, even a beautifully maintained convertible, wasn't considered a VIP. Well, she thought, things aren't always what they seem.

Hollywood, for instance. It was a geographic area but it wasn't really a place. It was a state of mind. And for Leigh, on this wonderfully blue-skied day, it was a Technicolor fantasy land where *anything* could happen.

As Leigh drove past the permanent sets—city blocks and smalltown neighborhoods—a flashing red warning light stopped traffic. Beyond her, a scene was being shot. She could see a second assistant director standing nearby talking into a portable phone. They were shooting a Western, and Leigh could see actors clustered on the wooden sidewalk in front of the saloon, horses and riders in the dusty street and a director riding with a Panaflex camera mounted on a crane.

It was organized chaos, a mesmerizing blend of reality and fantasy. This make-believe town on a Hollywood set would become, in a darkened theater, Abilene or Tombstone.

Leigh felt a rush of excitement just watching the scene. She loved it all. Since high school, she'd known this was what she wanted to do with her life—be one of the people who made fantasies come to life. She'd wanted it as badly as she'd wanted Rick McGuire to ask her to the prom. He'd asked a cheerleader instead, so that wish wasn't fulfilled. But the other was. Leigh was a director now, one of the dream makers.

Watching the man on the portable phone, she thought of the summer she'd worked at the same job. Being a second A.D. simply meant being responsible for getting people and equipment to a specific place at a specific time, to spare the director that mundane chore. Even with all the headaches connected with the job, Leigh had been thrilled to get it. She'd learned a lot—mostly that she wanted to be the person riding with the camera.

But her happy reverie ended when she glanced at her watch. It was getting late. And this was one meeting she wanted to be in time for. When the red warning light went off, indicating traffic could continue, she breathed a sigh of relief.

Driving to the executive office building, she scooted into an empty stall between a Mercedes-Benz and a Porsche. Quickly she ran a brush through her windblown hair. Then she glanced in the tiny rearview mirror. Her normally pale face was flushed with excitement, and her gray eyes glinted like quicksilver. Fierce determination and equally fierce uncertainty warred within her.

Calm down, she told herself. She took a deep breath to steady her nerves, then got out of the car.

As she walked away, she straightened her skirt. Jeans were more her style, but for this all-important interview today, she'd decided she should be as impressive as possible. In her usual attire, she looked all of twenty. Now she wanted to look every bit of her barely thirty years. So she'd dressed in a crisp white linen skirt and turquoise silk blouse. High-heeled white sandals added needed inches to her height. At five feet two inches tall, she was uncomfortably aware that she didn't exactly look imposing.

As she crossed the parking lot and passed the huge, dingy gray sound stages, there were butterflies in her stomach. She'd been on a major studio lot only a few times in her life. Despite the reality of the place—the old, unimpressive buildings, the lack of landscaping, the surprisingly quiet atmosphere—she still felt an uncontrollable surge of excitement. This was the place where dream merchants spun the fantasies that captured the imagination of the whole world. And she, Leigh Adams, was one of them.

When she reached the main office building, a receptionist directed her to the office of the particular vice-president Leigh had come to meet. Inside, a pretty young secretary smiled warmly and said, "Oh, yes, Mr. Jennings is expecting you. Go right on in."

The butterflies in Leigh's stomach suddenly took flight.

He's just another executive, and this is just another meeting, she told herself.

But her fingers tightened on the white leather clutch she was holding, and she had to bite her full lower lip to keep it from quivering. No matter what she tried to tell herself, the fact was this *wasn't* just another meeting. It was the most important meeting of her life.

Inside the small, rather Spartan office, a young man rose from behind a desk and extended a hand. "Leigh, it's good to meet you in person after all our phone calls. Please sit down. Can I get you anything? Coffee or a drink?"

Gary Jennings was the epitome of the New Hollywood. Young, not much older than she was, thin and wiry, he was dressed casually but with expensive good taste. He was one of a handful of top executives at the studio, a powerful man. But his friendliness reassured her, and she felt slightly less nervous.

"I'd love some tea, if you have it." She sat down in a comfortable overstuffed chair facing his desk.

"Okay." Buzzing his secretary, he asked her to bring in tea, then turned back to Leigh. "I saw in the trades today that *Intimacies* is one of the most successful low-budget films of the year."

Leigh, too, had read *Daily Variety* and the *Hollywood Reporter*, the trade papers that everyone in the film industry read religiously. She smiled. "I just wish I had points."

Gary laughed appreciatively. "A percentage of that kind of profit would be nice. Next time around I'll bet your agent will get you points."

The secretary came in with a tea tray and set it on a low table next to Leigh's chair, then left. Sipping the hot liquid, Leigh wondered why Gary was making small talk instead of getting to the point of the meeting—*Lodestar*.

As if reading her mind, he said, "We're just waiting for Zach Stewart. He should be here any minute."

With a jolt, Leigh realized she'd been naive in assuming the studio, in the person of Gary Jennings, would have final say about who the director of *Lodestar* would be. Her agent had told her that Stewart had optioned the script and persuaded the studio to finance it. Obviously he also had director approval.

The butterflies returned. It was one thing to win Gary's approval. He'd made it clear from the first of their many conversations that he was very impressed with her work on *Intimacies*, her first feature film, and thought she'd be perfect for *Lodestar*. But Leigh had no idea if Stewart had even seen her movie, let alone whether or not he liked it.

Desperately she searched her memory for any knowledge of Stewart. All she knew was what her agent had mentioned when the studio gave her the *Lodestar* script to read. Stewart had done a lot of movies for television, but this would be his first feature. She'd seen one of his movies, a romance that had less jiggle and more intelligence than most made-for-TV films.

That was the sum total of her knowledge about this man who would have the power to decide whether she got the chance to direct this movie that she wanted to do so badly.

Just then the intercom buzzed and Leigh heard the secretary announce Stewart. A moment later, he came into the room. The atmosphere, which had been rather calm, fairly crackled.

Ignoring Leigh, he strode to Gary's desk and faced him angrily. "Rein in your blasted business-affairs department, Gary! They're hassling Kline about his contract, and he's about to take another job."

"Zach, this is—"

Before he could finish introducing Leigh, Stewart interrupted, "He's the best art director in town, and I don't intend to lose him just because this studio wants to save a few bucks."

Watching him, Leigh felt surprise and something more. He wasn't at all what she'd expected. He was younger, for one thing, probably no more than thirty-five at the most. His faded jeans and blue V-neck sweater made a simple but powerful statement. Clearly he didn't need Gucci loafers and a designer shirt and slacks to bolster his self-assurance. And in contrast to Gary's studiously laid-back attitude, he was positively ablaze with emotion. The very way he held his tall, well-muscled body indicated a wealth of energy barely held in check.

"I'll talk to them, Zach. Don't worry. I don't want to lose Kline, either. Now if you'll let me, I'll finish the introduction I've been trying to make for five minutes.'' Flashing a smile at Leigh, he said, ''Leigh Adams, Zach Stewart.''

Finally Stewart turned to look at her. Her mind instantly registered details: sun-bleached blond hair, a deep cleft in a determined chin, faint lines at the corners of his eyes. At the same time, he assessed her with disconcerting forwardness. His gaze lingered on her unruly mane of hair, flicked to her gray eyes, moved quickly down her slim legs, then returned to focus on her eyes.

His eyes were so blue that they were astonishing. As they bore into hers, something blatantly sexual stirred deep within her. Startled, she wondered what on earth about him provoked such an unexpected response. While he was undeniably attractive, his features lacked the symmetry necessary to be considered really handsome.

There was nothing soft about his face or his manner. Certainly not that unsmiling, chiseled mouth. Yet something about him connected with something inside her. Was it energy—electrical energy? Like lightning. A positive charge coming into contact with a negative one. But lightning was as dangerous as it was brilliant, she knew. The thought made her hand tremble slightly as he clasped it in his larger, rougher one.

''You're prettier than I expected.'' The blunt comment wasn't softened by a smile.

So the attraction was mutual. For a moment, Leigh was flattered. But as quickly as it came, that flush of pleasure was replaced by irritation. She knew he wouldn't have judged a male director on his appearance. And she didn't intend to be judged on hers.

"My looks are totally irrelevant," she shot back.

For an instant, there was a stunned silence. Then Stewart burst into laughter. "Touché."

Laughter changed his entire countenance, softening the hard lines of his face, crinkling the corners of his eyes and revealing a flash of even white teeth.

He should laugh more often, she thought.

Sitting down in the chair opposite her, he continued to watch her thoughtfully.

Gary breathed an audible sigh of relief at the sudden lessening of tension. "Well, I just knew you two would hit it off. Now then, let's talk about *Lodestar*."

"What do you think of the script?" Stewart asked.

What she thought was that it was a compelling story with a magnificent setting and would make a memorable film. She'd give her right arm to direct it.

Aloud, she said, "It's a winner. It has all the right elements—strong story line, lots of emotion and tension. That Sierra Nevada high country has the same kind of drama the story has."

Leigh paused, wondering if she'd hit just the right combination of enthusiasm and blasé sophistication. She glanced nervously down at her hands then back at Zach Stewart. His blue eyes were riveted on her.

When he didn't respond, she added, "It's the tension that interests me. It should be taut as a guy wire throughout the film."

"Of course. That's what the story is all about—tension. Two people crashing in the back country of the High Sierras and making it back to civilization. Survival. Success. A good old-fashioned action-adventure."

He'd twisted slightly in his chair, moving that long frame so he faced Leigh. His entire concentration was on her, and it occurred to her that Gary Jennings wasn't part of this conversation at all.

She, too, ignored Gary as she responded to Stewart. "You're wrong, you know. This story is about a relationship between a man and a woman. They've lost their way and they're in deep trouble. The crash is just a metaphor for what's happened in their marriage. The theme is love. The title says it all—*Lodestar*. The beacon that guides the traveler. The love they once shared is what drives them to survive. And they find it again in the process."

Looking down again at her hands, she realized she was clasping them tightly. Her shoulder muscles felt tense and she had to force herself to relax. When she looked up, she deliberately included Gary in her glance, before once more facing Stewart.

The look in his blue eyes was strangely tender. And thoughtful. Did that mean she had a chance, she wondered. At the very thought, her heart accelerated.

"I'm glad you feel that way. This is really a story about two people who get in trouble, nearly lose each other, but are strong enough to finally survive. And succeed."

So he did understand. Of course, she thought. After all, he'd been sensitive enough to respond to the script, to pay his own money to option it, before knowing if a studio would finance the production.

After a momentary pause, he finished. "I saw your movie *Intimacies*."

Leigh waited for him to continue. She was dying
to know what he thought of it, but she wasn't about
to ask him.

There was a long pause, then he commented
matter-of-factly, "You're a hell of a director."

"Thanks."

Her tone was calm, but she actually felt tremendously relieved. If he'd said he didn't like her work,
that would have been the end of the interview.

"Was it your first film?"

"Yes—aside from a short film I did in U.C.L.A.
film school and a documentary I did at the American Film Institute."

A flash of surprise registered in his eyes. "That
was the sum total of your experience before
Intimacies?"

"Yes."

Despite her effort at self-control, Leigh's tone was
defensive. There had been some gossip about her relationship with Stan Munroe, the producer on *Intimacies*. Older, very experienced, he'd been her
mentor for years, and his advice and support had
been invaluable. The mentor-protegé relationship
was common in Hollywood. If she'd been a man, no
one would have thought twice about it. But because
she was a woman, some people automatically assumed the worst.

That was the special problem of women in the film
business—perhaps women in any business. Always,
in every way, they were limited by their gender. The
unfairness of the situation still rankled. Leigh forced
down her rising temper and reminded herself that
Stewart wasn't making an accusation.

He eyed her for a moment, then commented with deceptive casualness, "You were lucky the producer gave you a chance like that with so little experience behind you."

Leigh froze. She wanted to believe it was an innocent remark. But there was nothing innocent about Zach Stewart.

Clearly sensing trouble, Gary interjected, "Stan knew talent when he saw it. He gave Leigh a chance with *Intimacies*, and the rest is history. Leigh did a terrific job on a shoestring budget."

"Yes—but can you handle big budgets?" Stewart asked pointedly.

Leigh met his gaze without flinching. She had to control her anger as she answered, "I expect it's a great deal easier to make a film with a lot of money than a little."

"Not necessarily. It just gives you more money to waste."

"One thing I know, Mr. Stewart, is how not to waste money. Working on a limited budget teaches you that fast."

"There's a world of difference between a low-budget film and a major feature with a big budget and top people. You're in a whole different class then."

"Are you suggesting I'd be outclassed?" Leigh asked, hating the quavor in her voice. This self-confident man would most certainly mistake it for fear. But the quaver was from anger, which was building fast.

The look he gave her was appraising. "I'd say you're a pretty classy lady."

Before Leigh could respond that it was her directing ability in question here and not her pedigree, he went on, "How did you get along with the crew?"

"If you're asking if they resented working under a woman, the answer is yes. At first. But they got over that when they realized I was professional and fair."

"Of course you were working with people who knew they were lucky just to have a job," Stewart pointed out tersely. "It would be much harder dealing with people who know they're among the best in their field. They wouldn't accept you easily."

Leigh had tried to keep her temper in check. Alienating Stewart would mean losing the opportunity to direct this picture that she wanted badly to do. But the whole tone of his questions was growing more and more critical. It was obvious he thought the fact she was a woman mattered more than her ability as a director.

She'd come up against this for years, since she'd entered film school. And it had been especially hard to take when some people assumed she slept with Stan to further her career. Suddenly, she no longer had one ounce of patience with this man. Drawing a deep breath, she prepared to respond to Zach Stewart's insulting comments.

"Now, Zach," Gary began soothingly, "Leigh's highly talented—"

"Thank you, but I can speak for myself," Leigh interrupted angrily. Facing Stewart, she said, "I can direct the hell out of *Lodestar*. But obviously I'm not going to get the chance because you think a woman couldn't do it."

Rising, she looked down at Stewart and finished scathingly, "Good luck with your picture, Mr. Stewart. With your lack of imagination, you'll need it."

As she turned and strode out, she dimly heard Gary's feeble, "Leigh, please..."

Well, scratch one major feature film, she told herself dryly.

But the bravado she showed was only superficial. A sick feeling of intense disappointment was a lead weight in the pit of her stomach.

She was outside the building, heading toward her car, when she felt someone take a firm hold of her arm. Startled, she turned to look into Zach Stewart's blue eyes.

"I wasn't finished," he began quietly.

She pulled out of his grasp. "I was."

But as she continued walking, he remained beside her.

She looked straight ahead, ignoring him.

As she reached her car and fumbled in her purse for her keys, he went on in a reasonable tone, "I didn't mean to insult you. My questions and comments weren't personal."

She faced him then, ignoring her trembling legs. "Oh? Then I'd hate to hear you when you *were* being personal. Why don't you come right out with it, Mr. Stewart? You think the only reason I got the job directing *Intimacies* was by sleeping with Stan Munroe."

"All right, I admit I thought that was a distinct possibility. But after meeting you, I no longer think so."

"Thanks," Leigh said in a withering voice.

"Look, you're very young. What are you, twenty-five, twenty-six?"

"Thirty."

He seemed taken aback, then he smiled. His entire expression softened, became almost boyish in its appeal.

Leigh felt her breath catch in her throat. After a moment, she realized she was staring at him.

"Anyway," he continued, "you are young and you've only got one film behind you. You did a terrific job with it, but one film doesn't necessarily prove anything."

"I think it does. It proves I can turn out something pretty decent with limited resources to work with. You know that only one movie in ten earns a profit. I made a movie that earned a tremendous profit. I could do even better with *Lodestar*, but you're not about to hire me, are you?"

"No."

She wasn't surprised by the bluntness of his response. Already she'd learned that this was a man who didn't mince words.

He went on, "This is my first feature. A chance to prove to the industry that I can do more than turn out mindless TV pap. It means a lot to me. And I won't risk it with someone who's just getting started. I'm going with Ralph Hastings as director."

Leigh was furious. "Then why did we just go through that farce in Gary Jenning's office? Do you get your kicks by stringing people along, Mr. Stewart?"

"Calm down, Leigh. And for heaven's sake, stop calling me Mr. Stewart. You make me sound like a high-school principal."

"I'm tempted to call you something much worse," she shot back angrily.

Suddenly there was that smile again. "You are a feisty little thing, aren't you? Now, before you tell me exactly where to go, just listen for a minute. That meeting was Gary's idea. He really wants you for this project and hoped if I met you, I'd change my mind. I tried to tell him I was determined to go with Hastings, but he wouldn't listen."

"Why are you telling me all this now?"

"Because I hate the dishonesty we have to deal with so often in this business. I didn't want to leave you hanging, with the hope that maybe you'd get the job, after all. That wouldn't have been fair."

"Why Hastings?" Leigh asked flatly.

"Because he's been a director for thirty years and has never had a major disaster. Most of his films have been financial successes. I can depend on him to bring in *Lodestar* on time and on budget."

Leigh shook her head. "Maybe he'll do that for you, Mr. Stewart. But he won't bring in the kind of movie this deserves to be."

Surprise registered on his face, and his mouth tightened imperceptibly.

She didn't care if he didn't like what she had to say. Her dreams had gone up in smoke, as if tossed onto a bonfire. From the first page of *Lodestar* she'd thought of it as *her* script. She was meant to direct it. Fate, fortune, karma—whatever govered her destiny—had to grant her this wish. Why else did she feel such an empathy with the characters? Joe and Mary Beth Ramsey were as real to her as her best friends.

Why else would *Lodestar*'s locale be one of her most favorite places? Even now, standing on this lot, she could see the granite rim of the world above Yosemite National Park. Hear the wind sighing softly through the fragrant pines and cedars.

She'd lost her chance to direct this movie. What did it matter now if she lost her cool?

Angrily she continued, "I know Hastings's work. He thinks subjects, not images. Plays it safe, doesn't take chances or try for anything beyond a certain level. He'll give you a decent picture, all right. But he won't give you a great one."

Turning her back on him so he wouldn't see the hint of tears that shimmered in her eyes, she unlocked her car door and opened it.

But before she could get in, Stewart said, "Have dinner with me tonight, Leigh."

She was completely stunned. They'd done nothing but argue from the first moment they'd met. On top of that, he'd rejected her out of hand for a job he knew she wanted badly.

"What on earth makes you think I'd have dinner with you?" she exploded.

He grinned. "Now, Leigh, I could have asked you out, *then* told you I wasn't going to hire you."

He could indeed. That was normally how things worked in the film business.

"Since we've hardly had a civil word to say to each other in the entire half hour we've been together, why would you want to have dinner with me?"

"Because you're gorgeous. And smart. And talented. And whatever else our conversation has been, it hasn't been dull."

"Since you're such an honest person, tell me something honestly, Mr. Stewart. Would you expect to go to bed with me?"

He raised his eyebrows quizzically. "Expect, no. Hope, definitely."

"So I'm good enough to make love to, but not good enough to make your picture."

"Leigh..."

"Goodbye, Mr. Stewart." Her tone was final.

Getting into the car, she slammed the door, started the engine, then backed out. As she drove away, she didn't even look back. But it took all her considerable willpower not to do so.

CHAPTER TWO

ZACH LEANED AGAINST THE TALL BACK of his leather chair and listened as a young actor read dialogue. The role was that of a ranger, tending an isolated fire-lookout station, who was surprised when the *Lodestar* hero and heroine appeared from nowhere.

"God! Where'd you come from? And what's happened to you? You're the first people I've seen in...well, a long time."

Intense, concentrating on emoting, the actor was still frowning as he put down the script and looked up at Zach.

This was the part of casting that Zach loathed. The "don't call us, we'll call you" part. Actors had to bear rejection. That was part of the game. But he hated dishing it out.

Ralph Hastings smiled at the actor. "Good reading. Thanks for coming in. We'll be in touch."

When the young man had gone, Ralph enthused, "That guy's good. He'd be perfect for the part."

"Don't you think he was a little too intense?"

Ralph shrugged. "That's just his stage training." Then, glancing at the clock on Zach's desk, he continued, "How about lunch?"

"Okay. The commissary?"

"Fine."

Neither spoke as they walked across the lot. They continued on to the commissary, an elegant restaurant with potted palms and white linen tablecloths. Mirrors reflected the glistening art deco decor. After they were seated at a table in a corner, Ralph finally spoke, "I understand your concern about that actor, but we can't get too hung up over details like this one small part. The important thing is to bring this film in on time and under budget with as few problems as possible." Then, taking the menu a waiter handed him, he finished, "That guy's adequate."

That does it, Zach thought angrily. Adequate! He wanted a lot more than *adequate* on this film.

Since first starting preproduction, Zach had had a nagging feeling deep inside that there was something wrong. As he and Ralph hired the crew, auditioned actors and scouted locations, that feeling had grown stronger.

Ralph wanted to shoot all the interiors on the lot. Zach was determined they be done on location for a more realistic look. Ralph kept wanting the easy way, the convenient way. Damn, he wished Ralph would show some real concern about the movie.

Ever since Leigh Adams's fiery condemnation of the man a month earlier, Zach had watched for some expression of genuine enthusiasm from Ralph. He hadn't seen any. Ralph was a decent man, a competent director. But he had no sense of passion about this movie. Zach doubted that Ralph had been consumed by a burning vision of a film since his early days in the business.

Somehow, as he thought of passion, he thought again of Leigh Adams. He didn't think she'd be willing to hire someone who wasn't the best possible actor for the role. She wouldn't compromise or cut corners in any way. On the other hand, he thought with wry amusement, she also wouldn't be easy to get along with, since she would probably argue vehemently for what she believed in.

But just now, Zach wasn't so sure that was bad.

He remembered how she'd looked in that drab parking lot, a flame of fervor, passionate in her insistence that *Lodestar* could be great, that she could make it so. The image was intriguing—the petite young woman with the flamboyant red hair and wide-set gray eyes. Lavender gray like the color of dawn or twilight.

She was obviously intelligent and independent, very much her own person, unlike so many people in the movie business who tended to be sycophantic. Zach liked women who had brains, depth and a sense of self. She seemed to have all that and more.

He remembered how the coolness in those eyes had vanished when she'd realized he wasn't going to hire her. They'd darkened like a stormy sky. He wondered if they darkened like that when she made love. The thought strangely excited him.

Stop it, he told himself irritably. He had more pressing matters to think about at the moment than a young woman who'd gone in and out of his life in a matter of minutes. But as he scanned his menu disinterestedly, ordered, then talked to Ralph, Leigh remained at the back of his mind.

Back in his office after lunch, he found his secretary, Ruth, waiting for him. She was a statuesque, gray-haired woman who'd been with him since he produced his first movie eight years earlier.

"Mel Schuster called." Her voice was calm, as always. She wasn't easily ruffled. But the worried expression in her hazel eyes spoke volumes.

Mel was the agent for Kevin Marlowe, the star of the film. If there was a problem with him at this late date—if he was ill or just plain didn't want to do the movie—it could mean the end of the picture.

"Okay," Zach responded, his voice tight with concern. "Get him for me, will you, Ruthie?"

He strode into his private office. The large room was a reflection of the man. Everything about it was vibrant, contemporary, from the vividly colored David Hockney paintings on the walls to the stream-lined, chrome-and-ivory corduroy furniture.

But Zach was oblivious to his surroundings. Instead of sitting down, he turned on the speaker attachment and paced back and forth. When Mel came on the line, he dispensed with the pleasantries and asked, "What's up?"

"I imagine you heard Kevin got married recently."

"The whole world heard. I sent him a telegram of congratulations."

"Do you know his wife, Catalina?"

"I've heard of her, but I'm not familiar with her work."

"Well, she's gorgeous, of course. Any woman who could finally persuade Kevin to settle down would have to be a real stunner. But she can also act."

Suddenly Zach had an idea what Mel was getting at.

"Kevin knows you haven't cast the co-starring role yet."

Quickly Zach said, "Mel, we've just about signed someone."

Mel laughed. "Don't b.s. me, kid. I've been in this business since you were in diapers. I know that you haven't been able to get a major actress because the woman's role is overshadowed by the man's. And you're not happy with any of the lesser lights you've auditioned or you'd have signed someone by now."

"He wants us to hire his wife," Zach said flatly.

"You got it."

Zach exploded. "Why on earth can't he just buy her some extravagant present! Why does he want to buy her a part in my movie?"

Mel laughed. "Calm down. I know how you feel. But it's not as bad as you think. The girl can act, Zach. I'm not exaggerating. She's good. I'm representing her, and not just because she's Kevin's wife. Just meet with her and you'll see what I mean."

"I'll meet with her, to placate Kevin. But I'm not making any promises, Mel. I won't be blackmailed."

"I understand. When can I send her in?"

"This afternoon. Let's get this over with."

"Okay. She'll be there at four. And Zach—you're gonna be surprised."

Sure, Zach thought as he hung up.

At precisely four o'clock Ruth buzzed him to say Catalina O'Kelley was there.

"Send her in," Zach said, then leaned back in his chair. Beside him were Ralph and Gary. Normally Gary wouldn't have sat in on an audition. But because of the special nature of this particular addition, Zach had asked him to be there.

"We might as well keep this short, since we know we're gonna have to hire her," Ralph said wearily.

"No, we're not," Zach replied. "If she's bad, she's not getting the part. Period."

Ralph raised an eyebrow quizzically. "You know what that might mean."

Zach flashed an angry glance at Gary. "Will the studio back me up?"

After a moment's hesitation, Gary answered, "Yeah. We're not going to waste twenty million dollars on a movie doomed to failure because the female lead is a dead loss."

At that moment, Cataline O'Kelley swept into the room. She was even more stunning than Zach had expected. Tall and slender, she wore a cream silk dress that revealed a hint of lush curves in just the right places. Black hair with the sheen of polished ebony, cut just above her shoulders, contrasted with her light blue-green eyes. Her face was heart-shaped and a short, upturned nose gave an impudent look to her beauty.

The camera will love her, Zach thought. *She won't have a bad angle.*

"Gentlemen," she began in a dusky voice that was warm and appealing, "it's a pleasure to meet you."

She said it with such feeling that both Ralph and Gary seemed to take it as a personal compliment. Only Zach, who'd seen too many actresses to confuse ability with sincerity, remained unmoved.

"Please sit down," Zach invited. His coolness established an invisible barrier between them.

She did so, demurely crossing her long, shapely legs. She fixed her lovely aquamarine eyes on him and said with a smile, "I'm afraid my husband did a naughty thing. Generous, but naughty. He wants to help my career and I appreciate that. But he has no business trying to force you to hire me. So I want you to know all I expect is a screen test. If you don't think I'm right for the part, you don't have to hire me."

Zach expelled a breath of intense relief. "That's very considerate of you, Miss O'Kelley."

She flashed a dazzling smile. "Not at all, Mr. Stewart. I don't need blackmail to get this part. I'm good. Very good. I intend to prove it to you."

"What's your background?" Zach asked.

"I'm from New York. I've sung in a lot of night-clubs, done summer stock on the East Coast. I studied at the Actors' Workshop in New York."

"I know you've done some TV," Gary cut in. He looked a good deal less worried than he had five minutes earlier.

"Yes. Mostly small roles on series, and a movie of the week, *Daughters*. I did a pilot that didn't make it on the schedule."

"Have you read the script?" Zach asked.

"Yes."

"What do you think?"

"I think I can do some things that will flesh out the female lead. Mary Beth Ramsey is a bit of a cipher the way she's written."

Zach grinned. "All right, Miss O'Kelley. We'll arrange a test tomorrow morning."

"Thank you, Mr. Stewart. I don't think you'll be disappointed."

She rose and swept out of the room with the same aplomb she'd shown on entering. Watching her, Zach thought that Kevin, who was a notorious womanizer, had probably met his match.

SHE WAS RIGHT about not disappointing them. As Zach sat in a screening room the next afternoon, watching Catalina's screen test, he was impressed.

"She lights up the screen," Gary said excitedly.

"She does indeed."

"I'll tell business affairs to start negotiating with her agent. Just think of the publicity—Kevin and his new wife in a movie together."

"You think of the publicity, Gary. I'm thinking about the movie. And I think she's going to be great in it."

Beside them, Ralph said, "I just hope she can handle the physical problems of working outdoors, up in the mountains."

"She looks to me like a woman who could handle just about anything," Zach retorted. He was fed up with Ralph's constant allusions to the problems of shooting the whole movie on location.

Clearly sensing the dissension between his producer and director, Gary said soothingly, "Well, things are shaping up great. Just great. I think we'll have a solid commercial film on our hands."

"Exactly," Ralph agreed, focusing on Gary and ignoring Zach. "An exciting little action-adventure picture with no pretentions. Guaranteed fifty million at the box office."

That was basically how Zach looked at the picture—a simple, entertaining story. Yet somehow Ralph's words irritated him. It was time to clear the air. The antagonism building between them was rapidly approaching a point where it would be impossible for them to work together. Already Ralph was responding to the tension by going directly to Gary and ignoring Zach whenever possible.

But it's my picture, Zach thought firmly. *Ralph has to be reminded of that fact*.

As Gary rose and headed out of the screening room, Zach stopped Ralph. "We've got to talk," he said pointedly.

Ralph hesitated for only the briefest instant. "Okay. Your office?"

"Yeah."

An hour later, Ralph stormed out of the office, and Zach called Gary.

"I fired Ralph," he began bluntly.

"What?" Gary exploded.

"We can't work together. He doesn't give a damn about this picture. All he thinks about is making things as easy as possible for himself and collecting his salary."

Gary sighed heavily. "I've seen this coming. We're lucky he didn't have a play-or-pay deal. But, Zach, we're supposed to start shooting on June 1. That's in three weeks. Who on earth are we supposed to get to direct *Lodestar*?"

The thought that had been in the back of Zach's mind for weeks came into sharp focus.

"I know someone. It's a risk, but..."

"Who?" Gary demanded.

"Leigh Adams."

Gary laughed dryly. "Very funny, Zach. As I recall the way she looked when she left our meeting, she'll tell you in no uncertain terms exactly what you can do with your movie."

Zach smiled, remembering how Leigh had looked that day. She had a temper, all right. And passion. But passion was what *Lodestar* needed if it was to be everything he hoped it could be. He would just have to persuade her to put her passionate resentment of him into passionate involvement in his movie.

DRESSED IN OLD GRAY SWEATS, Leigh locked the door of her upstairs apartment and ran down the stairs, across the courtyard and out onto the street. Two minutes later, after dodging acrobats on skateboards, she crossed Ocean Front Walk, Venice's answer to the boardwalk.

Venice had been created decades earlier by a developer with grandiose dreams of recreating the Italian city in an area just south of Santa Monica. Many of his picturesque canals and bridges remained, but the small wood-frame cottages were rapidly being replaced by high-rise condominiums. However, there were still touches of the charming, bohemian colony it had once been, and that was what had drawn Leigh to it.

Negotiating the bike path that paralleled the beach, she reached the sand and removed her scuffed white running shoes. Then, carrying a shoe in each hand, she began to run along the water's edge.

A stiff breeze was blowing and, though it was late in the afternoon, there was still a radiant warmth from the sun, bright and yellow in the azure sky. The blue waters of the Pacific sparkled vividly.

Concentrate, she told herself. Run—don't think about which offer to accept...how to pay the rent...

Her legs and feet functioned properly, but her mind refused to obey. It was impossible to clear her head. She had to make a decision or one would be made for her and she'd lose by default. If she didn't accept one of the two offers available to her, the studios would simply choose other directors.

Unfortunately she wasn't excited about either project. The problem was she wanted to do *Lodestar*. And that was impossible.

Lodestar. The word echoed in her brain as first one foot, then the other, came down with rhythmic force onto the damp sand. Damn Zach Stewart, anyway! But her anger toward him was mixed with something else—another equally powerful emotion she didn't want to face.

Stopping, she took a deep breath, then looked back down the beach. Her tracks were clearly visible. Then she watched a swell build to a greater force than the preceding combers. The wave crested and surged toward the shore. The waters rushed over Leigh's feet and ankles and ran far up the sand. Then, as if obeying a command, the breaker reversed its thrust and rushed back to sea.

Leigh braced herself against the tug of the receding water as it pulled the sand from beneath her feet. Careful to maintain her balance, she watched the foam frothing on the beach. In just seconds, the path of her footprints was completely erased.

Startled, she whispered aloud, "Remember that. One quick wave and you're wiped out."

Then she laughed softly. *For Pete's sake*, she thought, *now I'm talking to myself. Out loud, yet*.

Spinning around to continue her run, she immediately collided with a small boy.

"Oh! I'm sorry," she cried, as she tried to regain her balance and catch the child before they both fell. She was unsuccessful, and they collapsed onto the wet sand in a tangle of arms and legs.

The brown-haired, brown-eyed boy, who wore a determined expression on his freckled face, clung tightly to a string.

"Are you all right?" Leigh asked as she stood and helped him to his feet.

"Sure," he responded, scrambling up and brushing sand from his bony knees. "I hope my kite's not broken." He ran toward the kite lying forlornly nearby, his short legs pumping hard to drive his feet through the soft sand.

Running after him, Leigh called, "I hope not, too."

The kite was bright red and yellow, a simple, two-stick affair. They boy picked it up, carefully holding it where the horizontal stick crossed the vertical, and examined it. There wasn't even a rip in the tissue paper. He shook the tail to rid it of the sand.

This kite, Leigh knew, was an Eddy Bow. Every spring of her life, she and her grandfather had made and flown all kinds of kites. One year they'd made a butterfly kite that Lucas had painted vivid yellow. It had won first place in a kite-flying contest, then hung from the ceiling of her bedroom for years afterward.

"It's okay," the little boy said.

"Good. I'd have felt absolutely rotten if I'd broken such a terrific kite. It was my fault. I wasn't paying attention to the traffic." Kneeling, she finished, "My name's Leigh. What's yours?"

"Robbie." The *R* was just a bit soft, revealing how young he really was. No more than six or seven, Leigh decided.

"I've been tryin' an' tryin' to fly it," Robbie continued, frustration evident in the slight pout of his lips and downcast dark eyes.

Quite far down the beach, Leigh could see a woman waving her arms, motioning for Robbie to return. The breeze blew her dress against her very pregnant figure.

"Your mother?" Leigh asked.

Robbie nodded. "She used to help me get my kite going, but now..." His voice trailed off on a woeful note.

"There's enough wind to fly this kite. All we have to do is catch it," Leigh said encouragingly.

Robbie's brown eyes brightened, and a wide grin revealed a missing front tooth. "Do you know how to fly a kite?"

Leigh nodded sagely. "I'm something of an expert, actually."

"Do you really think it will fly?"

"We won't know until we try, will we?"

Leigh waved reassuringly at Robbie's mother, who settled down again on the sand.

"Run with the string," she instructed Robbie. "I'll hold the kite and follow you. Run where the sand's hard."

Though they made several attempts, the boy simply couldn't run fast enough. Leigh looked about to see if there might be at least one able-bodied person over six and under ninety who could run with her. But except for the boy's mother, she and Robbie seemed to be it.

By this time, late in the afternoon, most of the beach was deserted.

Then she saw a man walking toward them. Dressed in jeans and a blue sweater, he held a pair of loafers in one hand. Even from this distance, she could see there was something about his bearing that translated as "confident."

Well, Leigh thought, *confidence is what we need right now*. Before she could think twice about it, she hailed him. "Hi! We need some help..."

But the words ended abruptly as she recognized the man.

Zach Stewart.

As he came closer, she saw that small cleft in the chin, the piercing light blue eyes, the deeply tanned skin. The deep V-neck of the sweater revealed a hard chest with a thick mat of curling golden hair.

Leigh's first thought was chagrin. She wished she'd done something with her hair instead of pulling it back in an old scarf. She wished she'd worn her new velour jogging suit instead of this comfortable old one.

Her second thought was anger. What on earth was he doing there, anyway?

When he reached them, he said, "Having a problem?"

Determined to be equally nonchalant, Leigh answered, "We're trying to get this kite airborne. Robbie, this is Mr. Stewart."

"Pleased to meet you, Robbie." Zach leaned over to set his shoes on the sand, then offered his hand to the child. "Call me Zach." Turning to Leigh, he asked, "A relative?"

"Friend."

"I see. Well, what role would you like me to play in this scene?" Zach asked. "Shall I lead and you hold the kite—or vice versa?"

Leigh bit her lip to keep from making a sharp retort. She'd been right about him. He was as self-assured as a riverboat gambler with aces up both sleeves. Still, as she saw a teasing grin curve his mouth and deepen that intriguing cleft, she had to admit that on him such confidence was charming.

"If you'll just hold this as high as you can," Leigh said, "I'll try to find a loose breeze."

"Okay." He winked at Robbie and gave him a thumbs-up sign as he took the kite. "Ready."

Once more Leigh raced along the beach. This time, she sprinted as fast she could, very much aware that Stewart was close behind her. All at once, she felt the kite lift into the breeze. It was flying, spinning out string.

"Thanks," she shouted at Stewart as she circled past him and ran back to Robbie. As she transferred the string to his tiny hands, she saw his face glow with happiness.

Like a living thing, the kite caught the breeze, then as the three of them watched, it found an updraft and soared skyward. Above, in the bright blue sky, it swooped and swirled as it rode the current.

As the delighted little boy raced toward his mother, Stewart smiled at Leigh. "Bravo," he said in a low, husky voice. The intimate quality of it reminded her of that day in the studio parking lot when he'd asked her to have dinner with him.

Startled at the sudden electricity between them, Leigh looked up at him. In her bare feet, she was a good head shorter than he was. At their first meeting, she'd at least had the trappings of sophistication to bolster her confidence in dealing with him. Now she was herself—period. She felt distinctly at a loss.

That put her on the defensive, and her words were sharper than she actually intended. "Fancy meeting you here in Venice. Somehow I would have thought the beach at Malibu would be more your style, Mr. Stewart."

To her surprise, he smiled. "I'd hoped you'd mellowed. Well, wrong again."

"If you'll excuse me, I have things to do."

As she started to brush past him, he reached out and took hold of her hand gently but firmly. The feel of his fingers, rough and strong, sent shivers up her spine. She stopped as something odd seemed to have happened to her knees.

"Leigh..."

He spoke her name as softly as if it were an endearment. As she looked into those penetrating blue eyes, she knew the moment for flight was past. She couldn't walk away from him now if her life depended on it.

"What do you want?" she whispered.

He hesitated for just a fraction of a second. When he spoke, she sensed the words weren't the first that had come to his mind.

"I fired Hastings."

The impact of the announcement sobered her. She pulled her hand out of his grasp and stood facing him. "I'm not surprised."

"Have you signed to do another movie?"

"Two studios are offering me projects."

"But have you signed a contract?" he insisted.

Reluctantly, she shook her head.

Zach breathed a sigh of relief. "Okay. Then let's talk about *Lodestar*."

"We don't have anything to talk about, Mr. Stewart. I'm not about to do your movie."

"Why not? Revenge for being turned down before?"

"I'm not into revenge."

"Then why won't you do it?"

"Because I don't think I could work with you."

He grinned. "Well, if it's a simple case of disliking me..."

"I don't dislike you," Leigh insisted, struggling to maintain her composure in the face of that disarming smile. "It's nothing personal at all. I have no personal feelings about you one way or another," she added for emphasis.

"So what's the problem?"

"Professionally speaking, you're obviously impossible to work with."

"Tough, I admit, but not impossible."

"You've fired one director; what's to stop you from firing another?"

The smile was gone now as he answered bluntly, "We're due to start shooting in less than three weeks. I don't have time to fire another director."

"You didn't think I was right before."

"I made a mistake."

The reluctant way he spoke those words indicated he rarely said them. Still Leigh hesitated.

"Let's continue talking about it over dinner." He paused for a fraction of a second, then added, "You owe me a favor. I helped with the kite."

When she hesitated, he asked huskily, "What do you have to lose?"

What indeed, she asked herself. But she wasn't at all sure she wanted to know the answer.

"I hear there's a place in Washington Square that serves terrific hamburgers."

She eyed him thoughtfully. "Do you ever take no for an answer?"

"Never."

There was a moment's silence, pregnant with anticipation.

Then Leigh's lips curved softly. "All right, Mr. Stewart. I'll let you buy me a hamburger. But that's all you're going to talk me into."

As he took her hand to lead her back across the sand, he said, "Call me Zach. After all, we're going to be working together."

Carrying their shoes, they walked across the beach to the pavement, then stopped to slip them on again.

"By the way, how did you find me?" Leigh asked curiously.

"I went to your house. Your landlady told me where you'd gone." He paused, then went on, "I was surprised to find such a lovely old Victorian house among the condos. When I think of Venice, I usually think of bikinis, roller skates and bicycles."

"And in that order, I suppose." Leigh's tone was dry.

But if she'd meant to needle him, she failed. He merely grinned and nodded agreement.

They had reached her house. As she paused to open the wrought-iron gate, she took a moment to admire the house. It was delightful, twin-gabled with a wraparound verandah. The horizontal clapboard was painted a soft gray. The second story, complete with a five-sided cupola, was sheathed in scalloped shingles weathered to a silvery sheen. The beveled glass of the wide front door, bright with the setting sun, reflected the showy clusters of violet jacaranda.

"How did you find such a gem?" Zack asked as they entered the courtyard.

"Marv. He told me the second floor was for rent."

When she didn't explain further, Zach asked, "Who's Marv?"

Surprised at his curiosity, Leigh glanced up at him. A hint of a smile teased the corners of his mouth, but his eyes were dead serious.

"Are we playing twenty questions?"

"No, just one."

Unsettled by his directness, she answered tersely, "Marv is a realtor. At least he was four years ago. I don't know what, or where, he is now."

Though she wasn't looking at him, she sensed his entire body relax.

They walked down the small side courtyard toward the outside stairs that led to the second story. A dwarf lemon tree and several pots of geraniums, red, pink and salmon-colored, sat near the staircase. Against the wall, under the shade of the jacaranda, hung a bamboo cage housing a pair of turtledoves.

There, on the bottom step of the stairs, was a white bouquet wrapped in tissue. It was the largest Leigh had ever seen—masses of roses, carnations, freesias and delicate baby's breath—all in white. Gathering the bouquet in her arms, she buried her face in the perfumed petals and willed her heart to behave. After a moment's hesitation, she looked up at Zach.

"Peace offering?"

He nodded, his eyes watchful. "Check the color. Truce?"

White was also the color of surrender, Leigh knew. At this moment, she wasn't sure at all which of them was surrendering.

Suddenly the turtledoves began cooing. Leigh couldn't suppress the laughter that burst from deep within her. "Perfect timing," she said, recovering her composure. An hour ago she'd been damning Zach Stewart to perdition. And now...

"Am I forgiven?" There was a glint of amusement in his eyes.

"I'll tell you after dinner," she teased. But as she smiled up at him, something in his expression changed, became less amused and more serious. She did not want to consider why.

Turning, she headed up the stairs, with Zach following closely.

"Are the doves yours?"

"My landlady's. Connie Cabot."

Just behind her, she heard his quick intake of breath.

"I thought I recognized her. Connie Cabot...she was one of the best editors in the business."

As Leigh paused to unlock her door, she looked at him. "Yes. She didn't do too badly...for a woman."

When Zach didn't rise to the bait, she continued, "I met Stan Munroe through her. He's her beau—to use Connie's word."

Zach said quietly, "I see."

Leigh didn't respond. She'd made her point.

Inside her apartment, she excused herself to find a container for the flowers. In the kitchen, she filled a large copper kettle with water and quickly arranged the bouquet. Then she carried it to the game table set up in the cupola.

Sunlight poured through the windows and across the flowers, glinting over the bright copper and onto the polished hardwood floor.

"I'll be just a minute," she called over her shoulder as she headed toward the bedroom.

Zach glanced at the robin's-egg blue walls covered with prints of Impressionist paintings and old movie posters. Then, walking past the white wicker furniture with matching blue cushions, he stood in front of a poster of *Gone with the Wind*, showing a ruggedly handsome Rhett Butler embracing a beautiful, disheveled Scarlett O'Hara.

"Interesting choice," he murmured.

Pretending not to hear him, Leigh went into her bedroom and closed the door.

Fifteen minutes later she emerged, freshly showered and changed into a white cotton gauze dress with a vibrant pink sash at the waist. Her legs were bare, and on her feet were bare little white leather sandals. She'd thought of wearing her heels, but knew it would be useless. Zach would still tower over her.

As she walked into the living room, Zach stood with his back to her, watching the sunset through the large window that overlooked the beach.

"Ready," she said, picking up the purse she'd left on a chair earlier.

He turned and for a moment simply looked at her.

"Remarkable."

"Because I was ready so quicky?"

"Because you can look so terrific with so little effort."

The words, so discreet and so obviously sincere, sent a rush of color to Leigh's cheeks. For a moment, she had absolutely no idea how to respond.

He cocked his head and eyed her quizzically. "Shy? Somehow, I wouldn't have thought that of you."

It took all her considerable willpower not to look away. She responded tartly, "Definitely not shy. Just weak from hunger."

He grinned and held out his hand. "Then let's go."

She hesitated. Something, some instinct for self-preservation, told her that if she took this man's hand there'd be no turning back. There was a challenge in his eyes that both excited and frightened her.

She reminded herself that she hadn't yet refused a challenge.

"All right," she agreed, and put her hand in his.

They went to a small restaurant on Washington Square. The square was actually a short street that dead-ended into the Venice beach and pier. The restaurant was unpretentious, with sawdust on the floor and a round, open fire pit in the center. But it served the largest, most delicious hamburgers Leigh had ever tasted anywhere, along with a huge mound of crisp French fries.

After they had ordered, and the waitress had brought a beer for Zach and iced tea for Leigh, Zach leaned his elbows on the table, crossed his arms and began without preamble.

"We're due to start shooting in three weeks. I need a new director fast."

"Why me?"

"Because I think you're the best person available. You did an excellent job on *Intimacies* with very little money. You said you could do an even better job on *Lodestar* with its bigger budget. I'm inclined to believe you."

"Why did you fire Hastings?"

Zach smiled dryly. "He's the first director I've ever had to fire."

"Why?"

"Creative differences. He wanted the film to go in one direction, I wanted it to go in another. We couldn't both be right. Naturally I prefer to think I am."

"Naturally."

Just then the meal was served, and by an unspoken agreement all talk of business was postponed until after dinner.

As Leigh was finishing the last of her hamburger, Zach said quietly, "Tell me about yourself."

"You know everything that matters. I studied hard to be a director. I directed *Intimacies*. I wanted to direct *Lodestar*. That's it...past, present—" she hesitated, then finished "—and I'm not sure about the future."

"That's not what I mean, and I think you know it. I want to know about *you*. Who taught you to fly kites?"

She wasn't normally reticent. But somehow with Zach she was reluctant to open up, to reveal much of herself. Perhaps, she realized, it was a defense mechanism. So far, he'd shown a disconcerting ability to get to her in a way that didn't bear close scrutiny.

Reluctantly she answered. "Luke taught me. And he bought my car so I could get from the valley to U.C.L.A. film school."

"Luke?"

"My grandfather. Lucas Adams." She smiled wistfully. "My crazy, wonderful grandfather. He was a magician in vaudeville."

Suddenly Leigh realized that Zach was listening with complete attentiveness. It embarrassed her somehow, and she finished almost in a whisper, "He told me that the secret of magic is to believe in it. He spent his life creating magic, and I want to do the same, in my own way."

Before she finished speaking, Zach reached across the table and covered her hand with his. She felt the pressure of his fingers as they gently squeezed her own. For a moment, she forgot to breathe.

"Now I know about you."

Something in his tone made her realize she'd given herself away to an extent she hadn't intended. It was unsettling to think he'd managed her so deftly, while she still knew almost nothing about him.

Pulling her hand away, she asked, "And what drives you, Zach? It can't be simply money or you'd have stayed in television."

Those blue eyes that had been so open, so filled with empathy a moment earlier, were shuttered in an instant. He shrugged. "What drives anyone?"

"In Hollywood, a lot of things—desire for power, prestige, perks. Like the best table at Ma Maison or invitations to the 'A-list' parties."

He smiled ruefully. "I've never eaten at Ma Maison. And I don't care much for parties."

"Ah, then it must be power. Do you lust after power, Zach?"

She was pushing him past the danger point, and she knew it. Though there was no good reason to do so, she couldn't help herself. She was suddenly very angry at him—at his rejection earlier, at the nonchalant way he came back into her life, at the clever way he got past her defenses and made her feel terribly vulnerable. And most of all she was angry that he could send her senses reeling with one touch.

"Spoiling for a fight, Leigh?"

She stared at him defiantly, but could think of nothing appropriate to say.

"Come on, let's go out to the beach and walk off your hostility."

Suddenly feeling chagrined in the face of his surprisingly even temper, she quietly let him lead her out of the restaurant. At the edge of the sand, she bent to take off her shoes.

"Let me."

He knelt beside her. As he did so, she put one hand on his broad shoulder to steady herself as she stood first on one foot, then the other. He undid the straps of the sandals, his fingers barely brushing her ankles. Yet the fleeting touch sent a frisson of excitement racing up her legs to lodge somewhere deep in her abdomen.

Taken unaware, Leigh drew in her breath and her eyes opened wide as she looked down at him. At that precise moment, he looked up at her and their eyes locked. She had looked into this man's face several times now. But suddenly, standing there on the beach that was bright now with a three-quarter moon, she felt light-headed.

What she felt showed in her eyes, for she heard the quick intake of his breath.

After a long moment, he stood and slipped off his own shoes, and the tension was broken.

Carrying their shoes, they strolled down the nearly deserted beach. It was a beautifully balmy night, not too cool as it often was on the coast, and filled with the sounds of lapping waves.

"Tell me," Leigh began, "who's in charge on your films—you or the director?"

"The director, of course, once shooting starts."

"And if there's a disagreement?"

He hesitated. Clearly he understood what she was getting at. Then he answered slowly, "On all my films the credits read, 'A Zach Stewart Production.' That isn't an empty claim."

The credits on *Intimacies* had read "A Leigh Adams Film" she reminded herself. She had been in charge. Only her. It wouldn't be that way with Zach.

She looked away, ostensibly at the water, ebony dark and smooth as glass. But it was Zach she was thinking of. There was no way they could work together and not have disagreement. When that happened, she'd have to fight him hard. She knew she could be tough when it came to her work, but she'd never come up against a man like him before.

"This film means a lot to me," Zach said quietly, interrupting her thoughts. "I wanted to break out of TV and into features. This is my chance. If I blow it, it could be my last chance."

"I understand," Leigh whispered. And she did. *Intimacies* had meant the same thing to her. A chance to prove herself creatively.

"But to be really good, a film has to be true to one guiding vision, not two, or, God forbid, several."

"The auteur theory?" he said sarcastically.

"No. I know that film requires the teamwork of craftsmen. But as the director, I have to take the material the writer has created and take the contributions of the art director and cinematographer and everyone else and add something new and alive that comes from within me."

Her soft voice had grown excited with the deep conviction of her beliefs. Struggling to find the right words, she went on, "As director, I'm not just a supervisor of the actors and crew. I have to be involved in a way that's, well…"

"Passionate," Zach finished for her.

She looked at him in surprise. She hadn't expected him to understand so well what she was getting at.

"Yes," she said quietly.

"That's just what *Lodestar* needs."

"And if we disagree?" she asked, meeting his look.

"We'll handle that if it happens."

"Oh, I think it's bound to happen."

He smiled. "I think you may be right. What's wrong, Leigh—afraid of a fight?"

With you, yes, she thought, strangely troubled.

"It's the opportunity of a lifetime for you." His voice was deceptively quiet, but the impact of the words hit her hard. He was right—it was the opportunity of a lifetime, one that might not come again for a long time. But there were very real drawbacks.

"I couldn't stand having you look over my shoulder while I'm shooting every scene."

"It wouldn't be that way. If I think there's a problem I'll certainly tell you. But you're the director, not me."

"We'd be at each other's throats."

He smiled briefly. "I don't think you give either of us enough credit for the professionals we are."

"But if we disagree?" she persisted.

"I'll be open-minded and willing to listen to your viewpoint. If we just plain can't reach an agreement, you'll have to give in."

Giving in wasn't something Leigh did often or well when it came to her work. She was silent for a long moment.

Zach continued patiently, "I'm the producer. I came up with the idea in the first place, hired a writer to bring it to life, persuaded a studio to finance it and found actors to star in it. Someone has to have final control. And that has to be me. I'm not a hands-off producer."

He was right, Leigh knew. Ultimately there could only be one boss.

Looking up at him, she caught the concern in his eyes. He was anxious for her decision, worried she might actually turn him down.

"I'd be stepping into a difficult situation—working with a crew I didn't hire, who would probably resent me."

"Yes."

"If I failed, people wouldn't remember that I stepped in at the last minute. They'd say I failed because I'm a woman and a relatively inexperienced one."

"Yes."

His bluntness was disarming. He wasn't trying to gloss over the problems to persuade her to take the job. Yet he obviously wanted her to take it.

She stood thoughtfully for several long seconds. She wasn't at all sure she could work with him. There'd be tremendous conflict. Though she didn't want to face it, she suspected that conflict had to do with more than the usual director-producer battle. It was man versus woman. Power. Control.

He said, "If you go through life avoiding situations where you might fail, you'll never accomplish anything. I think you've got more guts than that, Leigh."

She gazed into those eyes staring so intently into hers, and thought *it's not failure I'm really afraid of, it's you*.

She watched him for a moment—his hands thrust in the pockets of his jeans, the blue sweater hugging the rugged contours of his shoulders and back. His eyes held hers and though she wanted to turn away, she couldn't. She simply couldn't resist the attraction between them. And she realized she couldn't refuse to direct *Lodestar*.

"All right," she whispered. In an uncanny way, the words sounded more like a surrender than an acceptance.

Almost imperceptibly, the corners of his mouth softened. "I'm glad."

Extending her hand, she said, "Deal?"

In his clear blue eyes, she saw dancing glints of light. His expression had changed from relief to something else. Something that made her heart pound and charged the air with electricity.

He took her hand as if to shake it. But instead he raised it to his lips and gently kissed it.

Leigh's breath faltered as he turned her hand over and kissed the palm. Then, looking straight into her startled eyes, he moved his lips to her wrist and kissed it, as well.

"Deal," he echoed.

It was a moment longer before she wondered what had really happened.

CHAPTER THREE

AT EIGHT O'CLOCK the next morning, Leigh sat drinking the last of her breakfast coffee when the doorbell rang. Answering it, she was surprised to find a messenger with a copy of the *Lodestar* script. She'd expected Zach to send the script quickly, but not this quickly. As she took the heavy bundle, she smiled to herself. Clearly Zach Stewart moved fast.

Leigh carried the script to the game table and pulled out a chair. The early-morning sunlight streaming through the tall windows created a bright warmth, burnishing the copper kettle holding Zach's beautiful bouquet. It was absolutely huge! Almost sinfully so, she told herself as she gazed at a cluster of fragrant freesias—her favorite flower.

Leigh's gray eyes grew dreamy and a smile curved her lips as she recalled finding the flowers on her stairs, the conversation that followed and the incredibly ridiculous timing of the turtledoves cooing. The entire scene had been like something out of a 1930s romantic comedy, she told herself as she opened the script.

The first time she'd had it only long enough to read it hastily. Gary had requested that she return it to him as soon as possible.

This was her copy. Hers to interpret—to illustrate her vision. And hopefully to stamp *Lodestar* with her own special mark. She thought of last night and Zach Stewart's intensity. He considered this *his* script and meant it to reflect his vision. And he meant it to bear his signature.

Suddenly the memory of his slow and deliberate kissing of her palm and wrist assaulted her. She'd felt the warmth of his mouth and the shape of his lips as he'd pressed them against her flesh. Her heart had leaped in surprise. She wondered if he'd felt her racing pulse.

Of course he had, she admitted. He knew exactly what he was doing. If she believed that, she wondered why she didn't feel angry. Because, strangely enough, she didn't.

Two hours later, she'd finished going through the script scene by scene and had filled the margins with notes. She had decided exactly what the tone of the picture should be, and what kind of coverage— master shots, close-ups, et cetera—were involved. She knew exactly how she wanted the entire movie to look. Now it was theoretically only a matter of showing up on location and relaying her decisions to the cast and crew.

In reality, of course, filming would be much more difficult and complicated. Actors didn't always do as they were told without discussion and often argument. Problems could, and would, occur, usually at the most inconvenient times. Weather, a big factor on a location shoot, could be capricious.

Sighing, Leigh moved to sit in the deep, overstuffed chair and put her feet up on an ottoman. It was a major undertaking, all right. She would be responsible for a lot of people and a lot of money. Out of this experience could come anything from a blockbuster hit to a respectable effort. Or a dismal failure, ripped apart by the critics and ignored by the public.

Adding to the stakes was the fact that she was a woman, and few women were given the chance to direct a major feature film. The history of women directors in Hollywood wasn't great. Not one had built an enduring career.

If I land on my behind, Leigh thought wryly, *I'll just be another unemployed woman director.*

"Knock, knock."

Looking up, Leigh found Connie Cabot, her landlady, standing beyond the screen door. Leigh had left the other door open to let in the balmy early-morning sunshine and fresh sea air.

"Come in, Connie," she said, getting up to greet her visitor.

Connie Cabot was small, like Leigh herself, and thin, with the ageless beauty of exquisite bone structure. Though in her mid-sixties, she was an extremely attractive woman; in her youth, Leigh knew she'd been stunning. She wore her silver hair stylishly short, with sides swept back to leave her earlobes exposed. Thick and crisp textured, her hair had been silver since her early thirties. She'd told Leigh she'd picked up a severe infection while traveling in the South American jungles. For days she'd run a terribly high fever and as a result, her long dark hair had fallen out. When she'd recovered, her hair grew back as thick as before, but bright silver. She'd loved it. As soon as she could afford it, she had her ears pierced and bought herself the half-carat diamond-stud earrings she was never without.

Looking at Connie now, dressed in a bright red caftan that heightened the warmth of her clear hazel eyes, Leigh reflected again on how kind fate had been to send her this savvy lady for a friend.

"You look pensive," Connie said, giving Leigh a quick hug.

"I was just contemplating abject failure."

"Is this just free-floating anxiety or is there something concrete to worry about?"

Leigh handed her the copy of *Lodestar.* "This is pretty concrete."

"Leigh! You're going to direct it, after all?"

Leigh nodded. "Looks like it. Actually, the deal isn't made yet. But considering how badly I want to do it, I'm not about to let my agent play hard-to-get with the studio." Leigh grinned as she walked past Connie to the kitchen. "How about a cup of coffee?"

"Was that Zach Stewart who was looking for you yesterday evening?" Connie asked as Leigh disappeared.

"Yes," Leigh said, returning with the coffee. "It seems he fired the other director and wants me to take over."

As they sat down across from each other at the game table, Connie eyed Leigh speculatively. "He was much more attractive than you led me to believe when we talked about him before."

"Well, at that time he'd just turned me down for the job. Naturally I didn't think too much of him."

"Naturally. Considering how angry you were at him, I'm surprised you didn't tell him to go to hell yesterday."

Leigh grinned again. "I did. But he's a very determined man."

"Ah, yes. I could see that." She leaned forward to enjoy the fragrance of the bouquet. "His?"

Leigh nodded.

"Well, he certainly didn't stint, did he? I like a generous man." Connie leaned back in her chair and sipped her coffee.

Leigh smiled to herself as she observed how Connie's gorgeous pear-shaped diamond ring caught the sunlight. Besides the diamonds she wore in her ears, this ring was the other piece of jewelry she was never without. Connie had mentioned once that someone very special had given it to her and although it was a stunning stone, its worth, she'd confided, was in its intrinsic value.

Setting down her cup, Connie continued, "Well, Mr. Stewart is determined, generous and very attractive. Is he married?"

"Connie!" Leigh laughed at her friend's persistence. "This is a job, not a possible romance."

"Well, is he?"

"I didn't ask about his marital status. But it doesn't matter, anyway. How's your coffee? Need a refill?"

"My coffee's fine. Leigh Adams, is he or is he not married?"

"No," Leigh admitted reluctantly, "I think I read somewhere that he's divorced. But what has that to do with anything? We're going to be working together..."

"Intimately," Connie finished slyly. "I know about working on a film, young woman. You'll be living out of each other's pockets for several months.''

"Were you ever involved with someone you worked with?''

"That's an impertinent question.'' A sparkle in Connie's eyes took the sting from her words.

"Oh, and it wasn't impertinent when you were questioning me?'' Leigh was smiling broadly now.

Connie laughed. "All right. I admit there were one or two instances...'' She let the words trail off suggestively. "One very special instance.''

Leigh watched Connie's quick glance at the ring on her finger. Then she heard Connie say, "Well, I was never married, you know.''

But Stan Munroe was. And the father of four children, Leigh thought.

With a sigh, she said, "I'm much more concerned with making this movie a success than I am with Zach Stewart's availability.''

Even to her own ears, the words sounded rather hollow. Fortunately Connie didn't challenge them.

She did find Zach Stewart terribly attractive. More than attractive—compelling. And that fact was going to complicate things for her if she wasn't very careful. She really had to keep her act together to successfully direct this picture.

"Leigh, you're a good director. You've proven that. Just give it your best shot and go on from there. Whether the movie's a success or a failure isn't the crucial thing.''

"Somehow,'' Leigh replied, "I don't think the studio, or Zach, would agree with you. I'll bet that wasn't how you felt when you were editing. Didn't you—''

"What matters is doing your best," Connie interrupted. "And in your case, that's pretty darn good."

Leigh forced a smile. "Thanks, coach. But I may be stepping into a mess that no one can salvage. Most of the cast and crew are already hired. They're someone else's choices, not mine. They may very well resent the change in directors. Taking over at the last minute will mean problems, maybe insurmountable ones."

"Every picture has problems. There's no such animal as a problem-free picture. What's really worrying you? Here you have an opportunity that last week you'd have killed for, more or less. And this attractive, determined producer bringing you an armful of beautiful flowers..."

"Zach Stewart and I are going to disagree as sure as you and I are sitting here having this conversation."

Connie leaned across the table and took Leigh's hand in hers. "Disagreement can be healthy. A vigorous exchange of differing viewpoints can enhance art."

"That would be fine, if it were only between Zach and me. But there are so many more people involved—so many more to suffer the consequences. The director doesn't single-handedly make the film."

Connie squeezed Leigh's hand and then sat back in her chair. "My dear child, you've chosen a difficult, insecure profession. You know that, Leigh. And it isn't like you to step back from a challenge."

Leigh'd heard the same argument from Zach last night. And had yielded—agreeing to direct his picture.

"I thought you found challenge stimulating," Connie finished.

Recalling those blue eyes looking so intently into hers, Leigh thought, *I find Zach Stewart stimulating. Too stimulating.*

Connie fixed Leigh with a no-nonsense glare. "Well? Have we sufficiently reinforced your backbone with this little chat?"

Before Leigh could reply, the phone on the kitchen counter rang and she walked across the room to answer it.

"Hello?"

"Did you get the script?"

It was just like Zach to get right to the point. Shoving her free hand in her jeans pocket, Leigh responded, "Yes. I've read it and made notes."

"Good. I'd like you to come down to the studio right away for a meeting with the production staff. Say in half an hour?"

It was also just like him, she thought, not to bother with minor questions such as was it convenient for her to get to a meeting on such short notice. What mattered to him was making this movie. Everything else was beside the point.

"I'll be there."

"It's Building C. The guard at the gate will give you directions. Bye."

As she hung up, Leigh smiled wryly at Connie. "My master calls. I'm off to the studio, without even time to change."

"Well, get used to rushing around madly, because it isn't going to let up for several months."

"Is this what they mean by the high price of success?"

"I think so."

Though Leigh hurried, she didn't quite make it to the studio within half an hour. By the time she walked up the front steps of Building C, pulling a comb hurriedly through her hair, she was already ten minutes late. As she entered the lobby, the nervousness she'd felt since the night before washed over her like a flood. She was about to meet a group of people who had been hired by someone else, who probably were loyal to that person and not at all happy that Leigh was stepping in to take his place. It was the worst possible way to start a job where they would all be working closely together, under tremendous pressure, for several months.

Hardly ideal circumstances to begin production of her first major feature film.

In the *Lodestar* production offices, Leigh found Zach talking to a short, wiry man with graying black hair and a worried expression on his heavily lined face.

"Leigh, this is Arnie Archuleta, the production manager. Arnie, this is Leigh Adams."

Arnie nodded politely and murmured hello. But there was a distinct coolness about his manner, and he didn't extend his hand. Leigh felt her nervousness increase. If the first person she met wouldn't accept her, that could easily mean that none of the others would, either.

Forcing herself to meet Arnie's unfriendly eyes, she extended her hand and at the same time said, "I'm looking forward to working with you, Arnie. This is an exciting project, and with all our best efforts I'm sure we can make it a really special film."

He hesitated for a second, eyeing her soberly. If he didn't take her hand, Leigh knew there would be nothing but trouble to come.

Reaching out, he held her hand for a moment, then let it drop. "I think you just may be right, Ms Adams."

It took all of Leigh's self-control not to breathe a sigh of relief.

Zach had been watching the exchange. He shot Leigh a brief smile of approval, then went on in a businesslike tone, "Arnie and I were just going over the storyboard. I'll show you what we've come up with."

The storyboard, Leigh knew, was the bible of the production. How efficiently it was organized would affect the cost of the movie. She moved close to examine the series of cardboard strips with each scene from the movie numbered and laid out, not necessarily in chronological order, but in the order Arnie felt would be the most economical way to shoot them. She saw he'd grouped all night scenes together and all scenes involving subsidiary characters. Nodding her approval, she said, "That's good. The studio won't have to pay anyone to sit around while other actors are working."

Aware that this would be her first test of acceptance, Leigh said she could see that Arnie was very good at his job. She smiled and added, "For which I'm very grateful. Makes my job easier. However," she paused and considered her words carefully, "I do have a slight disagreement." The change in the atmosphere was immediate. Leigh could feel both men stiffen their backs and, she supposed, their resolve.

She kept her eyes on Arnie, but she felt Zach's gaze bore into her.

Refusing to look at him, she continued. "I think you've scheduled too much here and here," she said, pointing to some night scenes. "People just don't work as quickly at night as they do during the day."

Arnie disagreed, as Leigh had expected. The production manager's job was to save money, while the director's was to make the best possible picture. They often were at odds, and this time was no different.

"Ralph Hastings seemed to think this could be done," Arnie commented pointedly, when Leigh refused to back down.

"Ralph is no longer the director of this picture. I am. We're different people, and naturally we don't do things exactly the same way."

She waited for Arnie to respond. When he didn't, she considered giving her opinion of Ralph Hastings as a director, but immediately thought better of it. Instead she looked Arnie straight in the eye and said, "I know what I'm doing. Give me a chance to prove that to you."

The tension between them grew with frightening intensity. Zach cut his eyes from his manager to his director, then back again. Leigh deliberately turned so that she still faced Arnie, but her face was averted from Zach. *Please stay out of this*, she silently begged. If he had to come to her rescue in dealing with these people, she couldn't be effective. For better or worse, she had to make her own way with them.

Arnie looked at Zach, then back at Leigh. Finally he said, "All right, Ms Adams. You're the director."

He didn't smile, but there was an underlying respect in his voice that Leigh responded to gratefully. "Call me Leigh, Arnie. After all, we're going to be working together for quite a while."

The rest of the day passed in a hectic blur. There were meetings with all the rest of the production staff, from the cameraman to the wardrobe lady. Several times Leigh had to undo something Hastings had done, and there was more than one tense moment. Although Leigh sensed deep resentment toward her and knew that some of these people would never like her, at least she had the feeling they all respected her.

By the time she finished a private meeting with John Kline, the art director, she felt she had the difficult situation well in hand.

Leigh stood at the door of her office watching Kline walk away. He turned into his own office and, in just a few seconds, came out again carrying his jacket. He called good-night and hurried down the hall. Looking at her watch, Leigh saw that it was after seven. She must be the only one left on this floor. Perhaps in the entire building—except for the guard.

She stepped back into her office, sighing deeply. Gathering all her notes, she put them in a folder and tidied her desk. Then she sat down in her swivel chair and, lifting her arms high above her head, stretched luxuriously. Folding her hands in her lap, she propped her feet up on the desk, crossed her slim ankles and closed her eyes.

What a day this had been. Exciting, interesting, confusing. And more than a little scary. But that would be her secret.

She heard footsteps coming down the hall and knew they had stopped at her door. So much for being alone in the building. Opening her eyes, she saw Zach lounging nonchalantly in the doorway. He wore a white cardigan over a blue knit shirt that not only complemented his tanned good looks but his lean muscular build, as well. He'd obviously just freshened up—his hair appeared slightly damp.

When he smiled, Leigh noticed that the cleft in his chin deepened and his eyes brightened. He looked relaxed and pleased to see her still there. For a moment neither of them spoke. She watched as his gaze traveled over her disheveled hair, to her mouth, then he looked directly into her eyes.

She wished she'd had five minutes warning that he was going to drop in. The session with the art director had been intense, and as was her habit when nervous, she'd kept running her fingers through her hair. She was sure she'd chewed off all her lipstick.

She thought about removing her feet from the desk and assuming a more ladylike posture but decided against it. Once she'd relaxed, her fatigue had caught up with her.

"Long day, huh?" he said. "How'd it go?"

"Fine," she replied, her voice soft. "It's been a piece of cake." Then she grinned at him. "Can't you see how full of zest and energy I am?"

"What I see is a lady who's worked very hard all day."

"Isn't that the name of the game around here?"

"Well, yes. But some of us take time for lunch. I heard you stopped by a candy machine for a chocolate bar." He came into the room and sat on the corner of her desk. "Seriously, how do you feel today went?"

"Seriously," Leigh said, letting her happiness show in her eyes as well as in her smile, "I loved it. Every minute. Even the hard moments...and there were some, as you well know."

"Good," he said in that blunt way she'd heard before.

Leigh dropped her feet to the floor and stood up. "Well, I see by my watch and by the fading light out yon window that it's time to call it a day and go home."

Zach stayed seated on her desk, one foot flat on the floor, the other set in a gentle swinging motion. "Do you have plans for the evening—a dinner date or...some kind of date?"

Warily Leigh returned his gaze, then she shook her head.

He held out his hand. When she hesitated, he reached across the desk and took hers in his. "Do you believe in magic?"

Still wary, Leigh nodded, wondering what this unpredictable man was getting at.

Turning over her hand, he peered at it. "I see two things in your palm, young woman. Do you wish to hear what the fortune-teller sees?" His eyes were bright with pleasure as he watched her nod affirmatively. "Good. The first thing I see is that you are famished. You have taken a long journey today, and now you are in need of sustenance. Is this not so?"

Leigh tried to retrieve her hand. She was much too tired to match wits with Zach Stewart this evening. Yes, she was starved but she'd coped with all the emotion she cared to today.

"That is so, O Great Wizard," she said, going along with his joke, "but tonight is a night for going home and opening a can of chili and going to bed early."

"Exactly." He stood up and pulled her by the hand to the doorway. "Down about two doors is the ladies room, if you haven't discovered it by now. Go wash your face and you'll feel better. Come back by my office and I'll escort you to your car. It's time to close up shop for the day."

Leigh took time to get her handbag, then she followed his instructions. She was simply too bone weary to do otherwise. As she combed her hair and freshened her makeup, she chided herself. Why are you bothering, Leigh? You're just going home...alone. Still, when she'd finished, she felt refreshed and ready to face the drive home.

She was surprised to find the door to Zach's office closed. As soon as she knocked, he swung the door open wide. "Come in," he said, with a trace of laughter in his voice.

Leigh could see one of the chrome-and-glass tables was set for two. As she stepped hesitantly into the room, Zach removed a bottle of champagne and two chilled crystal glasses from the small office refrigerator and placed them on the table. Then with a delighted chuckle, he swept the lid off the silver chafing dish. "*Violà!* Chili from Chasens. I ordered this at five, to be delivered at six-thirty." He took her by the hand and led her to her chair. Picking up her napkin, he gave it a dramatic snap before laying it across her lap. "Your Luke's not the only one who can work magic for you, Leigh Adams."

Speechless, Leigh felt her heart do a wild flip-flop. There was no way he could have known she was going to tell him that she was going home to open a can of chili. She herself hadn't known that she planned to do that.

"Well," she said, trying to recover her equilibrium, "Ralph Hastings was a fool to argue with you."

"Believe me, Leigh, Ralph Hastings and I never shared Chasens' chili." As he poured the champagne he looked directly at her. "You and I will have disagreements. Probably we'll argue. But as long as we both believe in magic, we'll be all right."

His voice was low and soft, but he spoke with assurance. Offering her a glass of champagne, he took one himself and raised it in a toast. "To magic."

Accepting the champagne, Leigh was reminded of that first day she'd met him and the high-voltage energy that seemed to flow between them. And the night on the beach. Every time they encountered each other, their meeting seemed to end, for her, on a note of surprise. He was certainly a take-charge man. As she looked into those astonishingly brilliant blue eyes, she felt again that blatantly sexual awareness that sometimes happens between a man and a woman.

For now, she'd put away her concerns about holding her own. She'd enjoy. This had been a long day. And a long time in coming.

As crystal touched crystal, a bell-like chime rang out clear and sweet. Smiling joyfully, Leigh echoed, "To magic."

EARLY THE NEXT MORNING, Zach drove Leigh up to Kevin Marlowe's. The house was protected from public view by lush vegetation and clever landscaping. The building was situated on a hilltop, and its setting provided a gorgeous view this morning. Leigh knew that at night it would be stunning.

She was completely surprised by this interesting house. As they'd driven through Toluca Lake's impressive real estate, she'd formed an opinion of what this famous movie star's home would be like. A reflection of Kevin's public image...if not garish, certainly spectacular.

But she was wrong. It was a country house, designed by a noted contemporary architect, with simple lines and lots of sliding glass to take advantage of the view.

The maid answered their ring and invited them in. As they waited for her to announce their arrival, Leigh looked about. The living-room pavilion was a daring partnership of twentieth-century space and nineteenth-century elegance. It was a lovely room with generous intervals of glass and shelves. Bleached oak floors gleamed and Japanese silk draperies filtered the soft morning light. An immense ficus benjamina tree stood in one corner, and across the room was an ebony grand piano.

Just as the maid returned, Leigh noticed a magnificent Georgian console, beautifully and intricately carved. Besides a lamp and a stack of books, it held a basket filled with a large bouquet of deep pink hydrangeas.

As the maid showed them out to the terrace where they found Kevin and Catalina relaxing over coffee,

Leigh thought perhaps she'd made an invalid judgment of the man who lived in this house.

But if his house wasn't what Leigh had expected, Kevin Marlowe was. In person he projected the steamy sexuality that made him the hot male sex symbol that he appeared to be on the screen. Just short of six feet tall, with a lithe yet muscular build, he had dark brown hair and an olive complexion.

As Zach introduced them, he smiled at Leigh, and the white of his teeth beneath a thin mustache slashed the swarthiness of his face. But the smile didn't reach his eyes. Only his lips curved in a slightly sardonic effect. It was clear that the man himself was barricaded behind an invisible barrier.

He surveyed Leigh carefully; his eyes, as black as obsidian, were wide and alert. He appeared cool, cynical and very much in control. Yet instinctively Leigh sensed that he was coiled watch-spring tight, on his guard for...for what, she didn't know.

In spite of Kevin's aura of dangerous attractiveness, Leigh found that she was more interested in Catalina, his unknown wife. He was attractive, with that special appeal that had made him a superstar. But Catalina was more interesting. As spectacularly pretty as Leigh had expected, but with a great deal more depth. Zach had told Leigh he had great expectations for Catalina, and now she understood why. This wasn't just another pretty face. This was a woman of passion and intelligence, who would be very interesting to direct.

As they sat down at the white wrought-iron patio table, Leigh felt her excitement for this project grow. That excitement however, was shattered in an instant when Kevin began bluntly, ''I liked Ralph

Hastings, Ms Adams. I've already told Zach I think it was a mistake to fire him.''

Leigh started to respond, but Zach silenced her with a glance. This time, it was his fight.

"We've already discussed this, Kevin. I told you why I felt Ralph wasn't the best person for this picture. It wasn't personal. And it sure as hell wasn't a decision I made lightly. You've had a string of hits. And if *Lodestar* fails, it won't really affect your career. You'll just go on to something else that will probably be a success. I don't have that kind of safety net under me. My entire future is on the line with this film.''

"I'm aware of that, Zach. But...''

"There are no buts, Kevin. Leigh's damn good. Did you see that print of *Intimacies* I sent over?''

Kevin nodded, but it was Catalina who spoke. "We watched it twice.'' Giving Leigh an encouraging smile, she went on, "We both liked it. A lot.''

Leigh returned her smile gratefully. At that instant, she recognized a bond between them. Somehow Leigh was certain they would work very well together.

But Kevin remained unconvinced. Turning to Leigh, he said gruffly, "No offense, but you're not very experienced. I'm used to working with old pros.''

"I'm a young pro, Mr. Marlowe,'' Leigh shot back, her temper getting the best of her. She couldn't help being angry with Kevin. If he chose, he could deny her the opportunity to direct *Lodestar*. Desperately she searched for a way to reach him.

"When you were just starting out as an actor, did you ever ask someone to give you a chance to show what you could do?"

Clearly taken aback, he said, "Well, of course."

She leaned toward him and her voice quavered slightly as she said softly, "Well, that's what I'm asking you now. Give me a chance to show you what I can do. *Please.*"

There was a tense silence as Kevin thought it over. Finally he said slowly, "I'm not sure how good you are as a director, Ms Adams. But you have a lot of chutzpah. I know, because I have a lot of it myself. All right. I'll let you show me what you can do with this movie."

The sarcasm of the words was softened by a smile that had made millions of hearts beat like thunder. Leigh grinned in response. Inside, she felt as if the knot deep in her stomach was gently coming undone.

As the last of the tension dissipated, Catalina said brightly, "Well, now that that's settled, would you two like some coffee?"

THEY WORKED THROUGH LUNCH and on into the afternoon, running through the script. Kevin and Catalina read their parts, commenting on areas where they felt there could be improvement. The more she worked with Catalina, the more Leigh liked her. And the more she realized this was one actress who wasn't going to have to bask in her husband's reflected glory for very long.

As they drove away late in the afternoon, Zach said, "You handled that very well. Kevin's no push-over. I expected trouble from him, but I didn't say anything to you because I didn't want to make you nervous."

Leigh laughed. "Nervous! I don't think I could have been any more nervous. You didn't have to tell me there'd be problems with Kevin. I knew there would be."

"Well, you handled him perfectly. Do you really think he'll do well?"

"Of course. Did you think I was just stroking his ego?"

"Frankly, yes. Kevin has an amazing way of wrapping any director, male or female, around his finger."

"Not this director."

"What makes you so sure? He's had his way with more experienced directors than you."

"Because I know he's not a great actor. And Kevin knows I know. But I sense that beneath the easy charm, there's some depth that's never been tapped and I intend to bring that out."

"I hope you do. It would be nice to get good reviews as well as good box office."

"It's Catalina who really interests me, though," Leigh went on eagerly. "That woman can act. Why don't we do a rewrite on the script? Beef up her part, make it more equal to Kevin's..."

"Leigh, we start shooting in two weeks. There's no time. And no money in the budget."

"But you said yourself she's going to be great. She could do so much with a bigger role."

"Well, we can't give it to her at this late date. So don't even get into it."

Leigh bristled at his peremptory tone. "But..."

"Like I told Kevin, there are no buts about it. We can't do it. So forget it."

"Hold it, Zach. You sound like a parent talking to an unruly teenager."

"And you sound like someone who isn't facing reality."

"Why? Because I want to rewrite a good script to make it even better?"

"Because there's no time or money to do it."

Leigh was really angry now. How dared he shut her off as if her opinion didn't matter. "Damn it, there is time. On *Intimacies* we changed some of the script while we were shooting it."

"Well, then you were lucky it didn't come out looking sloppy. Winging it as you go rarely works."

"I wasn't winging it," she said tightly. "I knew what I was doing."

"What you were doing was making a low-budget film. If you blew it, if the last-minute changes didn't work out, it wasn't the end of the world. It's different when you're dealing on this level."

"I see. You're trying to tell me my business again. I'm beginning to wonder why you hired me since you obviously think I don't know very much."

By this time, they were at her apartment. As Zach pulled up in the driveway and turned off his car, his face was set in a stubborn expression. But Leigh's was no less stubborn.

"Zach…"

"Leigh…"

Each had spoken at the same time. They stopped and looked at the other. Finally Leigh went on angrily, "I know a terrific writer who's available—"

"No. Forget it. I'm not going to start hacking at this script at this late date. It's basically sound and you know it. And even if I didn't feel that way, there's no way the studio would go along with a rewrite."

"They could be persuaded."

"They're concerned enough as it is with the fact that I fired the director. That's turned this into a problem production, and they don't like problem productions. If I go to them now and say the script has problems and they need to fork over more money to fix it, they'll hit the roof."

"Aren't you willing to fight for what you believe in?"

"Damn it, Leigh, that's unfair and you know it. I believe the script is a lot better than most. You're the one who has problems with it."

That did it. Livid, Leigh opened the car door, then turned back to shoot Zach a scathing look over her shoulder. Without saying a word, she got out, slammed the door, then stalked up the stairs toward her apartment.

But with each step she took, she felt worse and worse.

What am I doing, she asked herself. *I claim to be a professional, then I behave like...like a damn fool. I'm being a spoiled brat who throws a tantrum when she can't get exactly what she wants.*

As she reached the landing, she stopped and came to an abrupt decision. Spinning around, she collided with Zach and would have fallen if he hadn't grabbed her.

For a long moment they simply looked at each other. There was still anger between them. They still didn't agree about this. But suddenly that wasn't the most important thing. What really mattered was not letting that anger overwhelm them.

He waited, watching her face.

"Were you coming up to fire me?" she asked with a hint of a self-conscious smile.

He shook his head. "No. I was coming up to convince you that you were wrong. I don't believe in walking away from arguments. I believe in fighting them out and reaching some kind of agreement."

"Well, how's this for agreement—you're right and I'm wrong. I'll do everything I can to flesh out Catalina's part while we're filming. But I won't insist on a last-minute rewrite."

Zach breathed an audible sigh of relief. Then he grinned. "That's a nice agreement."

"Of course. You win."

"No. We both win."

Leigh looked down at him. And suddenly she knew why she'd behaved so emotionally. Despite what she'd tried to tell herself, theirs wasn't just a working relationship. Zach touched her emotions in a way that frightened her. It was that fear that had made her run from him, and for one blind moment even consider throwing away the chance to make the picture.

Suddenly she became aware that he still held her. Sighing deeply, she smiled at him. "What we need now is for the turtledoves to start cooing." There was a gentle softness in her voice. "Do you think that would help?" she finished.

"Turtledoves rarely coo on cue," he said matter-of-factly, then grinned apologetically for his rhyme.

"That other time was a bonus. I think we're on our own now."

He didn't release her, and Leigh was strangely reluctant to step out of his grasp. His face was very close to hers, and she felt his hands tighten ever so slightly. Responding, she let her eyes meet his and read in them what she was sure he read in hers. Unhurriedly his gaze traveled across her face, studying her as if he'd never seen her before. Then she was confronted once again with those piercing blue eyes. He looked deeply, as if searching for an answer to an unspoken question. Then his gaze rested on her mouth.

Leigh held her breath, hoping he'd kiss her.

Am I crazy, she wondered. *This is neither the time nor the place. And it sure isn't in any way appropriate.*

But she remembered the warmth of his kisses on her palm and wrist and now, standing practically in his embrace, she wanted to feel them on her lips.

After a heart-stopping moment, he raised his eyes to gaze once more into hers. They stood so close together that she could feel his breath on her face.

"The first time I saw you in Gary's office," he said in a voice husky with emotion, "I saw your red hair and presumed your eyes would be green."

"Not all redheads have green eyes," she whispered. "Some have blue eyes, some have brown eyes and…"

"And some gray eyes that turn cool and distant—as yours did a few minutes ago," he teased, and as he smiled the cleft in his chin deepened and the corners of his eyes crinkled charmingly.

"And other times...?" Leigh knew she was playing the oldest game in the world, but she couldn't help herself.

"Other times, like now, they're soft and dreamy. And a man could..." He checked himself and released her left arm, but in doing so, raised his hand to brush against her cheek in a gentle caress. "That day in Gary's office when I said you were prettier than I'd expected, you told me your looks were totally irrelevant. Remember?"

Scarcely breathing, Leigh nodded. The smooth touch of his hand on her face was riveting.

"You were wrong," he said with mock severity.

Releasing her other arm, he cupped her face with both hands. His expression grew serious and his blue eyes narrowed speculatively as he said, "I think everything about Leigh Adams is relevant." Then he dropped his hands and, shoving them into his pockets, said, "Good night. I'll see you in the morning."

Turning, he hurried down the stairs and across the courtyard.

Leigh stood exactly where he'd left her until she heard the sound of his car driving away.

ZACH CUT OVER to Pacific Coast Highway and turned north toward Malibu and home. He was not part of the Malibu colony, but he did live in one of the canyons where he kept a couple of horses and maintained his privacy. Filmmaking was an exciting business, but an exhausting one. He looked forward to getting home in time for a long ride on Big Red. That would work off some of his tension.

But not all of it, he knew. A lot of the tension he was experiencing had to do with Leigh Adams. That diminutive lady had intrigued him since their first encounter—or should he say skirmish.

He thought of how fragile she'd felt when he'd caught her there on the stairs, and how difficult it had been not to take her in his arms. She was the first woman in a long time who'd made his heart pound and his breath grow short. She was slight, couldn't be more than five-two, but he knew that *fragile* didn't accurately describe her. She might look delicate but she was one tough lady. Her commitment to her work was formidable. Passionate! And while that was a welcome switch from Ralph Hastings's cavalier attitude, it was going to cause a lot of hassles between them.

She was going to fight him on every point of difference. As she had at that first meeting. He'd thought many times of her comment on Hastings. "He'll give you a decent picture," she'd said. "But he won't give you a great one."

She was right. And thank God, he'd seen it in time.

He'd called her feisty during that meeting. He wouldn't do that again. She wasn't quarrelsome, she was dedicated. He could appreciate that.

He pulled his car into the driveway of his house. The house sat on a small plateau ringed by hills. Zach had chosen the site for its isolation and a stunning ocean view. The architect he'd hired had taken advantage of both qualities by building a redwood-and-glass structure that was more glass than wood. From every room, there was a lovely view and a sense that the outdoors had almost been brought right into the house itself.

The decor was simple, almost Spartan. Pine tables, off-white Haitian cotton sofas and chairs, and a few carefully chosen contemporary paintings on the white walls.

But as Zach strode through the house to his bedroom to change into riding clothes, his mind wasn't on the comfortable, pleasant environment of his home. It was on Leigh. And later, as he rode his chestnut gelding, Big Red, along the crest of a hill, he thought of her again.

The sun would set in another half hour and twilight would fall. He dismounted and strolled along beside his horse. There was a lavender tinge to the sky near the horizon, and the sun was momentarily hidden behind a sweep of gray stratus clouds.

As Zach watched, the last brightness of the sun lightened the perimeter of the cloud mass with a soft glow. The luminosity reminded him of Leigh and those gray eyes he'd looked into this afternoon. It was true that when he'd first walked into Gary's office, he'd noticed that brazen hair and expected blazing green eyes. Perhaps, he told himself, he'd thought *blazing* because he himself had been so angry that day over the hassle Kline was getting.

Now that he knew her better, he realized there was an incongruity about her. It wasn't just the contrast of her flamboyant hair and alabaster-white skin, or her interesting face with its high cheekbones and wide, sensuously shaped mouth. There was a sereneness about her that balanced the fire of her personality.

"There's a hell of a lot more to that lady than meets the eye," he told Big Red as he mounted. Taking one last look at the streaks of brilliance along the horizon, he turned his horse. "Come on, boy, let's go home."

For the first time in years, he felt a strange loneliness.

CHAPTER FOUR

THE FOLLOWING DAY Leigh and Zach were sitting in his office finishing a hurried lunch of sandwiches before interviewing actors for the role of the young park ranger.

"All that's left to do is hire the second-unit director," Zach said, leaning back in his chair. "The guy I had in mind is ill. We'll have to find someone else. Do you have anyone in particular in mind?"

Leigh popped the last bite of her ham on rye into her mouth and chewed thoughtfully. The second-unit director was responsible for shooting the scenes that didn't involve the actors. In the case of *Lodestar*, that would mean sweeping mountain vistas and an action sequence involving the plane crash and a subsequent rockslide. Any number of lesser directors, or even assistant directors, could handle the job. But she knew immediately who she wanted.

"Jonas Cassidy."

Zach's eyes widened in surprise. "Cassidy! You can't be serious."

"Why not? He's not just good, he's great. Especially at action sequences. At one time he was the greatest living American director."

"That time is long past. He hasn't worked in years."

"Only because he hasn't been given the chance."

"He hasn't been given the chance because he's trouble." He regarded her quizzically for a moment. "Leigh, you must have heard that."

"I've heard. But I'm not sure I believe it. Just because he had high standards..."

"High standards!" Zach exploded. "The man was a fanatic. Everything had to be done his way and no other. He was right and the rest of the world was wrong. He wouldn't compromise over the smallest detail—"

Smiling slyly, Leigh interrupted, "I know someone else who fits that description."

Zach returned her smile self-consciously. "I'm not that bad. I can be flexible when I have to be. Cassidy was a holy terror to work with."

"Only the studios had problems with him. His casts and crews always got along fine with him."

"The casts and crew didn't have to worry about cost overruns because of his insistence on having it all his way."

"All studios care about is money. Cassidy was concerned with excellence—and he got it. Every picture he made was brilliant. And," she added for emphasis, "all his pictures made money for the studios."

"Leigh, what the hell gave you this idea, anyway?"

"Cassidy's always been my idol. I grew up watching his movies. I even did my master's dissertation on them."

"He's retired," Zach said flatly.

"Out of necessity, not choice. He's only fifty-eight. I'll bet he'd come out of retirement for this."

"There are a hundred people who'd do just as well and not cause headaches."

"There's no one else who does action as well as he does. Zach, you know how important it is to get it right. If it looks phony or unconvincing, the whole picture starts off badly."

"Don't lecture me," Zach snapped.

Until that moment Leigh had seen their conversation as a spirited discussion. Now she realized they were having a full-fledged argument. She picked up the commissary tray from where they'd placed it on the floor and began to stack the sandwich plates on it. She needed a moment to think and tidying up gave her the opportunity to do so.

Picking up the carafe, she looked at Zach to see if he'd like more coffee. When he shook his head, she added the carafe and their cups, saucers and napkins to the tray. This business of Cassidy mattered more to Zach than she'd realized. But it also mattered to her. It mattered a lot.

"He's the best person for the job," she repeated, her eyes meeting Zach's without hesitation.

"He's trouble. And I can't afford trouble on my first feature. The studio won't stand for it, and neither will I."

Her expression was deceptively calm. "So that's it."

"That's it. Let's figure out someone else we can both agree on." His voice was stern without a trace of yielding.

She lowered her lashes quickly to hide her disappointment and frustration. Leaning back in her chair, she crossed one knee over the other and concentrated on keeping her hands, folded lightly in her lap, from clenching into tight fists. She stared at the tip of her shoe and concentrated on her composure. *There was no way they could work together. No way she could win against Zach Stewart.* For the first time in her career, she felt acutely the disadvantages of her gender, her small stature. And even more disturbing, she felt an odd reluctance to fight this particular man.

When she felt in control, she looked up to find him watching her. The expression in his eyes did not match the sternness of his words. Though she was baffled by his uncompromising attitude, she did not doubt that he meant what he said.

"No." The word was uttered with a quiet finality.

Concern alternated with anger on his face. "What do you mean no?"

"I mean no. That's pretty clear, isn't it?"

"Leigh, this is stupid. Of all the things to argue about, Jonas Cassidy is the most pointless."

"We're not arguing about Jonas Cassidy. We're arguing about my status on this picture. Do I have real authority or don't I?"

"Of course you do. We've been over that."

"Yes, we've been over it. But apparently you didn't mean what you said when you assured me I would run this picture."

"I meant what I said. But I also said that in the case of a disagreement where compromise wasn't possible, I would make the final decision. Ultimately I'm responsible for the success or failure of this project."

"I share a great deal of that responsibility, Zach. I gave in on the rewrite even though I didn't entirely agree with you. Well, this time you're just plain wrong. And I won't give in.''

"Do you realize what you're saying?''

She nodded silently. She realized, all right. And it terrified her. But the alternative was to feel like a figurehead director, one without real authority. That was something she couldn't accept.

"You'd walk out on this picture?''

"Yes." *And on you*, a tiny voice deep inside added.

She went on desperately, "Don't you see, if I have to fight you every step of the way, then this just won't work. It will be a miserable situation for both of us.''

A deep and sudden sense of loss swept over her.

We haven't even begun to know each other and what we might mean to each other, she thought. *There is something magical that happens between us. But we'll never have a chance to find out what it is. Or if it's real.*

She felt a wrenching disappointment. And on top of that, tremendous guilt. Under normal circumstances, walking off a job was something she wouldn't think of doing. But these weren't normal circumstances. This movie meant too much. Even this man already meant too much.

"I can't tell you how sorry I am that someone else will get to direct *Lodestar*,'' she finished, and rose on shaky legs.

He rose, too. The anger in his eyes had slowly changed to thoughtfulness. There was even a hint of amusement around his decidedly appealing mouth. "You know, Leigh, I'm not often turned down. In fact, when it's a case of offering someone a job, it's never happened before." He went on, "I'm offering you a shot at directing a major film. Any other novice director would—''

"But I'm not any other novice director," she insisted urgently. "That's just the trouble," she added in a choked voice and turned away to pick up her handbag and folder.

Zach made one last desperate effort to heal the breach. "You can name anyone else you want—anyone." As he spoke he moved to stand behind his desk.

"I want Cassidy," she insisted, spinning around to face him across the expanse of oiled teak. "I'm convinced he's the best."

"You're wrong."

"Well," Leigh said with quiet firmness. "I guess we'll never know for sure who's wrong."

She stared at him coldly. "There's only a deal memo so far. The contract's still being drawn up and hasn't been signed, so there are no legal problems. Good luck finding someone else. And thanks for lunch." She turned and walked out the door. It took every ounce of self-control she possessed not to give way to the uncontrollable desire to run. As she passed out of his office, through the outer office to the hallway, then outside, she waited for him to call her back.

But he didn't.

APPROACHING THE HOUSE, Leigh could see Connie seated in the bay window of her living room, sipping tea and reading a book. When Leigh rapped lightly on the glass, Connie looked up and motioned for her to come in.

As Leigh sat down opposite her in an old, comfortable wing chair, Connie said with cheerful malice, "This is the biggest pack of lies I've read in a long time. Sheila Summer's autobiography. Really— the woman can hardly write well enough to sign her name to a contract. And as for her version of how she got started in the business...well, fairy tales are more factual."

Leigh forced a smile. "You worked with her, didn't you?"

"I did indeed. Want some tea?"

"No, thanks." She heard her voice, tight and controlled. She shouldn't have stopped. She just should have gone up to her apartment, slammed a couple of doors, tossed his bouquet into the wastebasket and been miserable by herself.

"Hey, what's wrong? I've been so caught up in Sheila's liberties with the truth that I've been unforgiveably dense," Connie apologized, closing her book and laying it aside. "You're upset about something. You're sitting there clutching your bag and that folder as if your life depended on it. For heaven's sake, drop them on the floor, kick off your shoes and relax. I'll be right back. You do need a cup of tea."

When Connie returned with the tea, Leigh thanked her and then, briefly, trying to be as unemotional as possible, related the argument with Zach. "The bottom line is," she concluded, "he doesn't have confidence in me. At least not enough."

"Did you tell him that? In clear concise language?"

"I told him...but I don't think he heard me. Oh, he watched my lips move and his ears received the words and forwarded them on to his brain. But I really don't think he heard what I said.''

"So you walked," Connie commented flatly.

"I walked. I can't do the job unless I'm authorized to make decisions. I have to trust my own judgment. How else could the cast be comfortable with me? And I with them?" Damn him, anyway, she thought as she sipped the hot soothing tea and felt a return of energy. He's not going to destroy my confidence in my ability.

Her gray eyes met Connie's in heartfelt appeal. "I really didn't have any choice. Did I?"

"No, you didn't have any choice. There are some things you can compromise on, but I can see why you couldn't on this issue. Sometimes—and this was one of those times—you have to stick to your guns. Otherwise your soul shrivels up and there's something crucial missing from your work.''

Leigh nodded. "Yes. I reached that point. I know I'm right, but that seems scant comfort at the moment.''

Connie smiled warmly. "Well, to quote Gary Cooper, 'A man's gotta do what a man's gotta do,' and a director's gotta do what a director's gotta do.''

"Why didn't he understand?" Leigh asked forlornly. She wasn't referring to Gary Cooper, and Connie knew it.

"Because he's scared, and like most men, he doesn't want to admit it.''

"Zach Stewart didn't look scared.''

"Of course not. In his business, he can't afford to let it show. But I'll bet he was very scared.''

"Of what?"

"Of taking a risk that might be bad for his picture. And of giving in to someone who's not only beneath him in the pecking order, but is a woman to boot."

"That's ridiculous!" Leigh fumed, suddenly furious. "If he felt that way, why did he hire me in the first place?"

"Because he knows you're good."

"Then why should the fact that I'm a woman matter?"

Connie grinned. "It will always matter, one way or another. And that's not entirely bad."

"We're talking about a business situation here, not anything personal."

"Oh?" There was a world of disbelief in that one innocent word.

"Strictly business," Leigh insisted defensively.

"Then why are you so hurt?"

"I'm not hurt. I'm angry at his behavior, and I'm disappointed that I won't be directing *Lodestar*, after all."

"Oh, Leigh, if there's one thing I've learned in a long and occasionally misspent life, it's to be honest about what I'm feeling. I don't hand out advice very often because most people aren't smart enough to take it. But I'm advising you to be honest with yourself. You're not just angry that Stewart wouldn't give you the authority you should have. You're hurt that he refused to consider your feelings."

Leigh didn't respond. There was no point, since Connie was absolutely right.

Connie went on, "The man's a fool, of course. I'm surprised. He didn't look like a fool."

"I'm the fool, Connie, for ever accepting the job in the first place."

"Now, don't talk nonsense. You had to take that job. If you didn't, you would never find out what you could accomplish."

"But I knew going into this that there would be conflicts."

"Tell me one relationship, especially where a man and a woman are concerned, where there aren't conflicts?"

Setting her empty cup and saucer on the coffee table, Leigh picked up her handbag and the folder. She hadn't gone back to her office or she'd have left it there. Now it seemed stuck to her like flypaper. She sighed and stood up.

"So...what do I do now, Dear Abby?"

"Stick to your guns. And hope that I was right about Zach Stewart not being a fool."

ZACH WATCHED THE SUN SET over the ocean. Malibu sunsets often were spectacular, and this was one of the better ones. Lavender and mauve were streaked carelessly across a burnt-orange sky. The ocean was slate-gray and still. It was a lovely, quiet evening, touched with the special serenity of the Malibu countryside, where houses were few and far between and the silver-green leaves of the giant eucalyptus stirred softly in the evening breeze.

But there was nothing serene about Zach's feelings. They were as turbulent as they got, and that was pretty turbulent. As he leaned against the stone wall surrounding his flagstone patio, he murmured, "The little fool."

She was absolutely wrong. Jonas Cassidy might have been a brilliant director—actually, Zach admitted reluctantly, he was quite brilliant. But he was known at least as well for his stubborn wrangling with studios. Zach had experienced enough disagreements with Ralph Hastings. He didn't want any more on this project.

Why couldn't Leigh see that? Why did she have to choose this particular thing to be stubborn about?

He took another sip of the deep red burgundy wine. For once, the wine wasn't doing a thing to calm him. Irritably he set the wine aside and stared out at the ocean. That, too, wasn't having its usual calming effect. He'd moved to the hills of Malibu because he didn't want to live amid the pressure of the city. This small ranch on a plateau overlooking the ocean was private and quiet. In a way, it was reminiscent of the much larger ranch he'd grown up on in the San Joaquin Valley, two hundred miles north of L.A.

But this evening the peace of his hideaway was spoiled by thoughts of one very headstrong young woman who refused to see reason.

It was easy for her to say there was nothing legally binding them, that he could hire someone else. Who else? He wanted Leigh, not some other director.

He was convinced she would see reason. She'd walked off in a huff but when she had time to think things over, surely she'd come back.

As the evening progressed, he waited for the phone to ring. It did several times, but not one of the people who called was Leigh. Finally he had to shower and change. There was a studio party celebrating a new release and, much as he hated to leave his phone, he felt obliged to attend.

Later, carrying his drink, Zach made his way around the crush of celebrities, near-celebrities and hangers-on. As he threaded his way through the crowd, offering his congratulations and exchanging pleasantries with friends, he found it difficult to concentrate on being cordial. He felt distracted and totally out of sync.

He was tired, he told himself. This had been some day. In fact, it had been some week. Then, once more, Leigh came to mind.

She's a damn fool, Zach thought for the tenth time since she'd walked out of his office. Too stubborn and inexperienced to realize what she was throwing away.

He took another swallow from his glass and told himself that Leigh Adams was an overconfident, idealistic young woman who had a lot to learn about doing business in the cutthroat film industry. If he'd insisted on having everything his own way, he'd never have gotten where he was.

And yet…she was good. Very good. There was a lyrical quality to her film that was almost like poetry in motion. And the performance she got from her actors—those kinds of performances didn't come easily.

Her passion for her work was unusual. It matched the sun-bronzed red of her hair and gave a glow to her wide-set gray eyes. He'd seen that inner fire in her smile…It promised something special.

Today, though, her gray eyes hadn't held any warmth when she told him to find another director. They'd cooled, then darkened like a stormy sea at twilight. But they had never turned hard. He remembered, too, how her full lower lip had trembled slightly, though she had tried to hide it.

All at once he caught himself. Was he going soft in the head? She had walked out on him. And if she didn't think over that foolish act and call him before he had to call Gary, the project was going to be in big trouble.

When he returned home Zach checked his answering machine for messages. Angry at the absence of the one he'd hoped for, he ignored the rest and went to bed.

Sleep didn't come easily. He kept thinking of Leigh, that irritating young woman who'd had the effrontery to turn him down, not once but twice. Try as he might, he couldn't dismiss her, though. The more he thought about the situation, the more he knew that she was the perfect person to direct *Lodestar*.

And, he admitted as he lay in the dark, she intrigued him. Very much.

Usually he got along smoothly with women. But this petite, soft-spoken, gray-eyed redhead who'd helped a little kid fly a kite one day, then challenged a superstar a couple of days later, confounded him.

Kevin said she had chutzpah. Well, Zach thought, Kevin might be right, but she also had integrity. Rare in any business, but especially rare in theirs.

It was a long time before he finally dropped off into a restless sleep, only to wake at first light. He got up, dressed for a dawn run and took the trail that led back into the hills.

The canyon was beautiful in the early-morning light, with the sun's rays brightening the mountaintops and the dewy freshness of the short grass, still May green. Usually he enjoyed this quiet beginning of the day, but not this morning. By the time he returned home, tired and sweaty, he'd faced the obvious—Leigh had no intention of backing down.

There was just one question—what was he going to do?

LEIGH WAS DEEP IN A DREAM about a strangely disturbing man who bore a remarkable resemblance to Zach, when a sound pierced her subconscious. Knocking. Persistent knocking. Moaning softly, she pulled the white down comforter over her head to stifle the sound. But it persisted. It was muffled, but it wasn't going away.

Opening one eye, Leigh stared sleepily at her alarm clock. Seven o'clock. She'd had a hard time getting to sleep the night before, tossing and turning until well past one o'clock. Six hours of fitful sleep weren't nearly enough.

Annoyed, she wondered who it could be, anyway. None of her friends would come by so early. And Connie wasn't an early riser.

Well, whoever it was wasn't going away, she realized. Thoroughly bad-tempered now, she flung off the covers, rose and pulled on a gray velvet robe. As she pattered barefoot to the door, she brushed her tangled hair out of her face.

Looking through the tall, narrow window next to the door, she saw Zach standing there. He wore a blue sweat suit and had an inscrutable expression on his face.

At the sight of him, in spite of the hour, Leigh instantly came fully awake. With unsteady fingers, she unbolted the door, opened it and stood staring at him, waiting for him to be the first to speak.

"You're not going to change your mind, are you?"

It wasn't really a question. Leigh merely shook her head.

"I was halfway up a mountain today when it occurred to me that maybe it was my turn to back down. If you want Cassidy, then that's it. You're the director."

Leigh felt a rush of intense emotion that was a great deal more than mere relief—or even victory. It was joy. Pure and simple joy. Her heart skyrocketed as she looked up into his face. He meant it! She could see it in those brilliant blue eyes.

Impulsively she threw her arms around him.

"Thank you for understanding."

Her words were muffled in his chest, and she wasn't sure he'd heard them. Suddenly she was only aware that he smelled and looked and felt very male. Very exciting.

She felt an immediate sexual response to him that completely caught her off guard. Startled, she pulled back.

But he wrapped his arms around her and, lifting her off her feet, spun her around and around. When he set her down and they stepped free of each other, he walked over to a small bookshelf and took out a Bible. Smiling at her, he held the book in his left hand.

"We've got to get this show on the road. So put your hand here and repeat after me."

Leigh added her hand to the Bible.

"Deal?"

"Deal," she echoed, laughing as gladness welled up within her.

They stood for a moment, staring deep into each other's eyes. The intense sexual awareness she'd felt a moment earlier returned, and she saw it reflected in his eyes. Somehow their casual state—his sweat suit clinging damply in places to hard muscles, her disheveled hair and loosely belted robe—only made the moment more erotic.

No, she told herself, stepping back to put distance between them.

He clearly sensed her retreat. Taking a deep breath, he slowly expelled it as he marshaled his own suddenly rebellious feelings.

"Well, the least I can do after getting you up so early is take you out to breakfast."

"Okay." Her voice was a little shakier than she would have liked, but at least now she was beginning to regain some of her composure. "I'll dress quickly."

As she turned to head back to her bedroom, he stopped her. "I'm sorry, Leigh."

She turned to look at him. "So am I. From now on I'll try to work things out instead of walking out."

"And I'll try to consider your point of view. I promise."

She accepted the smile and the hand he offered, but she couldn't resist a mischievous shot. "Do we need the Bible again to make that binding?"

CHAPTER FIVE

THURSDAY MORNING, as soon as she got to her office, Leigh called Jonas Cassidy's agent and told him she was eager to speak with his client. It was late afternoon before the agent called to say he'd finally located the elusive Jonas, but he hadn't been able to get in touch with him.

"Why not? Where is he?" she asked.

"Florida. His landlady said he probably wouldn't be in until evening, but I'll keep trying."

"Thanks," Leigh said. "If you'll give me the number, I'd like to call him myself." There wasn't a lot of time for a series of I'll-get-back-to-you calls. Besides, she'd wanted to be the one to ask him to be her second-unit director.

She stayed late at her desk, rereading the script and planning scenes. Every so often, she called the Florida number. Finally, at eight California time, Leigh dialed once again and Cassidy picked up the phone.

At first he asked if she was some smart-alecky kid being funny. When she convinced him who she was and what she wanted, he yelped with joy.

As soon as they terminated their conversation, she called Zach at his home.

"I finally reached Cassidy."

"And?" Zach asked.

"He said he'd be in my office tomorrow at four—on the dot."

"Four...? I'd have thought he'd be there by eight, nine, at the latest."

Leigh heard the implied criticism, but was determined not to react. "I told him four would be fine." Then she added, "I hope you can arrange to be free at four. I'm anxious that the three of us get together."

"I'll arrange it." His tone wasn't chilly, but neither was it warm. "I'm as anxious as you are about this meeting."

"I'm excited-anxious, Zach, not nervous-anxious." She spoke more sharply than she'd intended. But she was determined that Jonas Cassidy should no longer be the subject of any dispute. Forcing herself to speak more gently, she said she'd been here at her office long enough and was going to call it a day. "Night, Zach. I'll see you tomorrow," she said, and started to replace the phone in its cradle.

"Leigh..."

She heard him call her name and lifted the phone once more to her ear.

"Yes?"

"I didn't mean to bark. I am looking forward to meeting your hero." He hesitated a moment, then suggested she call the security guard to escort her to her car.

Her first impulse was to tell him she was neither a child nor an idiot who needed looking after. Then she realized his concern was thoughtful—rare in the marketplace these days. "I will," she promised.

Touched by his consideration, she relented and explained that the reason for the four o'clock meeting was the fact that Cassidy was in Florida and wasn't sure how early a flight he could catch.

"I'll probably be sorry I asked, but what's he doing in Florida? Just taking it easy?"

"No, he's working with an old friend, a retired naval captain who manufactures one-man minisubmarines. He tests their safety. Doesn't that sound interesting?"

"Well, it's not what I would have expected."

Then softly and hurriedly, she finished, "Thanks again, Zach. I can't tell you how excited I am about working wth Cassidy."

There was just the slightest pause, then in a deep and unexpectedly gentle voice, he responded, "You're welcome."

On Friday, Zach was waiting with her when Jonas Cassidy walked into Leigh's office promptly at four o'clock. He was wearing a navy watch cap and held an empty pipe clenched between his teeth. As soon as he stepped inside the door, he doffed his cap and stuffed it into his hip pocket. Removing the pipe, he dropped it into the breast pocket of his denim jacket. As he offered his hand to Leigh, he spoke in a slightly raspy voice. "Ms Adams, I can't tell you how happy I am to make your acquaintance."

"And I yours, Mr. Cassidy."

Looking at him, Leigh thought that none of the photographs she'd ever seen of him had done him justice. His smile was wide, his teeth strikingly white in a deeply tanned face. He wore his gray hair in a crew cut. His hands were big and, like his jaw, square. While she noticed the age lines around his mouth and dark eyes, he looked incredibly fit and energetic.

"This is Zach Stewart, our producer," she continued.

After the two men shook hands, they all sat down.

As Leigh briefly outlined the history of the production, filling Cassidy in on the cast, the crew and shooting schedule, she was acutely aware of Zach's presence. Though this meeting was being held in her office—with this man who was her choice—the fact remained that this was to be a Zach Stewart Production.

Cassidy asked a few pertinent questions and nodded at her answers. A couple of times, Leigh asked Zach if he wanted to add anything to what she'd said. Both times he just shook his head.

At the conclusion of the meeting, Zach stood and offered his hand to Cassidy, who rose to accept the handshake. "We'll get a deal memo to your agent." Then with a polite nod to Leigh, Zach said he needed to get back to his office.

When he was gone, Leigh pushed away from her desk and got slowly to her feet. "May I call you Jonas?"

"Of course. I've never cared much for formality."

"You haven't asked me why I hired you."

"Well, I'd be a liar if I said I wasn't curious. My stock's not too high in this town right now."

Leigh explained slowly, "When I was still in high school, a famous film director spoke at a special assembly for career orientation. He told us dreams are like stars...they seem abstract because we can't touch them. But like sailors who used the stars to navigate the vastness of the ocean, we can use our dreams to chart our course to our particular destiny.''

"We can see our dreams with our hearts,'' Jonas responded slowly, finishing the thought. "Yes...I remember that speech.''

"Do you remember what else you said? That our dreams—our visions—should be our stars.''

She walked from behind her desk to face Jonas. "You did that, didn't you? Dreamed dreams and charted your course by your visions.''

"Yeah,'' he said. Retrieving his pipe, he cupped the bowl in his big square hand and rubbed its glossy blackness with his thumb. "I did that. Sometimes I was called a visionary. And sometimes a pioneer.''

Leigh could see he was weighing his words very carefully. Clamping the stem of his pipe between his teeth, he rocked slowly back and forth on his heels. She could see the muscles in his jaw working. After a moment, he removed the pipe and studied it as if he'd never seen it before.

Then, considering her with an almost critical squint, he cautioned, "You gotta be very careful in this business. I hope I can still be called a visionary. But, Leigh, I'm no longer a pioneer. I came across that territory a long time ago...and the damn Indians almost scalped me. This picture with you is my second chance. I'm gonna be smart this time. If you dream big dreams...sometimes, kid, you have to settle for a little less.''

He smiled broadly and added, "Cut yourself some slack. As a director, you're gonna have to walk a tightrope between your dreams and the hard realities of this business.'' Holding out his hand, he said,

"I'm awfully glad you wanted me for this picture. I'll give it my best shot."

"I can't ask for more than that," Leigh said, placing her hand in his. As they walked to the door, she smiled and asked if he'd had time to collect his belongings and make an orderly departure from Florida.

"Wasn't much to collect," he replied. "I travel light these days." With a shrug, he added philosophically, "Our business is rough on relationships."

Then, telling her he'd see her Monday, he walked away.

She watched as he pulled his cap from his hip pocket and adjusted it to a jaunty angle atop that archaic crew cut.

Closing the door, Leigh leaned against it and smiled. She liked Jonas Cassidy. "Kid," he'd called her, and hadn't even been aware of having done so. She'd bet a nickel she'd hear that again because, as he'd said, he certainly wasn't one to stand on formalities.

Interesting that Zach hadn't said a word during the meeting. He'd been so opposed to Jonas that she'd expected him to have quite a lot to say. She hoped this meeting had assuaged some of his concerns.

Then, remembering the look in his eyes as he'd left her office, she thought of Jonas's caution. The real tightrope she'd have to navigate would be her growing feelings for Zach Stewart and her fierce desire to be a director.

THE NEXT TWO WEEKS passed in a blur of constant activity—meetings, auditions, more meetings. Leigh went to bed late and rose early. And loved every hectic minute of every jam-packed day. After years of study and hard work, after the hardship of trying to put together a good movie on a meager budget, she was finally where she'd longed to be. She had all the resources she needed to bring her artistic vision to life. *Lodestar* had an ample budget and a compelling story. This was the opportunity she'd waited for—the chance to show the world what she could do.

Whenever she felt a twinge of self-doubt, she beat it down quickly. This was no time to start wondering if she was really up to the job she'd wanted for so long. Fortunately, there were no more conflicts to shake her confidence. Things were going smoothly and everyone was working together as a team.

She said as much to Zach one evening when they went out for Chinese food after working particularly late. "I keep waiting for someone to blow up. Or make some monumental mistake. But it hasn't happened."

Grinning at her in that special way that affected her more than she cared to admit, he said, "We've had all the screw-ups, including mine, that the company can afford. It's time for everybody to get their act together and keep it that way." Then he went on, "I knew you and I would work well together."

"It didn't look like we would a couple of weeks ago."

"A couple of weeks ago we were finding our way. We've found it now. We're a good team, Leigh."

He was right, she knew. Once they'd gotten past the initial skirmishes about power and responsibility, they'd settled in remarkably quickly. She was no longer worried that working with him would be one battle after another.

Which was a tremendous relief. The movie would turn out much better if the director and producer could work together smoothly.

Then he went on, "By the way, I spoke to my mother today and she reminded me I promised to get home this weekend. There's a fund raiser for Uncle Ross at the ranch Saturday night. I assured her I'd be there and told her I hoped to bring you, too. She said she'd love to have you."

Uncle Ross. Quickly Leigh put it together. State Senator Ross Stewart, one of California's most powerful and charismatic politicians. Zachary *Ross* Stewart...why he was part of Stewart Enterprises. Land, money, political clout!

Leigh couldn't help her response—she burst out laughing. "So you're one of those Stewarts," she managed to say, looking up at him. "Oh, my. And I remember asking, that first evening we had dinner, what drove you."

"Your exact words were 'Do you lust after power, Zach?'" His eyes were filled with laughter.

"As I recall, you didn't give me an answer."

"As I recall," he said, disarming her with a conspiratorial smile, "we had more important matters to discuss. Well, will you come with me? We can fly up late tomorrow afternoon, then Sunday I'd like to fly on up to Yosemite to look over the location sites from the air."

Impatient for her reply, he urged. "Come on, Leigh, unless you have other plans for this weekend, say yes. Let's not get into another Mexican standoff.''

This man, Leigh thought, had the most amazing way of getting past her defenses. He'd yielded on what was to him a very critical issue—Jonas. How could she refuse him now? Anyway, she really didn't want to.

Nervously she ran her fingers through her hair and repeated, ''Mexican standoff!'' Then with a shrug, asked, ''Well what can I say to that?''

Leaning forward, he answered with a smile, ''You can say, 'Why thank you, Zach, I'd be delighted.' ''

Again, the enormous attraction of this man made her feel incredibly alive. Ignoring her earlier concerns about walking a tightrope, she smiled at him. ''Why thank you, Zach. I'd be delighted.''

As arranged, Leigh arrived at the Santa Monica airport at three the next afternoon. Following Zach's directions, she turned in to the lot adjacent to where the private planes were parked. She saw Zach standing on the tarmac, watching for her car. Returning his wave, she proceeded, looking for an empty space.

Parking in the space beside his mint-condition 1966 Porsche, she reached in the back seat of her VW and pulled out her totebag. Then she locked her car and hurried to where Zach stood beside a sleek white aircraft.

''Hi,'' she said, walking around the plane. ''Well, I see this isn't just an ordinary puddlejumper. Nice— very nice.'' She stood on tiptoe to peer inside, so Zach opened the door for her to see the interior.

"Color coordinated, yet. Love that rich brown interior."

He grinned as he reached to take her bag. "Yeah, I think so too. It's a Cessna. Cruises about 140. Gets me where I want to go."

Then surveying her with some amusement, he changed the subject. "You're all dressed up." He was teasing, but a bold appreciation showed in her eyes.

Leigh wore a linen suit of pale green. Her silk shirt was also green but a slightly more intense shade. She knew what this color did for her hair and eyes. Today she wanted to be as pretty as possible. "Well, I did throw in a pair of jeans and a sweater for tomorrow."

Glancing down at her high-heeled sling-back pumps, he said, "And something to walk in, I hope. Although what you're wearing does a lot for your—" he caught himself and finished "—outfit."

As he took the totebag from her, he raised an eyebrow quizzically. "That's all you're bringing?"

"You said we'll only be gone overnight."

"I always thought women needed to take a lot of things in case they change their mind about what to wear."

"That's a myth, and anyway, I rarely change my mind."

"So I've noticed."

His face was perfectly straight, but Leigh caught a twinkle in those blue eyes. She smiled briefly in response.

It struck her how marvelous he looked in light tan slacks and a short-sleeved white shirt. She noticed he had a tan blazer folded over his arm, but didn't appear to have any luggage. He either kept clothes at the ranch or had stored them already.

Zach tossed the bag onto one of the back seats and helped her inside, next to the pilot's seat. Leigh wasn't entirely surprised when he sat in the pilot's seat. Zach explained, "My parents' ranching operation covers about ten thousand acres. And the acres aren't all in the same place. They always had a light plane to get around in."

"Beats a horse, I suppose," Leigh quipped.

Zach grinned. "Sure does. Anyway, I took flying lessons as soon as I was old enough. I loved it. If I hadn't gone into this business, I think I'd have been a professional pilot."

"Not a rancher?"

"No, not a rancher. I like my beef served rare on a platter, not on the hoof."

Handing her a headset, he explained that if she liked she could listen to music. It wouldn't interfere with his communication to the tower. Or, he added, she could just use them to talk with him through the intercom system. She put them on, but declined his offer of music.

As Zach put on the earphones and began talking to the control tower, Leigh buckled her seat belt and leaned back. It was nice to feel comfortable with Zach. After the terrible strain of their disagreement over Jonas, Leigh had feared they would never get along. But all that was behind them now, she told herself. When she felt a twinge of doubt, she repeated silently, *all over.* Whatever problems came up during the shooting, they would work them out somehow without either walking out on the other.

They flew north over the barren brown Santa Monica Mountains, then the taller, even more barren Tehachapis, and finally reached the San Joaquin Valley. Broad and flat, surrounded by the foothills of the massive Sierra Nevada range on the east and the coast range on the west, it looked like a patchwork quilt. Fields, orchards and pastureland were blocked out in squares and rectangles of varying colors. They valley was huge, stretching to the north as far as Leigh could see.

"It's the richest agricultural area in the world," Zach commented, descending slowly to a lower elevation.

"I know." Amused, Leigh smiled at him. "Even though I grew up in the San Fernando Valley, I'm very much aware of this one." Then she asked, "How long have your people been here?"

"My grandfather Stewart was one of those who came to the valley in the thirties. It took hard men to survive the hard times, but survive he did. Not only that, he built a small empire. Cattle first, on the eastern side of the valley, up in the foothills alongside the river. That's where the ranch headquarters are. Later he expanded into farming cotton on the west side of the county."

He went on to say that while his Uncle Ross left the ranch to go into a legal career, his father loved everything about ranching—and so did his mother. They met at U.C. Davis. "Dad always said it was sheer luck that he fell in love with a woman majoring in business."

"What's your mother say?"

He grinned. "She says luck had nothing to do with it. She knew all about the Stewart ranch.... What better way to get a good job than to marry the boss's son?''

"Ah, a neat role reversal. I think I'm going to like your mother. Do you have brothers and sisters?''

"Got one of each. They're both married, have children and are part of Stewart Enterprises.''

"What does your family think of your choice of career?''

"My father always told us, 'You can do anything, be anything you wish if you're willing to pay the price. Just always do your very best.'''

Zach was silent a moment, then he continued, "From my father, I learned how to work. I never wanted to be anything but a film producer. But I've worked at every job in the business, I think, except wardrobe mistress. And I always gave my best effort. And I expect the same from everyone who works for me.''

"I see.''

She did, indeed, see. This was a man who had a great deal to live up to. No wonder the success or failure of *Lodestar* meant so very much to him.

"What about your family, Leigh?''

"They're not like yours. No empire. No overwhelming drive to succeed. Just two very nice people who were thoroughly happy with each other and what life gave them.''

"That sounds quite nice, actually.''

"It was. I had the most normal, middle-class upbringing you can imagine. The only unusual note was Luke.''

"Your grandfather, the magician.''

Leigh's expression softened as she remembered her grandfather. "Yes, the magician. He was very, very special. He inspired me to dream of more than being queen of the prom.''

''I suspect your parents weren't entirely approving.''

Leigh grinned wryly. ''No. They loved me and wanted me to be safe. There's nothing safe about a movie career. When I talk to them, my father always asks me if I'm working. And my mother always asks if I'm dating anyone special.''

Zach grimaced. ''I get the same questions, if it's any consolation.'' Then, looking out the window, he went on, ''We're here.''

Below, Leigh saw the private airstrip at the Stewart Ranch. When they landed, they met a ranch hand waiting in a four-wheel drive that turned out to be surprisingly luxurious.

''I can see I'll have to revise my assumptions about ranch life,'' Leigh teased.

''My grandfather used to say we were all getting soft. Of course, he was out riding around the place by himself, sleeping on the ground with nothing but a bedroll when he was in his eighties.''

The ranch hand, a wizened little man with coarse gray hair and skin like leather, piped up from the front, ''Mr. Stewart was one of a kind, all right. Tough as they come. Drought, flood and the depression couldn't lick him.''

Zach smiled warmly at the man. ''He was tough, all right. He could be a real pain in the neck, though. Expected a lot from people. How did you stand working for him so long, Nate?''

Nate shrugged. ''Wasn't hard. Just did what he said an' stayed out of his way when he was mad.''

''What did he get mad at?'' Leigh asked curiously.

Nate grinned laconically. "Aw, nothin' much—just rain. And drought. And wind. And cold. And heat. Failed crops, and crops that were so plentiful he couldn't sell 'em all. People who crossed him, and people who didn't have the guts to stand up to him."

"Is that all?" Leigh asked wryly.

"That about covers it," Zach responded. "He was definitely a man of strong feelings."

Leigh couldn't tell if he'd cared for his grandfather. One thing for sure—it gave her an entirely new light on Zach Stewart, film producer.

They turned off the narrow, paved road that had led from the airstrip onto a two-lane drive leading up to the house. The setting and the house itself were magnificent. Built on a very slight rise a few hundred yards from a slowly moving river, it was surrounded by massive oak trees and a green lawn that covered several acres. The rolling foothills in the distance were dotted with grazing cattle fattening on sweet meadow grasses.

The two-story house was white with a red tile roof and a broad veranda running along the front. It certainly wasn't Leigh's idea of a ranch house. The headquarters of Stewart Ranch was a picturesque setting of wealth and power.

They stopped in front of the double oak doors. Zach took their bags out of the car, then Nate drove off.

"He's an interesting character," Leigh commented.

"He's a character, all right. Been here forever. No one's sure exactly how old he is, and he won't say. I think he's afraid we'll make him retire."

At that moment, the front doors opened and Zach's parents came out to greet them.

The father he admired so deeply threw his arms about Zach in a bear hug. "Glad to see you, son." Then he stepped aside and Zach leaned down so his mother could kiss him, before he enfolded her in a fierce hug.

"Dad...mom, I'd like you to meet Leigh Adams. She's the lady I've been telling you about."

His mother stepped out of Zach's embrace to offer her hand to Leigh. "We're so glad to meet you and just delighted that you could come." Her greeting was warm and sincere.

"That goes for me, too," Zach's father said, taking her hand in his and leading her inside. "Come on in. We've just got time for a short one before you have to get ready for tonight's shindig."

As she followed her hosts, already dressed for tonight's party, Leigh could see where Zach got his blond good looks and his charm. On the flight up, she'd learned where he got his confidence. The senior Stewart was, like Zach, tall, lean and strong looking. His white dinner jacket was impeccably tailored and he wore it with ease.

Mrs. Stewart was also fair, although now her hair was a mixture of blond and silver. She wore it in a casual cut that Leigh recognized as classic, as was her simple yet elegant gown. It was from her that Zach had inherited those astonishing blue eyes. Hers were now intensified by the sapphire blue of her dress. She was tall and slim and moved with confident grace. Not your average little ranch wife, Leigh thought with humor.

The house was furnished with a great deal of both taste and money. Yet it was comfortable and homey rather than pretentious looking. After giving Leigh's bag to a maid to take upstairs, Zach's mother led the way into the den, while Zach and his father followed, discussing the ranch.

After everyone had been given a glass of white wine, they sat down and spent a short time getting acquainted. They asked how the movie was progressing and talked a bit about how Ross's campaign was shaping up. This evening's fund raiser would give him additional momentum.

"This family is very supportive," Zach's mother explained. "The entire clan gathers at the drop of a hat." With a smile, she added, "I like it that we do. But enough of us. I'm sure you're anxious to freshen up. I'll show you to your room."

She showed Leigh upstairs to a guest bedroom that overlooked the grounds behind the house.

"I think this is one of the most pleasant rooms in the house," she said. "It has such a nice view of the river. At night, you can hear it moving slowly past, and the sound is quite relaxing."

"Thank you, Mrs. Stewart."

"Call me Caroline. We don't stand on ceremony much around here. See you at the festivities."

When she had gone, Leigh examined her dress the maid had unpacked for her. She was relieved to see it hadn't wrinkled during the trip.

When she was dressed and ready to go downstairs, she walked to the window and looked down at the party preparation. Obviously a large crowd was expected. Leigh estimated there must be fifty round tables set under the spreading oaks. Each table was set with colorful china, crystal and silver. White paper lanterns were strung throughout the grove of beautiful old trees. A portable dance floor had been laid, and as she watched, a dance band was setting up.

Glancing back to the river, she could see swans gliding gracefully up and down. Across the river, the foothills, heavily dotted with oak, rose higher and higher.

It was a gorgeous place to live. No wonder Zach spoke affectionately of his home. It was solid and secure.

They came from different worlds, she thought, giving thanks, as she often did, for Luke. He'd taught her to value her talents and strive to make the most of them. Her parents, she reflected as she stood looking out on that scene of affluence, had been content to settle for much less.

They chose to be comfortable rather than to risk. They were good people, but never in a million years would they understand what drove her. Even if she told them it was wonderment of life itself and one's potential to embrace it, they wouldn't understand her any more than they had understood Luke.

As she turned away from the window, she thought Luke and Zach's grandfather had something in common. She sensed she and Zach did, also.

Picking up a small silver clutch bag, Leigh opened the door. Zach stood at the head of the stairs, leaning casually against the banister, waiting for her. Like his father, he was dressed in a white dinner jacket and looked devastatingly handsome.

"Am I late?"

"No," he said in a low and incredibly intimate voice, his boldly approving gaze adding so much more to his words. "What you are is...beautiful."

Her dress, a glistening silver silk jersey, was deceptively simple and demure. Cut high in front, it had tight-fitting elbow-length sleeves. The handkerchief hem stopped at midcalf. It was the back that made the dress stunning and downright sexy—it was slashed to the waist.

The striking color made her gray eyes look more intense than usual. She'd bought it in a fit of extravagance when she'd been hired to direct *Intimacies*, but until tonight, she hadn't had an occasion to wear it. With it went sling-back silver heels and dangling silver earrings.

"Beautiful," Zach repeated as he held out his hand.

Feeling so, and happier than she'd been in a very long time, Leigh put her hand in his and they walked out to the patio.

Leigh was surprised to see the crowd that had arrived in the time she'd been upstairs. She'd heard planes flying in, but she was unprepared for the number of cars parked on both sides of the long drive and even along the road leading to the airstrip.

As she sat down at a beautifully decorated table, she mused aloud, "I wonder what we'll have."

Zach laughed. "Beef," he whispered, leaning close to her ear. "At this house—count on it."

He was right; the main course was medallions of beef with béarnaise sauce. The superbly catered dinner began with an orange consommé and ended with a heavenly rum trifle. Fine California wines complemented each course.

The evening passed in a whirl. She met Zach's close-knit family and found them attractive, fun people. The senator was charming and obviously much admired by his supporters.

She met so many people that she gave up trying to remember anyone's name. She danced with Zach's brother and brother-in-law and his uncle. When she danced with John Stewart, and she complimented him on his home and family, he was charmingly modest. "My father started it all. He deserves the credit," he said, then added, "He sure gave us Stewarts a mark to aim at."

Leigh wanted to say something to the effect that at least one of his sons took that mark seriously. But instead she smiled at him and as the number concluded, commented on the music.

"That reminds me..." He led her over to the band leader and requested a particular song. Then he led her back to their table.

John Stewart held out his hand to his wife as the band leader announced their host had requested the next number.

Dancing with Zach a moment later to "Sweet Caroline," Leigh watched his parents' obvious pleasure in dancing with each other. Seeing him interact with his family made it clear where his determination came from. It was rooted deep in Stewart Enterprises. Not just the land and power, but also in the values his family represented. And obviously respected.

On the flip side, she could understand, too, why he was determined not to fail. Why he needed to succeed.

Held in his arms as they glided about the floor, she found herself wondering what had caused his marriage to fail. Whatever it was had certainly made an impact. According to his bio, he had been divorced for several years. Had the unaccustomed failure left a bitter aftertaste he couldn't quite swallow? Somehow Leigh couldn't imagine the family-oriented Stewarts taking a divorce in stride.

But her wandering thoughts were quickly replaced by a vivid awareness of what a marvelous dancer Zach was. He was much taller than she was, but he was a strong leader and she followed him easily.

"Enjoying yourself?" he asked.

"Immensely. Thank you for bringing me."

"My pleasure. This is the best evening I've spent in a long time."

When the song had ended, they were left at the edge of the dance floor. It was darker there because the lantern overhead had lost its light.

Leigh sensed he was looking down at her, but she did not dare to look up into his face.

He's so close, she thought. *Too close*.

But she couldn't deny she liked dancing with him, liked being held in his embrace.

Taking a small breath, she stepped back and risked a glance at his face. Even in that dimly lit corner, his eyes were intensely blue.

Trying to diffuse the suddenly highly charged atmosphere between them, she made small talk. "Tonight," she began, "not only is the music divine, but the quality of my partners has been superb. I feel a bit like Cinderella."

"Why should you feel like Cinderella? You're Leigh Adams, film director. You'll never sit on a hearth, waiting for things to happen."

As the band's female vocalist began to sing a torch version of "The Man I Love," Zach pulled her into his arms and they began dancing again. He drew Leigh closer and leaned his face toward hers. "Don't you have everything you want?" His voice had dropped to a husky whisper.

"Does anyone?" Her voice sounded too soft and tremulous. And because she was affected by the moonlight and this attractive man, she asked, "Do you?"

With his hand spread against her back, she felt the touch of his fingers on her bare skin. Releasing her hand, he cupped her chin and forced her to look up at him. "Not yet, but I'm closer than I've been in a long time."

Leigh scarcely breathed. They were just a moment away from a kiss and suddenly she wanted nothing more. It wasn't only a response to the moonlight and the suggestive music. From the moment she'd first met him in Gary's office, and felt the chemistry between them, she'd wanted to know his kiss.

Just then, another couple came twirling across the floor and collided with them.

"Oh, terribly sorry," the man said as they untangled themselves.

"Please forgive us," the woman called as the music ended and they walked away.

All at once, Leigh realized she'd let herself get out of hand. She'd gone too far—and it was too soon.

Before she could suggest they return to the table, the last dance was announced.

Zach led her back into the center of the floor and held out his arms as the band began its theme song...''All the Way.'' Unable to stop herself, she burst out laughing, and after a moment, Zach laughed with her.

When the party was over and everyone had said goodbye, Zach asked if she'd like to stroll down to the river before turning in. The last of the lanterns had been extinguished, and only a pale moon lit the oak grove and the river.

They strolled hand in hand, not talking, just listening to the gentle lapping of the water against the banks. Then Leigh said, ''It's lovely here, Zach.''

He didn't say anything but she felt the slightest increase of pressure in his fingers. Their silence was companionable as they walked along. She wanted to extend this beautiful evening, but she knew that wouldn't be wise.

''Well, I'd better get back,'' she began.

He stopped her with a look. And suddenly the silence between them wasn't companionable. They stood facing each other, bathed in moonlight, pulled inexorably toward each other.

It would have been so easy to step into his arms, to lift her face to his, to taste the kiss she'd yearned for. But something deep within her held back. A warning signal flashed. And though she couldn't quite identify the danger, she knew it was there.

''*Leigh*.'' His voice flowed over her, enveloping her in an invisible cloak of warmth and sweet seduction.

"I think I hear the clock striking twelve," she said nervously. "I need to go in now or I'll turn into a pumpkin."

He let his gaze travel over her face, her hair, then focus on her eyes. The message in his own eyes was perfectly clear. "You're running away."

"I'm not running away!" she snapped. She was angry at herself for her deep ambivalence and angry at him for causing it. "We have to get up early in the morning to fly over the locations..."

"Forget the locations. Forget the movie. It's just you and me, Leigh. And right now, nothing else matters a damn."

That was the danger, she realized. That in giving way to what she felt for him, she would lose herself—and lose what she'd worked so hard for. She couldn't let herself fall in love with him. Not now, not when she was so close to achieving what had always been the most important thing in her life.

It would mean dividing herself just when she most needed to focus all her energies on one difficult job. And it would mean making herself vulnerable in a way she'd never been before. That scared her more than all the fears of failure she'd ever endured.

"This movie is all that matters right now," she insisted desperately. "It has to. Can't you understand?"

He looked at her intently, and for a moment she was afraid he wouldn't respect her feelings. If he simply pulled her into his arms, she knew she wouldn't resist. But she would be lost, and that thought terrified her.

Her fear shone in her luminous eyes, in the quiver of her full lower lip.

Taking a deep, ragged breath, Zach pulled himself together.

"All right. But you can't run forever, Leigh. Sometime you'll have to stop. And when you do..."

He didn't finish the thought. He didn't have to.

With a violently mingled sense of relief and disappointment, Leigh turned back toward the house. Zach walked beside her. After a minute, he slipped his arm lightly about her shoulders. Smiling down at her, he said, "I'm sure glad that you're directing *Lodestar* rather than Cinderella. It's the coach that turns into a pumpkin. She merely loses her shoe."

And her heart, Leigh added silently.

THEY LEFT AFTER LUNCH on Sunday.

"How far is Yosemite from here?" Leigh asked as the Cessna lifted off the runway.

"About twenty minutes."

He didn't speak again, and neither did she. She'd made a point of avoiding him all morning, as much as possible. Though she felt more than a little awkward now, sitting next to him in the close confines of the plane, she was relieved that he wasn't picking up where they'd left off the night before.

They flew over the foothills for just a few minutes, then they were flying over the mountains.

"In *Lodestar*, this is the flight path Joe and Mary Beth followed," Zach commented.

Leigh thought about the story line of the movie. The couple had quarreled and Joe offered to fly Mary Beth to Reno for a divorce. They crashed en route. Leigh thought about an opening shot while the titles rolled. Preferably it should go far toward explaining what had happened between them immediately before.

Then they were over Yosemite Valley and she marveled as she looked down on the granite peaks and domes, waterfalls, streams and lakes, meadows, forests of pine, fir and hemlock.

Down there, she knew were three groves of the giant sequoia redwoods. Yosemite was part of her growing-up years. Her parents had enjoyed camping here, and they'd come several summers.

"You mentioned once you've been here before," Zach said.

"Yes. A friend and I backpacked for a week in that high country down there. Set up a base camp at Tuolumne Meadows."

Zach glanced over at her. Clearly he was startled by her words. "How long ago was that?"

"Two years. You sound surprised. Why?"

He shrugged and, after a long silence, said, "I guess I was surprised. I'm not sure why. You keep throwing me curves—catching me off guard."

Precisely what you do to me, she wanted to respond, but didn't.

Looking back over her shoulder as Zach headed south again, she said, "There's Tenaya Lake and Tioga Pass. Whenever I drive that road over the crest of the Sierras, I feel like I'm right on the rim of the world." As she settled comfortably in her seat again, she finished with, "I love everything about this high country. That's one of the reasons I wanted so much to direct your picture. This place means a lot to me. I...well, I guess I respond to it in some elemental way."

When she glanced over at him, he was looking at her with such a strangely gentle expression that Leigh felt her heart lurch as if they'd hit an air pocket and dropped several thousand feet.

When, after a moment Zach asked if she'd seen enough, she nodded.

Neither spoke again until they crossed the foothills of the San Joaquin Valley. Then Zach said, "When you get a closer look at the locations we've selected, I think you'll be happy with them." He shot her a meaningful look. "But if not—"

"I'm sure they'll be fine," she interrupted.

"Don't feel like you have to accept something you're not satisfied with."

"Do you really think I would?"

He smiled. "No. I should have known better than to even suggest such a thing. You and Ralph Hastings are opposites in that regard."

"Which is why you fired him and hired me."

Leigh laughed and expected Zach to as well. But he didn't.

Instead he glanced at her with that same strangely gentle look she had seen in his eyes just before.

After a moment he said with a touch of humor, "Whenever I start to think you're being just a wee bit difficult, I'll remind myself of that."

And I'll remind myself how important it is to keep my head on straight, Leigh thought soberly. *I can't fall in love with a strong-willed man and handle* Lodestar *at the same time.*

The next six weeks in beautiful Yosemite were going to be difficult in more ways than one.

CHAPTER SIX

THE FOLLOWING WEEK, Leigh sat in the back seat of a station wagon, driven by a card-carrying member of the teamsters' union, heading toward Yosemite. In less than an hour, *Lodestar*'s company would be on location.

Filming on location required a regular convoy. Many big trucks were required to haul the generators, the crane that raised and lowered the camera, the props, wardrobe and the "honey wagons" (portable bathrooms). The Winnebagos that would be the actors' dressing rooms had been delivered, and the complete convoy had left yesterday late in the afternoon so they could travel in the park at night.

The movie crew and cast had all driven up from L.A., starting out at dawn, in a logistical exercise the U.S. Army would have been proud of. All this came under the watchful eye of Arnie Archuleta, the production manager.

Arnie, Jonas Cassidy and John Kline, the art director, were making the trip with Leigh. Leigh had enjoyed the trip with these men who were all much more experienced than she was in the art of movie making. They'd been good company, sharing stories of other on-location filming.

Just then they rounded a curve and drove into the Wawona tunnel. Blasting through solid granite, the tunnel was almost a mile long. When they came out of it, Yosemite lay before them.

"Let's stop for a minute," Leigh told the driver. A moment later, they were standing on the edge of the lookout area. Patches of blue sky could be seen through the clouds that dominated the mountains, obscuring the view. Suddenly the clouds parted, and the midday sun illuminated the great rock forms. The cliffs, peaks or domes, from three thousand to five thousand feet high, rose from the forested valley floor.

Talk about magic, Leigh told herself. Even the names of the mountains conjured up enchantment: El Capitan, Half Dome, Clouds' Rest. She could see Bridalveil Fall, which fell six hundred twenty feet. It was nourished by a lush hanging valley and got its name because the wind-tossed water, resembling a bridal veil, seemed to dissolve in a shifting mist. She'd spent many happy moments watching the afternoon rainbow climb the column of Bridalveil Fall.

But they couldn't stand there forever admiring the magnificent view. They had a major motion picture to make. With a sigh, Leigh turned back to the car.

It was past noon when they finally pulled into the parking lot of the ruggedly beautiful six-floor Ahwahnee Hotel. This was where the seventy people working on the movie would stay for the six weeks they were scheduled to shoot it.

Gazing at the fifty-eight-year-old hotel, Leigh thought that it almost looked as if it had been there forever. But she knew that its tenure was transitory compared to the aeons amassed by its neighbors, Half Dome and Glacier Point.

Since Zach was busy handling some last-minute details in L.A. and wouldn't be up until that night, Leigh took care of checking everyone in. Kevin and Catalina, as befit their status as stars of the film, had the finest suite in the hotel. Everyone else had a room that was large or small, private or shared, depending on his or her position.

Because this was the busiest time of year in Yosemite, not everyone could be accommodated in the hotel, the manager explained apologetically.

"I hope you won't mind being in a cottage," he went on. "They're quite close by on the hotel grounds and very nice."

"That sounds fine," Leigh responded politely. Actually she was glad it had worked out that way. Now she would have at least a minimal degree of privacy and solitude. As the shooting progressed and tension and pressure mounted, both privacy and solitude would be hard to come by.

The manager explained that, according to Zach's request, they had reserved a small banquet room for the company to use as a screening room. The tables had been taken out and more chairs brought in to accommodate the various people who would want to view the dailies—each day's film footage.

Leigh arranged with the manager to use the bulletin board in the lobby to post information updating each day's shooting schedule. This would keep the company informed as to where everyone was supposed to be and at what time.

In addition, there was a daily call sheet. Everyone, from actors to grips, from camera operators to gaffers, would have to consult it each night. It was a plan of the next day's shooting schedule, listing

A | FIRST CLASS OPPORTUNITY FOR YOU

♦ **Grand Prize** – Rolls-Royce ™
  (or $100,000)
♦ **Second Prize** – A trip for two to Paris
  via The Concorde
♦ **Third Prize** – A Luxurious Mink Coat

The Romance can last forever… when you take advantage of this no cost special introductory offer.

4 "HARLEQUIN SUPERROMANCES®" – FREE!

Take four of the world's greatest love stories – FREE from Harlequin Reader Service®! Each of these novels is your free passport to bright new worlds of love, passion and foreign adventure!

But wait… there's *even more* to this great *free offer*…

HARLEQUIN TOTE BAG – FREE!
Carry away your favourite romances in your elegant canvas Tote Bag. With a snap-top and double handles, your Tote Bag is valued at $6.99 – *but it's yours free with this offer!*

SPECIAL EXTRAS – FREE!
You'll get our free monthly newsletter, packed with news on your favourite writers, upcoming books, and more. Four times a year, you'll receive our members' magazine, Harlequin Romance Digest®!

MONEY-SAVING HOME DELIVERY!
Join Harlequin Reader Service® and enjoy the convenience of previewing four new books every month, delivered right to your home. *Great savings* plus *total convenience* add up to a sweetheart of a deal for you.

BONUS MYSTERY GIFT!
P.S. For a limited time only you will be eligible to receive a *mystery gift free!*

TO EXPERIENCE A WORLD OF ROMANCE.

How to Enter Sweepstakes & How to get 4 FREE BOOKS, A FREE TOTE BAG and A BONUS MYSTERY GIFT.

1. Check ONLY ONE OPTION BELOW.
2. Detach Official Entry Form and affix proper postage.
3. Mail Sweepstakes Entry Form before the deadline date in the rules.

H·A·R·L·E·Q·U·I·N
FIRST·CLASS
Sweepstakes

OFFICIAL ENTRY FORM

Check one:

☐ Yes. Enter me in the Harlequin First Class Sweepstakes and send me 4 FREE HARLEQUIN SUPER-ROMANCE® novels plus a FREE Tote Bag and a BONUS Mystery Gift. Then send me 4 brand new HARLEQUIN SUPERROMANCE® novels every month as they come off the presses. Bill me at the low price of $2.50 each (a savings of $0.25 off the retail price). There are no shipping, handling or other hidden charges. I understand that the 4 Free Books, Tote Bag and Mystery Gift are mine to keep with no obligation to buy.

☐ No. I don't want to receive the Four Free HARLEQUIN SUPERROMANCE® novels, a Free Tote Bag and a Bonus Gift. However, I do wish to enter the sweepstakes. Please notify me if I win.

See back of book for official rules and regulations.
Detach, affix postage and mail Official Entry Form today!

134–CIS–KAVR

FIRST NAME_____ LAST NAME_____
(Please Print)

ADDRESS_____ APT._____

CITY_____

PROV./STATE_____ POSTAL CODE/ZIP_____

"Subscription Offer limited to one per household and not valid to current Harlequin Superromance® subscribers. Prices subject to change."

ENTER THE H·A·R·L·E·Q·U·I·N
FIRST·CLASS *Sweepstakes*

Detach, Affix Postage and Mail Today!

Harlequin First Class Sweepstakes
P.O. Box 52010
Phoenix, AZ 85072-9987

which scenes were to be shot and who was supposed to be in them.

When all the details were taken care of, Leigh went to her cabin, escorted by the manager himself. He was a very self-possessed middle-aged man who mentioned with studied casualness that he had played host to everyone from Queen Elizabeth of England to the president of the United States. In a subtle way, he made it clear he wasn't about to be awed by a mere movie company. But beneath his urbane exterior, Leigh sensed there beat the heart of an avid movie fan. He made a point of saying what an admirer he was of Kevin's movies. Before long, she thought with amusement, he would be asking Kevin for an autograph. Monarchs and presidents came and went, but bona fide movie stars transcended time itself.

"Now this is your cottage, Miss Adams," he said, unlocking the door and motioning her inside. It had a sitting room and a bedroom and bath and was utterly charming, especially with its stone fireplace. Leigh immediately felt she would be comfortable there.

"Mr. Stewart is in the cottage next door, as he requested," the manager went on. "If you need anything, please don't hesitate to let me know. We pride ourselves on our service. Good afternoon."

When he was gone, Leigh continued standing just inside the sitting room, looking extremely thoughtful. So Zach had requested that they have neighboring lodgings. What, if anything, did that mean?

She shook her head irritably, as if trying to physically clear her mind of disturbing thoughts. She was being foolish, she told herself. After all, she was the director of *Lodestar*, Zach was the producer. They would be working very closely together during the shooting. There would be meetings nearly every night, often lasting quite late. There would be a hundred things each would have to consult the other about. Obviously for convenience sake, it would be a good idea for them to be in close proximity.

As she had done many times before, she told herself that her relationship with Zach was professional and must remain so, that they both had a great deal at stake on this project.

But now, for the first time, she felt a conflict between being a woman and being a director. The director in her wanted to focus all her energies on this film, to make it good—better than good, excellent, a piece of perfect craft and exquisite passion. But the woman in her thought of Zach—his hands—large, masculine, yet infinitely tender. His mind—an exciting mix of stubbornness and flexibility.

The woman in her wanted to explore this man, to let him explore her. The director in her knew that for the duration of this project the only appropriate outlet for her emotions, especially her passion, was on the screen.

Remember that, Leigh told herself firmly. *Keep your mind on business. Forget that dance at his parents' ranch. Forget that kiss that almost happened.*

A tiny voice inside answered sarcastically *Sure. Easier said than done.*

Determined to ignore it, Leigh strode into the bedroom where her bags had been deposited by a bellboy earlier, and began unpacking.

She placed her marked-up copy of the script on the table next to the bed, then called room service to order a large pot of coffee and a tray of sandwiches and fruit. There would have to be a meeting as soon as possible of the key members of the crew, and the meeting was likely to last well into the afternoon.

Leigh called the production manager and asked him to notify those key people that she was waiting for them. Over the next several minutes, they arrived, one by one. When the small sitting room was filled by the production manager, art director, wardrobe mistress, cinematographer and others, Leigh began the speech she'd silently rehearsed to herself on the drive up from L.A.

"I'm looking forward to working with all of you. This is a special project, one I'm sure we're all going to be proud to be a part of."

As she went on, she sensed the reserve on the part of many of the people present. Most of them, perhaps all of them, had never worked with a woman director before. Some appeared to be merely curious about her, but others were distinctly cool. She'd suspected from the start she would have to prove herself to these people. The slightly wary atmosphere in this room now only proved that.

When one or two people questioned her decisions, she tried not to take it personally, but to answer matter-of-factly. If she was at all emotional, she knew, many of these people, especially the men, would consider it a fault. Directors came in many guises, but all the good ones had one thing in common—they were definitely in charge and didn't allow their authority to be questioned.

Nevertheless, it was hard not to make some biting retort when the stunt coordinator suggested that she might not fully appreciate the danger of one of the scheduled stunts.

Forcing herself to pause long enough to get her temper under control, she asked, "Are you suggesting that only a male director understands danger?"

The man hesitated, then answered with a noticeable lack of sincerity, "No, of course not."

"Good. Because obviously facts would prove you wrong. I know of a good many male directors who've mishandled stunts. People got hurt, even killed. While it's true there are just a handful of women directors, not one has had a problem with stunts."

There was a tense silence in the room. Feeling that she'd made her point, Leigh went on to another subject.

Toward the end of the meeting, Jonas came in. Leigh had left a message for him to stop by about five o'clock, and as with their first meeting he was right on time. She couldn't help smiling at his punctuality. If Zach had expected the worst of him, so far he was proving Zach wrong.

Jonas stood unobtrusively in a corner while Leigh finished the last of her business with the key crew members.

"I guess that's all for now," she said wrapping up. "See you all first thing tomorrow."

They went out, talking among themselves. When they were gone, Leigh leaned back in the comfortable, overstuffed chair in which she'd conducted the meeting and sighed heavily.

Crossing the room, Jonas sat in a matching chair opposite her and smiled. "Well, you faced 'em down. So far, I'd say it's woman director one, crew zero."

Startled by his perception, she asked worriedly, "Was it so obvious how nervous I was?"

He shook his head. "Nope. You were as cool as the proverbial cucumber. I just know what you're going through because I've been through it so often myself. Every time out, you have to prove yourself to the company. Make it clear you're in charge and you know what to do."

"I think most of them were just waiting for me to slip up and reveal that I'm really incompetent."

"Probably. Just remember—they can kill you but they'd have no place to hide the body."

Leigh burst out laughing. Suddenly all the tremendous tension she'd felt throughout the long meeting dissolved. "Thanks," she said softly.

Jonas shrugged. "It's okay."

Eyeing him thoughtfully, she asked, "Have you been expecting me to slip up?"

"No. I saw your movie. It was damn good. You can handle this job."

It was an understated compliment, but it warmed Leigh considerably. She sensed that it was the highest accolade Jonas Cassidy could give.

"So you're not prejudiced against women directors?" she asked with a wry smile.

"Nope. I'll tell you something I don't talk about much. My first movie was a clinker. It just plain didn't work. It wasn't a bad story and the actors were terrific. But somehow I couldn't bring it all together. The first time I looked at all the film together in the rough cut, I knew my career as a director had started and ended right then and there."

"But your first movie was *Men at Arms,* wasn't it? And that was a classic. Not to mention a big hit."

"Sure. But only because of a woman editor who fixed my mistakes and somehow made something out of nothing. In the process she taught me more about how to make a movie than anyone else I've ever met in this business. Connie Cabot's her name."

Leigh's face shone with excitement. "Of course! I remember she told me about that once. But she didn't think you did such a bad job."

"You know Connie?"

Leigh nodded. "I sure do. She's my landlady—my friend, really."

"I'll tell you something. That woman could have been one of the best directors Hollywood's ever seen. But she was a woman. And in the thirties and forties, that meant she didn't have a chance. It's different for you, young lady."

"Yes. In some ways." After a moment's hesitation, Leigh went on, "Can I ask you something very frankly, Jonas?"

"I'd prefer that to beating around the bush. Fire away."

"You've been making movies since before I was born. Do you resent the fact that I'm in charge here and not you?"

He hesitated, clearly marshaling his thoughts. When he finally responded, he chose his words carefully. "The fact is, Leigh, when you called recently, my career was over. Not because I'm not still one hell of a director. But because I couldn't—or wouldn't—get along with the right people. My agent continued to represent me because he has something you don't run into very often in Hollywood—loyalty. But try as he might, he hasn't been able to get me a job in three years.''

Jonas leaned forward, clasping his hands together between his knees. His eyes bored into Leigh's. ''I know it wasn't Zach Stewart that wanted me for this job. And certainly not the studio.'' He waved aside her quick protest. ''You went to bat for me. Which showed a lot of guts for someone who doesn't have any clout yet. You're giving me a second chance. I appreciate it more than I can say. And I won't let you down.''

''I know you won't.'' She was more touched than she could say by the blunt sincerity of Jonas's gruff words.

But as she struggled to find the right words to express her gratitude to him, he went on in a more businesslike tone, ''Well, enough of this maudlin stuff. We've got a movie to make. You wanted to talk to me about the second unit. I've got them ready to start first thing in the morning.''

''Good. I can't wait to see what you do with that plane crash scene. No one handles action better than you.''

He smiled, pleased. ''You know something? You're right.''

They both laughed.

Then as Jonas rose to leave, he asked, ''Any last-minute orders?''

''No.'' She cocked her head and gave him a frank look. ''Any last-minute bits of advice?''

He squared his shoulders and answered firmly. ''Watch out for Kevin. He's the one you're likely to have problems with.''

''Because he's the star?''

"Yeah. But more than that, he's a man without a great deal of self-confidence."

"Kevin?"

"Oh, I know he's one of the biggest stars around and he acts like he's God's gift to the movies. But I worked with him once, a while back. And I learned something important. All that confidence is a facade."

"Why?"

Jonas shrugged. "Who knows? I decided a long time ago that most actors are just scared kids at heart. Kevin's all right, as actors go. But like I said, he's pretty insecure."

"It's hard to believe."

"Yeah. But I know for a fact it's true. You have to decide how you want to handle him. I'm just suggesting you tread easy, that's all."

"Thanks for the advice, Jonas."

"It's all right. I'll check in tomorrow evening to let you know how things are going with the second unit."

"Okay."

As he started to walk out the door, Leigh put her hand gently on his arm and stopped him. "Jonas— I'm glad we're working together."

He grinned. "Me too, kid."

Then he turned and strode jauntily away.

For the remainder of the evening, Leigh was too busy to order supper, let alone go to the hotel dining room. Instead she munched on the remaining sandwiches and fruit.

At ten o'clock she changed into a burgundy silk nightgown and matching velvet robe. The set had been an extravagant present from Connie.

After glancing over her notes regarding the first scene to be shot in the morning, Leigh went into the bathroom and washed off her makeup. She was about to take off the robe, when she was surprised by a knock at her door. She wasn't expecting anyone else tonight and had no idea who this could be. Her immediate thought was that something had gone wrong already, before they'd even started shooting. Tension made her queasy as she opened her door.

To her complete surprise, she saw Catalina standing there.

"Hi. I saw your light still on and decided to stop by for a minute. Everything's moved so fast we haven't really had a chance to talk, to get to know each other. I hope I'm not intruding."

"No, of course not. Come in."

Catalina wore jeans, a gorgeous white angora sweater and, surprisingly, well-worn hiking boots. She explained unnecessarily, "I was out walking. I try to do it every day. It clears the cobwebs, y'know."

As they sat down in the twin chairs where Leigh and Jonas had sat talking earlier, Leigh responded, "I understand. I like to run. It's going to be hard to work into the shooting schedule, but I'm going to try."

"Good for you. Kevin told me a little about what to expect. For six weeks we'll all eat, sleep and drink *Lodestar.* It'll take over our lives. Then one night there'll be a wrap party and the next day we'll go our separate ways. For the actors, at least, and most of the crew, it'll be history. Finis." Her mouth curved with impudent humor. "A strange way to make a living."

"Yes, it is that. A short, intense experience. We become like family for a while, but when it's over most of us will never see one another again."

Catalina nodded in agreement. "That's why it's so important to have a permanent family to provide a sense of continuity. That's why I married Kevin. And why I want to have children." She looked at Leigh. "What about you? I know you're single but were you ever married?"

"No. I didn't want to get married unless I was very sure it would last. Divorce just isn't something I want to go through."

"I know what you mean," Catalina responded with feeling. Then, with a frankness that caught Leigh off guard, she went on. "I know what a lot of people have said about my marriage. Most of them say it was a fluke that I persuaded Kevin to settle down. It can't possibly last. But you know what? They don't really know Kevin. And they sure don't know me. I intend to live happily ever after with that man."

Catalina's voice was as silky soft as usual. But Leigh detected a barely discernible undertone of determination. Catalina might be thoroughly feminine and breathtakingly beautiful, but that didn't necessarily mean she was a marshmallow. Although Leigh had heard rumors of this kind, she had always doubted them. Now she felt a new respect for her.

Catalina continued, "My parents have been happily married for thirty years. I intend to follow their example. I've seen most of my friends go through divorce and remarriage. It seems to me they were no better off the second time around, more often than not."

Leigh smiled softly. "I know. Sometimes it all seems like a childish game." She weighed her next words carefully. "But the reality is that this business is hard on marriage."

"I know. But my mother taught me that determination is ninety percent of anything. I'm determined to make my marriage last. And I'm determined to make a success of my acting career. I won't let the two be mutually exclusive, because I need both."

That was a statement Leigh had no intention of responding to. Instead she said, "I'm going to do all I can to focus on your role in this movie. I think you can do a lot with it. People are really going to be surprised."

Catalina's lovely face was suffused with pleasure. "Thank you. But I'm not the only one who's going to be a surprise. I meant what I said the other day about *Intimacies* being so great."

As always when she was complimented, Leigh felt an odd shyness steal over her. She was never quite sure how to handle it.

"It's really a kick, isn't it?" Catalina said. "The first major film for both of us."

Leigh grinned. "It is a kick, all right. When I'm not caught up in the million and one details and swamped by the pressure of coming in on time and under budget, the fact is I feel that making movies is the most fun imaginable."

Catalina rose and stretched tiredly. "Well, I'd better let you get to sleep or you'll be so tired tomorrow you won't find it much fun. And if I don't get enough sleep, the makeup girl will have to spend hours erasing the bags under my eyes."

As she went out the door, she called back breezily, "Night, Leigh."

"Good night, Catalina."

Closing the door, Leigh turned and headed toward the bedroom. Kevin Marlowe, she thought with amusement, had better hang on to his hat.

She had slipped off her robe and was turning down the bedspread, when she heard another knock at her door. It must be Catalina again, she thought, wondering what Catalina had come back for.

Not bothering to put on her robe, she went to the door and opened it.

Zach stood there.

For a moment Leigh felt nothing but pleasurable surprise. Then, as his eyes flicked rapidly from her face down to her bare toes, then up again, she remembered she was barely dressed.

"Oh! I...I wasn't expecting you. I thought you were Catalina." Realizing that she was babbling, she pulled herself together and said, "Come in. If you'll excuse me, I'll just slip on my robe."

With as much dignity as she could muster, she forced herself to walk, not run, into the bedroom. When she came out a moment later wearing her robe, Zach still stood near the door. And his mouth was still slightly curved in an amused smile.

He explained, "I just got in. I won't keep you, but I thought I'd better check in and make sure everything went okay when you arrived."

"Yes, of course." Her voice was less than composed. *Damn!* Leigh thought, thoroughly irritated with herself. She sounded like a flustered virgin caught in a state of dishabille.

Clearing her throat nervously, she said, "I met with everyone, including Jonas. Everything's all set for tomorrow."

"No problems?"

"No problems."

"Oh, by the way, we definitely signed Maurice Rincon to do the score."

Rincon was a famous French composer who'd scored many top films over the past twenty years. Zach had told her early on that they hoped to get him but weren't sure if he was available. For a few minutes she and Zach stood there discussing the type of score they hoped Rincon would create.

Then as Leigh tried unsuccessfully to suppress a yawn, Zach finished, "Well, I'd better go." Turning, he opened the door behind him. "I'll meet you on the set about midmorning. If you need me before then, I'm just in the cabin next door."

"Yes, I know." Somehow the words seemed to convey a meaning Leigh hadn't intended. Refusing to meet Zach's eyes, she glanced outside through the open door as if there were something utterly fascinating about the pitch blackness.

"Well, good night, Leigh."

"Good night."

She breathed an inward sigh of relief and told herself she hadn't made such a fool of herself, after all.

Then, just as she was about to close the door, Zack called back over his shoulder, "That's one hell of a sexy nightgown."

In a moment, he had disappeared into the darkness.

CHAPTER SEVEN

EARLY THE NEXT MORNING, Leigh was on location. She marveled that they'd been allowed to use this particular place. When Zach had said their location site was back of Mirror Lake, at the edge of Tenaya Canyon, she couldn't believe their good fortune.

She knew Mirror Lake well. Leigh remembered coming here at sunrise with her parents and Luke to see the mountains reflected in the crystal-clear surface of Mirror Lake. She knew that shiny rock surfaces were common in Tenaya Canyon. Luke had taught her about them the summer she was ten when her family camped there together.

Recalling that happy summer, Leigh looked about her and felt her throat too full to swallow. She was moved almost to tears remembering that she had last been here with Luke.

Here, she thought, *almost in this same place where we're going to film* Lodestar.

Now as she looked about—at the trees and the terrain—she could see how right it was for this movie.

Thank you, dear Luke, she said silently. *Just when I need to remember your magic, you come back. Today I start making mine.*

The caterers already had the breakfast fires burning in the big truck. Leigh had been too keyed up to eat at the hotel. Now she realized that two cups of coffee probably weren't enough to keep her going until lunch. She ordered scrambled eggs and toast, ate quickly, then joined the director of photography, otherwise known as the cinematographer, and his assistants where they were setting up for the first shot.

Brady Delinski, the cinematographer, was a slight man with sparse gray hair, pale hazel eyes narrowed in a permanent squint and a perpetual worried crease in his forehead. Though he'd been hired by Ralph Hastings, Leigh approved heartily of the choice. Brady had made nearly a hundred movies, some of them less than masterpieces, but every one well photographed.

Brady and his assistants would be the first people on the set each day, making sure they had enough film and checking to see that the cameras were working properly. There were three altogether, though most of the time only one would be used.

The cinematographer was second only to the director in importance on a film. If he didn't do his job well, the all-important mood and atmosphere of a scene, or even an entire movie, could be ruined. Leigh was very glad she had a professional the caliber of Brady working with her.

"Morning," she said as she walked up to him.

He nodded. From the beginning, he'd been very reserved with her. Though he didn't say anything, Leigh sensed strongly that he was one of the many people on this crew who would have to be convinced of her ability. The only way to do that was simply to get to work and show them that she knew what she was doing.

She glanced at the set. "Everything looks ready. Liz tells me she has the crash set up pretty well."

Liz Bramley, the young first assistant director whom Leigh had personally chosen, walked up just then. A petite blonde with a clipboard held tightly against her chest, she had ambitions of becoming a director herself one day.

Now she and Leigh walked over to inspect the mock-up of a wrecked plane. The first scene they would shoot would involve Kevin and Catalina, injured but alive, dragging themselves out of the wreckage.

The wreck was almost frighteningly realistic looking. Remembering her recent flight with Zach in his light plane, Leigh felt a shiver of trepidation. She knew she would remember this scene every time she flew in the future.

"This is great, Liz. Very realistic."

Liz's pale face flushed with pleasure. "Thanks. John Kline and I went to the FAA and looked at some of their photos of crashes to get an accurate idea of how this should look. The art department did the actual setup."

Leigh smiled. "Good work. I'm impressed."

Just then Kevin and Catalina, who had been in the hands of the makeup, wardrobe and hairstylist people for the past hour and a half, walked up. For this scene, both had their faces smudged, their clothes slightly torn and raw gashes painted over Kevin's forehead and Catalina's arm.

"So much for glamour," Catalina quipped.

"It could be worse," Kevin responded. "I spent one of my earlier, less memorable films in nothing but a loincloth. And the temperature never got above fifty the whole time we were shooting.''

Catalina shot him a sly glance. ''I'll bet you did more for that loincloth than Johnny Weismuller.''

''Maybe. But the ape in that movie had all the good lines.''

They all laughed, and Leigh felt herself relax. *It's going to be all right,* she thought. So far, everything looked great. No problems. If it could just stay that way for forty-five days, *Lodestar* might turn out very well indeed.

''Okay,'' she said to Kevin and Catalina, ''let's block out the scene.''

With Brady watching carefully to see where he should train the camera, Leigh rehearsed the scene, showing Kevin and Catalina where their marks were. Marks were literally lines on the ground made with tape, showing the actors where to move. Without them, an actor might move out of frame without even knowing it.

When Kevin and Catalina knew what to do, they left the set. Then their doubles took their places, standing patiently while the final lighting was set.

''We're lit to the marks,'' Brady announced to Leigh, who'd stood off to one side, watching carefully.

''Okay. Liz, get Kevin and Catalina.''

Five minutes later, the two stars had returned, been powdered down a final time and had assumed their positions inside the cockpit.

''Now, Catalina, I want you to be slumped forward. Kevin, you're leaning against the door of the plane.''

They arranged themselves as she described, and she went on, "Catalina, you come to first. You're dazed. For a minute you don't know where you are or what's happened. Then you realize you've got to get out of the plane before the engine explodes. You get up and drag Kevin, who's still unconscious, outside. Got it?"

Catalina nodded but Kevin was frowning. "Wouldn't it look better if I drag her out, instead of the other way around? After all, it's more appropriate for the man to save the woman."

Leigh had to stop herself from responding that this was not just another in Kevin's long line of macho-hero, beautiful-but-helpless heroine action-adventure pictures. Such an observation would only alienate Kevin immediately. This was the very first scene and already they were having a disagreement. How she handled it would affect the rest of the picture.

"You're right that the audience might expect that of you because you've always played the larger-than-life hero. But, Kevin..."

She hesitated, searching for just the right words. Out of the corner of her eye, she caught Catalina waiting, holding her breath. She might be just a bride still, but she already knew her husband's overweening ego. Clearly she was concerned how Leigh would deal with it.

Leigh went on, "But that's the special thing about *Lodestar*. In a lot of ways, expectations will be turned upside down. You won't play the same character you've always played. You'll show the vulnerability you're capable of, but have never been allowed to use. People will be really touched."

Kevin looked less resistant. "You have a point. I guess it's about time I tried something different. But are you sure I'll come off in a positive light?"

Leigh knew that what he was really asking for was reassurance that his masculinity wouldn't suffer. She smiled warmly. "As a woman, I guarantee that nothing is more appealing than a strong man who is temporarily vulnerable. I'll bet Catalina will agree."

Catalina nodded enthusiastically. "I do, indeed."

Kevin smiled at his wife. "Okay."

Leigh breathed a sigh of relief. "Great. Let's do it."

She looked around quickly to make sure they were all set. The shiny boards were set up to reflect light on Kevin and Catalina, and the cinematographer had taken his meter readings and distance measurements. Nodding approval, Leigh turned and climbed the crane with Brady, while the camera operator and the focus puller stood by. Then, when she was seated, she said, "Okay, let's make a little magic."

The camera operator said, "Rolling."

"Quiet everybody!" Liz shouted.

The sound engineer, stationed a few yards away behind a computerized console, checked his dials and said, "Speed." The second assistant director walked forward and smacked the clapboards together to give a sound-track cue.

"Action!" Leigh called authoritatively.

As she watched Kevin and Catalina with a critical eye, she felt a rush of adrenaline. *Lodestar* had begun.

By midmorning Leigh had said, "That's a wrap," and they had completed the first scene. It had only required four takes.

The second scene involved Kevin coming to enough to mumble, "Duffel bag. Get duffel bag."

Catalina had to run back to the plane and plow through a jumble of luggage, searching for it. All the time she was weeping, almost hysterical. Catalina had improvised in this scene and Leigh was impressed by her obvious skill and natural acting ability.

Complimenting Catalina on her improvisation, Leigh told her she was certain she got several takes she could use. Already it was becoming apparent that Catalina had a lot of ideas that would add to her character.

"Well, I tell you for sure, if I found myself in that predicament," Catalina said, acknowledging the compliment, "I'd improvise, too. It just seemed right—once I got caught up in the scene."

As they took a break for lunch, someone quipped that the studio would be relieved to know that so far they were on schedule.

Later, while they were waiting to get set up for the third scene, Zach walked up. Like everyone else, he was casually dressed in jeans, and he had on a light blue shirt with the sleeves rolled up and cowboy boots. He looked much more like a ranch hand than the stereotypical film producer. Leigh could picture him dressed just this way, riding around his family's ranch.

"How's it going?" he asked. There was no trace of concern in his expression, yet Leigh knew it was there.

She smiled confidently. "A page down. Two to go."

Zach nodded approvingly. Shooting progress was measured by pages of script. If they could shoot an average of three pages a day, they would come in on schedule.

"It's incredible, you know," he responded thoughtfully. "In television movies, we shoot as much as a dozen pages a day. This pace is a luxury."

"Don't talk to me about luxury," Leigh responded wryly, taking off her felt hat and wiping her sweaty brow with a handkerchief. "The temperature may not be all that high, but my tension thermometer readings must be in the high eighties and climbing."

Her white T-shirt was plastered wetly between her shoulder blades.

Zach's blue eyes seemed to take in every inch of her small body in one long, lingering gaze...the outline of her breasts through the thin cotton T-shirt, her small, round derriere under snug-fitting, faded jeans.

His eyes narrowed and his look became even more provocative. Not one more word was said. They were surrounded by the organized chaos of a movie set—dozens of people bustling around, talking, shouting, laughing, working. Yet it was almost as if there were an invisible force field around the two of them, separating them from everyone else, from the entire rest of the world.

As their eyes locked, Leigh fell under the spell of his erotic message. Moments earlier she had complained about heat—now goose bumps chased across her skin.

At the same moment, she felt a sharp stab of fear. All morning she'd been in charge, confident, able to stand up to anyone, including her insecure, temperamental star. Now one look from Zach left her shaken to her very toes. It confused and angered her—and it excited her.

She opened her mouth to say something, but no words came. Closing her mouth she turned on her heel and strode away, forcing herself not to look back.

For several minutes, she concentrated on setting up the next scene. When she finally dared to turn around, Zach was gone.

Leigh breathed a sigh of relief—and disappointment.

IN HIS COTTAGE, Zach stood under the stinging spray of the shower. Leigh Adams, he thought, visualizing her as she'd looked this morning. A pint-size package of dynamite. She'd looked so small in that cluster of technicians around the camera, but when she'd called "Action!" "Cut!" and "That's a wrap!" there could be no doubt that she was in charge.

Zach turned off the water and began toweling himself dry.

As he dressed, he reflected on how Leigh had looked today in her working clothes. He'd noticed her hiking boots. They were well broken in. She'd spent a lot of time in those. The hat, probably her hiking hat, showed a lot of wear, too. Today she'd looked as beautiful in jeans and a T-shirt as she had in that silver dress she'd worn at his parents' party.

He wished now he'd gone ahead and kissed her that night, in spite of the touching vulnerability that had shown in her eyes. He needed to kiss her. To hold her in his arms...so he'd quit thinking about it so much.

From their first meeting, something had been building between them. She knew it, too. But she was afraid of it. He wasn't sure if she was simply afraid to get involved with him because of their positions on the movie, or if she was afraid to get involved with anyone, period. He wondered if she'd been hurt. Or worse, disenchanted.

You can heal from being hurt, he thought, but once you discover enchantment is only an illusion—well, it was a bit like trying to believe in the tooth fairy once you knew where the quarter really came from.

He hadn't intended to get involved with her. All along he'd been aware of his attraction to her, but had told himself it was something that would have to wait. *Lodestar* was the first priority. Suddenly his priorities were shot to hell. He hadn't felt such intense desire in a long time.

It wasn't just the normal, natural drive that motivated his relationships with other women after his divorce. It was something more profound, more immediate. After that walk by the river, when he'd come so close to kissing her, he knew she was well aware of his feelings.

And he was just as aware of hers. She wanted him every bit as much as he wanted her. Compared to the fierce attraction between them, the fact that he was the producer and she the director on a film that meant everything to both of them just didn't matter.

THEY WORKED UNTIL SIX O'CLOCK EXACTLY, the official quitting time. Leigh made sure they didn't go over. She didn't want to run up the budget on the first day with expensive overtime for the crew.

"Good thing we got everything done today that we were s'posed to," Brady said laconically. "The second unit's due here first thing in the morning to shoot the explosion of the wreck, isn't it?"

Leigh nodded. Her gray eyes met Brady's hazel ones. "There was nothing to worry about. I had no intention of going over schedule today and causing problems tomorrow."

For a moment he simply stood there. Then a touch of humor showed in his slight smile. "Well, you've started out all right, I guess."

As a compliment, it was hardly effusive. Yet it warmed Leigh tremendously. In his own understated way, Brady was granting her his approval.

"See you tomorrow, Brady," she responded with a broad grin.

He nodded, once more quiet, as usual.

Kevin had left an hour earlier, but Catalina had remained behind to finish some close-ups. Now she and Leigh rode back to the hotel together.

"I've never felt so tired and yet so keyed up at the same time," Catalina said, leaning back in the seat.

"I know exactly what you mean," Leigh replied. "I guess we'd both better get used to it. It'll be this way for a while."

"How do you think it went today, Leigh? Honestly."

"Good. In fact, if I weren't so afraid of sounding overly confident, I'd say it went great."

Catalina's lovely face broke into an appealing smile. "I thought so, too. You know, I haven't said anything to anyone, including Kevin. But the truth is, I was nervous about working with him.''

"Don't be. As soon as I met you, I suspected you wouldn't be overshadowed by him. After today, I'm sure of it. You've got the same special quality Kevin has. That indefinable something that makes a camera worship you.''

Catalina threw back her head and laughed. "Now there's a compliment. Be careful, or you'll have two stars with enormous egos.''

She was joking, yet the words were touched with real affection. She might poke fun at Kevin, but she clearly adored him.

"I was a little nervous about dealing with Kevin at first," Leigh admitted.

"I know. But you handled him just right. I'll tell you something about Kevin, if you'll promise it won't go any further.''

Leigh held up her hand. "I promise.''

"A lot of people think he's conceited. The truth is just the opposite. He's secretly convinced that his success is a fluke that could disappear at any moment. He's never thought himself all that attractive or all that talented. That's why he worries so much about how he's going to come off, why he felt so threatened today when you suggested he not play his usual hero.''

"I thought so. It's precisely that vulnerability, which he tries so hard to hide, that will make him even more popular.''

"I think you're right." Catalina's face softened. "It was what made me fall in love with him. I suspect he thinks I was drawn to his image of superhero. The truth is, I thought the Kevin Marlowe I'd always seen on the screen was a macho bore.''

Catalina was thoughtful for a moment, then she continued, ''There's something I think you need to understand about him. He was a change-of-life baby, the last of five boys. He was lonely as a child, never felt that he was a part of the family. I think he felt unwanted. Now he needs to prove he's special, a big success, so his parents won't be sorry they had him. Do you understand, Leigh?''

Leigh knew exactly what Catalina meant. Though the motivation was different, Zach, too, needed to prove himself to his family.

''I know what you mean, Catalina,'' she said slowly.

''I thought you would. You know, Kevin told me that good directors have four things in common—compassion, a good mind, a strong point of view and the ability to listen. I think you have all four.''

Leigh was pleased but embarrassed by the tribute. As the car pulled up to the hotel, she said, ''I'm glad we had a chance to talk. See you tomorrow morning.''

''Will the dailies be ready?''

''I'm not sure. I'll have to ask Zach.'' But as soon as she said that, Leigh began to feel apprehensive. She hadn't seen Zach since that brief, unexpectedly charged meeting at midmorning. Somehow she was reluctant to seek him out now, even though she, too, was anxious to find out when the dailies would be available to be seen.

As she entered her cabin, she thought about calling Zach and discussing it over the phone. Which was downright silly, she knew, since he was right next door. Sitting down, she thought very hard for a few minutes.

She had to come to terms with this attraction she felt for him. He'd be on the set every day, and they'd be thrown together constantly at meetings and viewing the dailies. She simply couldn't continue letting his mere presence get to her as it had today.

Thoroughly irritated by what she perceived to be an untimely weakness, she gave herself a good dressing down. All that mattered right now was this picture. Not her feelings for that man. She would regard him as a professional and stop getting sidetracked by an engaging smile and compelling eyes. There would be no dancing together, no long walks in the moonlight, no more thoughts of throwing caution to the wind. And there would be no more embarrassing scenes in full view of the entire crew, when she completely lost her position of director and let herself be just another woman profoundly attracted to a man.

It was a convincing speech she gave to herself, and at the end of it she felt like a football player who had just been given a really inspiring pep talk. As she stood up and headed for the door, she felt ready to take the bull by the horns.

She knocked purposefully at Zach's door, determined to reinforce her resolve. The sun had gone down and dusky twilight had settled over everything. The heat had turned to the sudden coolness that comes so abruptly in the mountains. Leigh hadn't bothered to put on a sweater over her T-shirt, and now she shivered.

From the cold, she told herself. Only from the cold.

Then Zach opened the door. His expression was surprisingly serious. There wasn't a hint of the amused smile that so often softened his face.

"I wanted to ask you about the dailies," Leigh began.

"Come in," he responded, opening the door farther and stepping aside.

"No, I...that is, I've got to get back to my cabin and call Jonas to find out how the second-unit work went today. I just wanted to ask you about the dailies right now."

"It would be a lot more comfortable to discuss it inside where it's warm," Zach insisted. When she still hesitated, he said gruffly, "Don't be a little fool. You're shivering."

There was an element of anger in his voice that she didn't begin to understand. But it made her mad. Determined not to be baited, she simply repeated her request. "The dailies, please."

A long tense pause followed before he answered. "Certainly. I've arranged to have the film driven down to the Fresno airport every day, then flown to L.A. for processing. It'll be delivered back here the following day. So we'll be seeing dailies a day late."

Leigh nodded curtly. "All right. Thanks." Then she turned on her heel and strode away.

She hadn't gone six feet when she felt a hand roughly grab her arm and spin her around. Zach stood facing her. His eyes glittered with a powerful emotion that might have been either anger or passion. Or both.

"Damn it, Leigh, we have to talk!"

"Then call a meeting."

"That's not what I mean and you know it."

She knew exactly what he meant. But she wasn't about to admit it. "I don't know what you're talking about."

"I'm talking about the fact that I can't get you out of my mind. I'm talking about what's been building between us from the first moment we met. I lay awake half the night thinking about you being so close."

"Just why am I so close, anyway? Why did you arrange for us to be next to each other?"

"I told myself it would be more convenient. The truth is, I wanted you near me. I wanted you as close as possible so it would be easier for us to make love."

Leigh felt her heart pound as the impact of the words hit her. Looking into Zach's eyes, she saw raw desire. And knew that the same desire was reflected in her own eyes.

She felt terrified and exhilarated. His words slid past her defenses, taking hold of her senses, promising the fulfillment of something irresistible.

In a voice that was a mockery of her normal one, she stammered, "I...I have a dozen people to talk to tonight, so if you'll excuse me."

"Like hell I'll excuse you!"

And with that, he pulled her into his arms and kissed her deeply.

Leigh forgot the lecture she'd just given herself, forgot everything but his lips against hers, the satiny thrust of his tongue. Fire shot through her veins and licked at the edges of her heart, white-hot fire that melted her resistance. She had no choice but to give herself up to his overpowering hunger and her own.

His arms went around her, molding her body to his own. She responded with an instinctive movement that left nothing to the imagination.

Zach tightened his embrace, forcing Leigh's hips against his thighs. The powerful contact obliterated all her thoughts as wave after wave of pure desire washed over her.

It seemed forever before he finally held her at arm's length; forever before her breathing returned to normal. Finally she opened her eyes and raised them to his. What she saw in those blue depths thrilled her as nothing else in her entire life had done.

"This isn't wise," she whispered helplessly.

A smile lit his eyes. "Maybe not. But it's inevitable. Come inside, Leigh."

CHAPTER EIGHT

A FIRE WAS BURNING in the fireplace in Zach's cabin. Leigh was grateful for the fire's warmth as she and Zach sat down on the facing sofa.

He turned her to him. This time she didn't lower her gaze and try to avoid his. It was too late for that. What she'd tried so hard to deny was out in the open now, for both to see. There was no use pretending she didn't want him. Her determination not to become romantically involved with this man had disappeared the moment his lips met hers.

"I've been wanting to kiss you for weeks, since that first argument in the studio parking lot."

"I know," she whispered. "I wanted you to kiss me. So many times I almost let you. But I resisted."

"I understand. Getting personally involved while we're making this movie complicates things."

"Yes, it does that." She smiled ruefully. "Oh, it definitely complicates things."

"I told myself it would be better to wait until the movie was finished before telling you how I felt. But I'm afraid patience has never been one of my virtues."

The look in his eyes, so direct and so intense, started a slow, irreversible sensation deep within her.

"Something very special is happening between us, Leigh. You feel it, too, don't you?"

She didn't need to answer.

Pulling her into his arms, he kissed her again and again, until they were both breathless. He wanted her. God, how he wanted her! He'd waited all these long weeks, day after day, night after interminable night.

"I can't wait any longer," he whispered hoarsely.

Picking her up as easily as if she were a rag doll, he carried her toward the bedroom. Her arms went around his neck and her gray eyes, wide with both apprehension and anticipation, stared into his. Suddenly she was as nervous as a new bride.

"Zack, wait..."

"*No.* We've waited long enough, Leigh."

There was no light on in the bedroom. The room was lit only by the soft light filtering in through the open door from the sitting room. As he placed her on the bed, she made one last attempt at reason. "This is reckless..."

"Oh, yes. And unless you tell me right now, this moment, that you don't want me, then we're going to be very reckless."

Her arms were still around his neck. Smiling seductively up at him, she whispered, "Would you believe me if I said that?"

He shook his head. "No."

"Then I won't bother to lie."

He threw back his head and laughed lustily. Then, smiling down at her, he said, "I knew you were the kind of woman I could laugh with in bed."

And without further hesitation, they indulged in an ecstatic explosion of long pent-up desire. Somehow their clothes were off, discarded carelessly on the floor, and they lay in bed together, naked.

Zach's fingers entwined in Leigh's hair as he kissed her over and over, brushing his lips against her forehead, her eyelids, the curve of her cheeks. Then his hands slowly moved down her back, past her waist to the tiny indentation at the base of her spine.

As a shock wave rippled through her, his hands roamed across her derriere. His lips were nuzzling the slender curve of her throat. He mumbled choked, unintelligible words of longing. Through it all, only a few words were clear—"Leigh, darling Leigh"—again and again.

Then he buried his face in her breasts. Her head fell back as she arched her neck and breasts to receive his hungry mouth. She was on fire, her entire body smoldered with a passion that demanded fulfillment, that would let her hold back nothing from this man.

Leigh knew he must feel the rapid beating of her heart. She felt his own heart pound as her hands moved to his shoulders, her fingers kneading the hard, corded muscles. A heavy ache deep in her abdomen intensified as his lips drank in the soft fullness of her body.

She needed him so, needed to be part of him.

"Now," she whispered urgently.

Zach raised his head and looked deeply into those soft gray eyes. It would be so easy to do as she asked. For it was what his own body demanded, as well—immediate gratification. But he fought for control over his rising passion. They'd both waited too long to let this be anything less than absolutely perfect. He wanted to erase whatever lingering doubt she had, so that no matter what happened between them she would never regret this.

"I won't let myself take you quickly. You deserve more than that."

"Zack, I want you."

"I know, sweetheart. I want you so much it's all I can do not to take you right this minute. But I'm going to give you more than that. Much more."

Her lips curved in a seductive smile. "More?"

"More," he promised. Then his lips moved to the pulse beating madly at the base of her throat. "There's still so much of you to discover. And I intend to take my time doing it."

Her voice was a breathless whisper. "Zach…"

Tenderly he pressed his fingers against her lips. "Shh. I'll show you the journey's not over yet."

He was right, she quickly learned. It had only just begun.

She'd never felt anything like the sweet agony that filled her as his hands and lips roamed her body in slow, sensuous circles, pausing here…there…then moving on to explore another secret place. There was no resistance in her at all as she opened up completely to him. She wanted to feel his exquisitely gentle touch everywhere. As long as possible, Zach reined in his own desire to bring her to a level of feeling that was almost excruciatingly intense.

Then gradually his gentleness turned to urgency, and the ache deep within her grew enormous, nearly to bursting point. She began to move wantonly against his hands and mouth. At the same time she murmured words of longing and desire. The meaning lay not in the words themselves but in the timbre of her voice.

Now, he thought, as reason began to slip away, to be replaced by pure feeling. *Now…*

She welcomed him with open arms, drawing his body down against her smaller, more vulnerable one. They moved together, slowly, slowly, then faster and faster, in perfect unison, until they were rocked by an explosion that rent heart and soul and they were no longer separate.

As they floated back down from that intense level of awareness, both knew they'd been touched in a way they'd never been touched before. And both knew they'd shared the only real magic—the magical feeling of falling in love.

They lay together for several minutes, neither speaking. Zach's arm lay across Leigh's breasts possessively. Her head rested on his shoulder. This had been a shattering experience for her, yet she didn't ever remember feeling such contentment, such inner peace. She knew without asking that it had been the same for him.

For a moment she almost thought she might fall asleep. Then the moment passed and suddenly she was wide awake. Reality hit with a vengeance as she realized what it meant to have made love this man. Her first inclination was to run.

Oh, God, she thought, *it's too late to run.*

"Zach..." Her voice was soft but intense.

He raised up on one elbow and looked down at her. "Yes, my love?"

"I'm not sure you understand why it's so dangerous for me to become involved with you."

He smiled gently. As far as he was concerned, their joining was not only inevitable but right. "A little late to worry about that, isn't it?"

But she didn't return his smile. "I'm serious. There's a very real problem."

His smile faded as he realized how concerned she was. "I understand. You're afraid you'll lose credibility with the cast and crew."

"They'll think I slept with you to get this job, and they won't respect me no matter how well I do."

"I know how that would hurt you, Leigh. Believe me, I've never forgotten my stupid comment about how you got the job directing *Intimacies*. I'll never forget the hurt in your eyes."

"It would be the same now. The set would be full of gossip and innuendo. I couldn't deal with that and at the same time concentrate on the movie.

"I know that."

"And what about the studio? I'll bet they'll be concerned that we'll lose our objectivity."

"What are you getting at, Leigh?"

"We could keep our relationship to ourselves."

He frowned. "You mean a secret."

She nodded.

Zach was thoughtful for a long moment. Everything within him rebelled at the request. He was used to being his own man, not playing it safe and taking the path of least resistance.

Then another thought occurred to him. "What is it you're really afraid of, Leigh?"

"I just told you…"

"Yes, but I'm not sure that's the whole truth."

He was right, Leigh realized guiltily. It wasn't the whole truth.

She spoke slowly, unable to meet his piercing gaze, "I think I'm afraid of having a serious relationship. I never have before. Not…not one like this, where I feel so much. Where the person matters so much."

Sitting up, she pulled the covers beneath her chin and locked her arms about her knees. Eventually she risked looking into his face. "Zach, it's taken me longer to get where I want to be than it has you. Since I was a kid, I've dreamed of being a director. Now I've got the chance and I don't want to blow it."

Zach gathered her in his arms and pressed her against his bare chest. "Oh, sweetheart, I know it's scary. But we can work it out."

She heard his words and believed that he meant them. But it wasn't so simple.

"We'll work it out," he repeated. "I promise you."

She laid her fingers lightly across his lips. "Please. What I feel for you is very special. But, Zach, I've been very careful not to get myself into a position where I have to divide my—" she paused for the right word, then finished "—energies."

"You mean commitments." He captured her fingers and kissed them, one by one. "Trust me, Leigh. I understand how you feel. We've found something very rare. We just have to hang in there and make it work for us. If we're clever enough to make movies, surely we can manage something as wonderful as falling in love."

"Oh, if only you're right. But I've never tried to divide myself between directing and being seriously involved with someone. What if I fail at one or the other? What if, in trying to have both, I fail at both?"

Zach's lips brushed her forehead in a tender kiss. "You seem so brave on the outside, but inside you're just as afraid of failure as I am. Well, sweetheart, I promise you, you won't fail at either. You're a brilliant director. And you're the woman I've been looking for, needing, for so long. Everything will be all right. Trust me.''

She gave him a rueful grin. ''Where do you get that awesome confidence?''

''Partly from you. All I have to do is look at you, touch you, feel what you do to me, and I know without a doubt we're right for each other. And that's all that matters.''

''Oh, Zach, if only it were that simple.''

''It is.''

''What about the other problems?''

''Such as?''

''I might be tempted to give in to you when we argue, instead of fighting for what I believe in.''

He smiled warmly. ''Oh, I doubt that. One thing I've learned about you is that you have the courage of your convictions. You don't give in easily. It's one of the things I admire about you, when I'm not mad at you because of it.''

She didn't return his smile, and it slowly faded as he realized there was something more she wasn't saying. ''Is there more?''

She hesitated. This was the hard part and there was no easy way to say it. ''I'm afraid that with two temperaments as strong as ours, emotional involvement could lead to an explosion as destructive as it is passionate. Look how we argued about *Lodestar* at first. Oh, Zach, you know how willful we both are. Compromise doesn't come easily to either one of us. And what's a relationship without it?''

''So we'll both just have to learn to compromise. It's not impossible. Nothing's impossible.''

No, she thought, *nothing's impossible. But some things are very, very hard.*

"But we don't need to complicate things for ourselves. For now, can we please keep our relationship between the two of us?"

He hesitated. He didn't want to do this. But he knew how much it meant to her.

Finally he agreed reluctantly. "All right. For now. But when *Lodestar*'s finished—"

"I'll kiss you in front of Mann's Chinese Theater at high noon," she interrupted to tease him. Then she went on, "You know what we need right now?"

Amusement glinted in those bright blue eyes. "A couple of thick steaks and a bottle of wine?"

She considered the suggestion. "Mm, sounds good. Actually I was thinking about a bath. A nice, steamy hot, leisurely bath."

"Together?"

"Is there room?"

"We'll make room."

While Zach phoned room service, Leigh ran a hot bath. She had just sat down at one end of the tub when Zach joined her.

"It's lucky both of us aren't tall," she quipped as he maneuvered his long legs around her shorter ones.

Then, sighing contentedly, she leaned her head against the back of the gleaming white porcelain tub. "How long can I luxuriate here before room service interrupts?"

"An hour. They're pretty busy at the moment, apparently."

"An hour? I'll starve."

"Is food all you can think about?"

Shooting him a provocative glance, she responded, "Not after tonight."

For a few minutes they were silent, enjoying the relaxing warmth of the hot water and the nearness of each other. When they finally stepped out onto the white bath rug, Leigh allowed herself the luxury of letting her gaze roam over Zach's body.

It was the slim, hard body of an avid runner. The smooth chest tapered to a narrow waist and sinewy thighs. His skin was golden brown, and it glistened now with beads of water.

As Zach began to dry off, Leigh stopped him. "Here, let me."

She took the soft, fluffy towel from him and began slowly, gently drying him.

"I warn you, I'm easily spoiled."

"I'm not surprised."

Through the towel, her hands felt the hard planes and angles of his body. She dropped the towel and, encircling his waist with her arms, began to kiss a path across his shoulders.

Unlocking her hands, he turned to pull her against him, bare skin against bare skin. As her breasts were pressed against his chest, she felt a ripple of renewed desire. The feel of his skin was enough to make her want him again already.

"I knew you'd be as passionate about lovemaking as you are about your work," he said. "But I didn't realize you'd be so generous and uninhibited. That was an unexpected bonus."

"You make me want to give in a way I've never done before," she admitted slowly, half embarrassed. Then suddenly feeling the seeds of doubt, she added, "I suppose you've been told that before."

She tried to make the words sound light, but she knew her underlying anxiety showed through. She simply wasn't experienced enough about this sort of thing to sound glib.

He paused, then said with conviction, "This isn't just another affair, Leigh. You're the kind of woman a man can spend a lifetime looking for and never finding."

Leigh was so deeply touched that she had no idea what to say. She stood there, speechless, her eyes locked with Zach's.

His lips curved in a suggestive smile. "And unless we get dressed immediately, I'm going to make love to you again, here on this rug."

She smiled up at him, suddenly too shy to speak. But her eyes revealed that she wouldn't mind one bit if he did just that.

Gazing down at her, he went on in a more serious voice, "Stay with me tonight."

It was what she wanted, as well, to sleep with him all night, to feel him close—and to make love again.

She nodded. Then she turned away and began dressing.

THE NEXT MORNING Leigh rose early, went to her cottage, donned her jogging clothes and headed across the meadow near the hotel. It was a bright, cool morning. No one else was about and the only sounds were those of nature.

Then, as Leigh passed through a small stand of trees, she saw Zach running toward her. He'd risen even earlier and left a note saying he hadn't wanted to disturb her. Now he was on his way back. Her heart sang at the sight of him.

"Good morning," he said with a grin. "I almost woke you up to ask if you wanted to join me, but I wasn't sure you'd appreciate being wakened so early."

"I wouldn't have minded. Are you going back now?"

"I hadn't gone very far, actually. I could stand running a couple more miles."

"Okay."

They set off together, neither speaking as they ran side by side. Zach slowed down and matched his long stride to Leigh's shorter one. It was nice sharing the morning with him. More than nice. It was something she could get used to very easily.

When they returned to their cabins, he asked slowly, "Want to run every morning?"

When she hesitated, he added, "Unless, of course, you want the time alone. If you do, I understand."

"No. I...I'd like that very much. I guess I'm just concerned about people seeing us together and jumping to conclusions."

"Jogging in broad daylight is hardly clandestine. I don't think anyone will think anything of it."

She grinned. "Okay, I'll stop being paranoid."

She started to turn toward her cabin, but Zach reached out and stopped her. "Leigh..."

The tone of his voice was different now, lower and much more suggestive. There was none of his earlier breezy bonhomie.

Her eyes met his slowly, almost unwillingly.

"If we weren't out in the open, I'd kiss you. Since we are in plain view and I see that people are beginning to turn up, I'll just say this—I want you. More than any woman I've ever known."

Leigh shivered. The tremor went right through her sweat shirt to his hand on her shoulder.

Then she turned and went into her cabin. It wasn't until she'd closed the door behind her that she finally expelled the breath she'd been holding.

Late that afternoon they were ready to shoot one of the most crucial scenes in the movie. The character, Mary Beth, was supposed to fall over a cliff while running away from a rattlesnake. They shot the scene with a close-up of Catalina recoiling in horror from the snake, then turning and racing blindly toward the cliff. But just before she reached the edge, Leigh yelled, "Cut!" and "Time for the stunt double."

Catalina grinned. "Better him than me. It's a long way down that cliff!"

The stuntman, a slim young man who often doubled for actresses in action sequences, came onto the set. He wore the same jeans, shirt and jacket that Catalina wore, plus a dark wig and makeup. In a long shot, as this would be, he would easily pass for her.

Leigh carefully checked everything one last time. The scene absolutely had to go right for the first time. If it didn't, they'd have to reshoot. It would be time consuming to set up and might make them miss the right light. If they didn't finish and had to try it again tomorrow, that would put them behind schedule and therefore over budget, after only two days of shooting.

Finally Leigh was confident that everything was ready. She nodded to the production assistant holding the clapboards, then she cued the stuntman.

The young man ran to the edge of the cliff. His timing and careful placement of his steps were like the choreography of an intricate ballet or a champion pole vaulter. As he reached the edge of the cliff, he went flying over. The camera angle Leigh had chosen showed him going over the cliff and falling down. They stopped rolling just before he hit the bottom.

The audience would think the Mary Beth character had fallen on hard ground. In reality, the stuntman doubling for the character fell on an inflated, twenty-foot-square heavy plastic air bag. The stunt coordinator stood near it, just out of camera range.

Because everyone was aware of the potential for an injury, first-aid supplies and a stretcher were kept ready. When the stuntman landed exactly as he was supposed to, then immediately jumped lightly off the mattress, Leigh sighed with relief. "All right, that's a take!" she shouted happily. Then, as a smattering of applause and murmured approval died down, she added, "And we can wrap early today."

The crew members, who'd been on their feet for nearly eight hours, were happy to hear that. They grinned and chatted happily as they began to dismantle the equipment.

As Leigh turned to head back to the administrative trailor that was parked nearby, she saw Zach standing in the background. When she reached him, he smiled warmly. "You know the way to the crew's heart. Let them off early."

"They deserve it today. And that stuntman deserves a bonus. He saved the studio thousands of dollars by getting it right in one take."

"I'll pass your suggestion on to Gary Jennings. Are you busy at the moment?"

"No. I was just going to make sure the schedule was ready for tomorrow."

"I already checked with Arnie. It's ready. By the way, I'm not sure he's ready to admit it yet, but the truth is, he's impressed with what you've done so far."

"We've just started, really."

"But a good start is important. It's hard to overcome a bad one."

As members of the crew passed by them, heading toward the cars and vans that would take them back to the hotel, Zach went on in a lower voice, "Come on. I've got something to show you."

"What is it?"

"You'll see. Trust me."

"Do we have enough time for me to go back to the hotel for a shower? I feel absolutely glued into these clothes."

"On you a glued-on T-shirt looks good." Grinning at her, he winked and said, "Sure. You have time for a shower and change."

Zach waved Leigh's driver on and opened the door of his car for her. "Get in. And don't worry that we'll start a rumor by returning from the site. I'll act important and you act cowed," he said with a laugh.

"That'll be the day!" Laughing with him, she suggested, "I'll act important and you act cowed. Then we'd really have an interesting rumor floating around."

Arranging to meet by the pool as soon as they'd showered and changed, Leigh hurried to her cottage. Quickly she peeled off her boots and dusty clothes and stepped into the shower. Zach had said he'd be waiting with a glass of white wine in fifteen minutes, so she hurried.

Dressing in a pair of lavender slacks with matching sweater, she brushed on lavender eyeshadow and touched her lashes with mascara. A hint of blush on her cheeks, gloss on her lips, and she was almost ready. She touched the inside of her wrists, the lobes of her ears and the hollow at the base of her throat with Joy, her favorite perfume. Then—for good measure—she added a touch to each temple.

Studying herself in the mirror, she saw that her mass of curls softly framed her face. She looked into the reflection of her own eyes and acknowledged that she positively glowed. *Know what, my friend,* she told herself. *You're falling in love.*

And whether it was wise or foolish didn't matter because there was nothing she could do to stop it.

Because she hadn't the faintest idea of where they were going, she slipped her feet into a pair of comfortable, low-heeled pumps, ones she could walk in almost anywhere. Outside, she locked the cottage door and dropped the key into her handbag.

Holding two glasses of white wine, Zach leaned against the railing of the small footbridge that led from the hotel lawn to the cottages and watched Leigh approach. His heart turned over when he saw happiness brighten her face as she spied him waiting for her.

"Thank you," she said, smiling softly as she took the glass from him. Sipping the wine, she looked about, then asked, "What's going on with all these people?"

"A wedding, I think," Zach said.

Indeed, a wedding party was gathering under the spreading limbs of a huge oak not far from where they stood. A middle-aged man, casually dressed except for his clerical collar, spoke in a strong Irish brogue, calling the wedding guests together.

A band of musicians began to play. Their music was lively: jigs and reels and Irish folk tunes. There was an assortment of instruments: a tin whistle, a guitar, fiddle, flute and a set of Irish bagpipes. Everyone, guests and musicians alike, stood, except for one young woman who sat in a folding chair and held a lap harp.

Then the last sound of the pipes faded away and the young woman with the lap harp began to play. The melody was plaintive and sweet. While it played, the bride's attendant came through the solarium doors. She was followed by the bride on the arm of her father, walking slowly toward the man who waited for her.

The final notes of the music soared in the clear afternoon air, then seemed to settle over the couple like a silken cloak.

Zach felt absolutely entranced and somehow he knew that Leigh felt the same enchantment he did. He felt sure she did not realize that she'd clasped his arm. He looked down and studied her fingers lying against the sleeve of his jacket. Her fingers were surprisingly long and slender for someone as petite as she was.

Suddenly he thought of the ring his grandfather had left to him. Zach had been divorced for several years when his grandfather died. In an envelope addressed to Zach had been a note and his grandmother's wedding ring. The note simply said that Zach had learned some sense about women now. And he was to have this ring that his grandmother had worn with love and pride for more than fifty years. His grandfather had closed by saying that as his first grandson—and his namesake—he sincerely hoped that Zack would be as fortunate as he had been in choosing a wife to wear the ring.

Because it was his grandfather's way, he'd closed with a jest. "If you get real lucky, you might even find a wife with the same name. Then you'll only have to add your own wedding date." The ring, Zach remembered, was eighteen carat and unusually wide. And engraved inside were the words: "Love forever. Z to L, 6-6-1919."

His grandmother's name had been Lily.

I'm going to marry Leigh, Zach thought quietly. *And put our wedding date on my grandmother's ring.*

At the same moment, Leigh's thoughts were less confident. This open, exuberant celebration of love they were witnessing was bittersweet, in a way. For it made her question herself and the life she'd chosen as she'd never done before.

For years she'd known exactly what she wanted to do—to be a film director. And she'd pursued that dream with a determination that made up for the many moments of self-doubt. Then came *Intimacies*, and suddenly after all these years of hard work, the dream was a reality. Now, with the chance to direct *Lodestar,* she was well on her way.

Had she gone overboard in her commitment to directing, she wondered. It didn't seem enough now, especially after making love to Zach. She wanted everything they could possibly share together—marriage, children. But combining marriage and a demanding career would be very, very hard. She'd seen many of her friends run into serious problems trying to do that very thing. All too often either the marriage or the career suffered.

Leigh's thoughts were interrupted by the conclusion of the ceremony as the musicians burst forth with music and someone called for the bride and groom to lead in an Irish jig. Everyone joined in—men, women and children.

For a moment, Zach and Leigh stood watching. Then he said, "We'd better get started on my surprise or we'll be late for the dailies."

Smiling, she nodded.

While Zach drove, Leigh leaned back in the seat and relaxed. It had been a long and busy day. Besides, she never tired of looking at the scenery. Now in the late afternoon, the tall pines and firs seemed to hold their arms open to the last of the sunlight, and here and there were the dogwoods with their beautifully fragile white blossoms. Along the river the cottonwoods' newly green leaves shone brightly as they caught the reflections of sunlight.

When they reached Glacier Point, Zach pulled into the parking area, which was empty except for their car. Taking a small picnic basket from the back seat, he opened the lid to reveal its contents. "The surprise. Prepared by the chef at the Ahwahnee."

"Mm, it all looks marvelous. I don't know whether to eat first or admire the view."

"You and your insatiable appetite. Come on. Let's watch the sunset first. We can eat later."

They walked the groomed trails to stand at the guardrail overlooking the valley, almost three thousand feet below. Holding hands, they stood silently as their eyes swept the breathtaking vista of the High Sierra.

After a moment, Leigh walked a few steps away from Zach. "When I'm in the valley," she said, "I'm so aware of the magnificence of the place that I'm awed."

She paused, then continued, somewhat embarrassed. "When I'm up here looking across range after range of mountains that began centuries ago, I'm humbled." She walked back to stand close beside Zach, slipping her arm through his. "Just think—all that we see began aeons ago. And they're still here for us to appreciate now. In comparison, our lifespans, even if we live a long life, are like the blink of an eye. I said I feel humble, but also," she whispered, "inspired."

She glanced up into Zach's face. "Do you ever feel like that?"

"Sure. Especially, when I'm up in the High Country." Then he took her in his arms and added tenderly, "But at the moment, you take my breath away more than this magnificent view ever could."

Leigh leaned back in his arms to look up at him. Instantly his mouth came down on hers. He kissed her long and deep, then released her to enfold her once more in a tender embrace, his cheek against her hair. They stood in silence, the two of them locked in each other's arms and listened to the roar of the Nevada and Vernal Falls as they dropped down the Giant's Stairway. A light stir of wind blew across their faces. It was as if they were the only two people in the world.

"Leigh."

Something in his tone warned her that what was to come was serious. Looking up at him, she said, "Yes?"

"There's something I want to tell you about. I think it's...necessary."

She waited. Whatever it was, it was obviously hard for him to talk about, and he would have to do it in his own way.

Finally he was able to say, "You probably know I was married once."

She nodded. She'd hoped he'd tell her about his marriage sometime. But she wasn't sure he ever would, certainly not so soon in their relationship.

"It was a long time ago. And it didn't last very long. But it made me reluctant to get involved seriously again. Until I met you." Zach placed a tender kiss on the top of her head and Leigh snuggled closer.

"Leigh, I want you to understand about my marriage."

She listened, saying nothing. Right now, all that Zach needed was her attention, not questions or comments.

"Her name was Daisy." He smiled but there was no warmth of humor in his smile. "Right out of *The Great Gatsby*. Which is appropriate since I felt the same adulation toward her that poor, dumb Gatsby felt for his Daisy."

Leigh felt Zach's arm tense around her shoulders. She sensed how hard this was for him, and waited patiently for him to continue.

"She was an actress. Not really talented, but so beautiful you didn't notice. Someone said once that she was a younger version of Marilyn Monroe. She had that same unusual combination of vulnerability and sexuality.''

Suddenly Leigh knew who Zach was talking about. Daisy Benton, the premier sex goddess in Hollywood. She'd even made a movie with Kevin once.

Zach continued, ''We were both just twenty-two when we met. I'd just dropped out of college to do the only thing I'd ever wanted to do—make movies. Daisy had just come from the East Coast. I thought she was the most beautiful woman I'd ever seen. I thought I loved her. Three weeks later, we were married. Three months later, I filed for divorce.''

''What happened?''

Zach was thoughtful for a moment. ''In a way, it's hard to say. On the surface it seems simple enough. Daisy was ambitious. She wanted to be a star. And she was willing to sell herself to get what she wanted.''

''Even after you were married.''

''Oh, yes. I couldn't handle it. Which, oddly enough, surprised her. She told me I was naive.''

Leigh wanted to comfort Zach, to tell him how sorry she was for his shattered illusion of love. But she sensed he knew that, so she simply waited for him to finish.

''I realized I had been infatuated with her, but didn't know her well enough to love her. We were absolutely wrong for each other. Divorce was the logical solution. The hard part was coming to terms with my feeling of failure. No one else in my family had ever gotten a divorce. Telling my parents was hard. And as for my grandfather...well, he just said I'd been a damn fool.''

"You were very young," Leigh whispered. "Everyone's entitled to one mistake."

"Not if you're a Stewart," he responded dryly.

Then, looking at Leigh intently, he said, "I don't talk about it normally. And I don't intend to talk about it again. But I thought you should know."

"Why?"

"Don't you know why?"

She shook her head.

"Because I intend to marry you. I even have the ring."

Leigh stood back, stunned.

Zach grinned, and the traces of deeply buried sadness left his face. "I suppose I should have asked you, but since I don't plan to take no for an answer, there's not much point."

Leigh opened her mouth to speak, then closed it again when she realized she had absolutely no idea what to say.

"This is what every producer dreams of," he teased. "A director who doesn't argue back."

Leigh found her voice. "But...but the picture."

"What about it?"

"Damn it, Zach, that's what we're supposed to be concerned with right now."

"We're going to make one of the best films that's ever been made. We're good together, Leigh." Lightly he ran one fingertip down the curve of her throat, sending her pulse racing. "Or hadn't you noticed?"

When she didn't speak, he went on in a voice filled with tenderness, "I can't imagine life without you. I want to share everything with you—the good and the bad. Together there's nothing we can't accomplish."

Leigh's joyful heart leaped in response to this very special man. Without taking her eyes from his, Leigh could tell they stood in the last radiant light of the glorious sunset. It was as if here, close to the heavens, they were receiving a golden shower of blessing.

He drew her back into his arms and kissed her hungrily. As his kiss deepened, Leigh realized that everything he'd said was true...they were good together in every way. There was nothing they couldn't accomplish together. Then the fire of Zach's kisses caught her own banked desire and she gave herself up to him.

CHAPTER NINE

LEIGH AND ZACH walked into the screening room together. Leigh noticed Kevin and Catalina sitting next to John Kline, the art director, in the second row of folding chairs. The editor, Bill Regan, an intense young man wearing wire-rimmed glasses, sat at the end of the same row of seats. In front of him were Arnie, Liz Bramley, the cinematographer and the camera operator. In the fourth row, Jonas sat with his second-unit crew.

Leigh and Zach slipped into the first two seats in the back row, directly behind Bill Regan.

At the rear of the room, on a raised platform, the projectionist waited to be given the cue to roll the film. The can of film had just arrived from being processed in L.A., and the tension and expectation in the room were palpable.

Leigh felt it the moment she walked in. This was the moment of truth for all of them. What had seemed wonderful when they were shooting it might easily turn out to be disappointing on film.

As Leigh and Zach sat down, they smiled and nodded at everyone. On Leigh's part, the smile was forced. She was nervous. And she sensed Zach was, too.

He gestured to the projectionist to roll the film. As the lights in the small room went out, Leigh leaned toward him and whispered, "Why do I feel like a Christian about to be fed to the lions?"

He chuckled softly. "Don't worry. You're more than a match for any lion."

Reaching over, he squeezed her hand reassuringly, then continued to hold it in the dark.

The first scene was one directed by Jonas. It was the crucial plane crash that came very early on in the movie. Leigh hadn't wanted to resort to the usual trick of showing a plane disappearing behind a hill, followed by an explosion. But they couldn't actually crash a plane in Yosemite itself.

To resolve the problem, Jonas had filmed an actual plane crash in another location that looked similar to Yosemite. Then he'd carefully placed props made to look like the wreckage on the set.

It worked beautifully. As Leigh said to Zach, no one could handle action sequences better than Jonas. He made it all look absolutely real and therefore very exciting.

"This will put the audience on the edge of their seats from the very beginning," she whispered to Zach.

"All right, I know what you want to hear. You were right and I was wrong about Jonas."

In the pale light of the movie screen, she caught his wry grin.

There were more shots of the same scene, from different angles, then came the film Leigh had shot the day before. It was two short scenes and a longer one, where Kevin regained consciousness and kissed Catalina.

In the longer scene, Keven had most of the dialogue. The man's role was definitely the focal point of the script. Yet, as Leigh knew she would, Catalina managed to steal the scene. She could do more with a look than most actresses could do with a monologue. There was a glow about her. Though Leigh knew it sounded corny, she felt it was the glow of stardust.

Neither Leigh nor Zach spoke. In fact, the entire room was unusually silent. But there was a feeling in the atmosphere that Leigh recognized. Everyone in that room was caught up in watching Catalina. At that moment, Leigh was certain, a star was born.

The final scene was on the screen now. It was the one where Kevin and Catalina kissed tenderly. As it played, Leigh felt herself transported. Suddenly she wasn't seated beside Zach in the screening room. She was back at Glacier Point, held in his arms, feeling the strength of him and tasting his lips on hers. She'd wanted him so. Even now she could feel the intimacy of his kisses and the fire of desire that he aroused in her.

While she tried to concentrate on watching the film, she found herself thinking about the man beside her. Never before had she felt so abandoned with a man. But Zach was unlike any other man she'd ever known. He made her want to throw caution to the winds, to fulfull her most secret fantasies. Here, in this darkened room, it was all so clear. She wanted him. Wanted him as badly as he wanted her.

She felt him stir as he shifted his legs, and his thigh brushed hers lightly. Even through his gabardine slacks, Leigh felt the taut muscles of his thigh. She was startled by a sharp jolt of desire that made her senses swim.

For a moment she had the uncanny sensation that he was thinking exactly the same thoughts. She looked at him, but it was too dark to see his expression.

So lost was she in her sensual reverie, Leigh almost felt stunned when the last scene ended and the projectionist flipped on the light. Leigh blinked as she pulled herself together.

Without looking at her, Zach rose and moved to where Jonas stood.

"Great stuff, Jonas."

Leigh saw Jonas's transparent look of pride.

At the same time, several of the other people in the room were telling Catalina how great she'd been.

"Incredible!" John Kline said in his emphatic way.

"Thanks," Catalina responded, half embarrassed.

"The camera loves you," Brady Delinski said. "You make my job easy."

"You just plain steal the scene," Bill Regan added enthusiastically.

Suddenly there was an awkward silence as everyone realized what Bill's comment said about Kevin. Seeing Kevin's pride in his wife rapidly turn to consternation, Leigh said quickly, "You two are terrific together. Such chemistry. Kevin, you must have taught Catalina some of your tricks for getting an audience in the palm of your hand.''

But the words of praise didn't seem to soothe Kevin's bruised ego. With a barely polite smile in response, he rose and said to his wife, ''We'd better go. We both have an early call in the morning.''

Catalina, trying very hard not to show how concerned she felt, followed obediently.

''Did I say the wrong thing?'' Bill asked.

''No, dear boy, you said the *worst* thing,'' John replied. ''Never compliment a scene stealer in front of the victim.''

Zach and Jonas, along with Jonas's crew, had joined the others. Zach said flatly, ''The only important thing is how well it looks. And it looks great. We can all be very optimistic.''

''It really does look fantastic, Leigh,'' Jonas added.

''Now we'd better all turn in,'' Zach said. ''There are a lot of long, hard days ahead.''

As the crew separated to go to their rooms, Zach and Leigh headed toward their cottages. It was a dark, cold night. Leigh's sweater wasn't nearly warm enough. When she shivered, Zach shrugged out of his brown corduroy jacket and placed it around her shoulders.

''You'll be cold,'' she protested.

''The last thing on my mind right now is the temperature.''

The underlying meaning of his words told Leigh instantly that she'd been right in the screening room—he was thinking about her then every bit as much as she was thinking about him.

When they reached her cottage, Zach held out his hand for her key. She handed it to him. Inside, he closed the door, then turned and kissed her. He didn't bother with the light at first. Not until they'd finally pulled apart, both shaken from the force of their desire, did he turn on the light.

"It was all I could do not to drag you out of there," he murmured as his lips nuzzled her throat tenderly.

"I wish you had."

"You'd better not say that. Tomorrow night I might just do it."

"Mm, that certainly adds spice to the ritual of watching dailies."

Then he swept her up into his arms and moved toward the bedroom. "We're going to have it all, you and I. Exciting work and even more exciting love."

It was a heady thought, and as he set her on the bed, Leigh's heart and mind soared with happiness....

THE NEXT DAY they shot one of the most important scenes in the movie. The location on this day was a small meadow with a stream running through it. Leigh blocked out the scene as Kevin and Catalina listened intently.

· "Joe and Mary Beth have been trudging through the mountains for a couple of days by this time. They're tired and filthy. And more than a little scared, though Joe won't admit it. But already they've begun to look at each other in a new light. They've only survived this long by depending on each other, helping each other.''

"Which is rekindling the old flame," Kevin concluded.

"Exactly. In this scene, Mary Beth is bathing in the stream. She isn't aware that Joe is watching her. Joe has climbed up to a higher ridge trying to get a better look down the canyon they're following. He's just returned to where they're camped and spots Mary Beth in the stream."

Leigh finished the walk-through, showing Kevin and Catalina where their marks were.

"It's going to be a memorable scene," she said enthusiastically. "We'll be shooting Mary Beth from Joe's point of view. He's reluctant to make his presence known. After all, we've established that they've been estranged for some time and it's been several months since they've made love. He circles around, watching her, feeling a newfound desire. She continues bathing, taking her time, completely innocent."

Kevin said nothing, but he looked thoughtful.

Leigh was afraid he was concerned about his wife doing a nude scene and she hastened to reassure him. "Catalina will keep her body stocking on the whole time. I don't want this to be too explicit or we'll have an R rating. I don't want that, and neither does the studio."

Kevin nodded. Yet somehow he didn't seem reassured. After a moment, he said, "I take it the camera will be behind me and I'll be in the scene most of the time.''

"Well, no, not exactly. We'll start out with you in the frame, then cut to Catalina. Except for brief cuts back and forth to register your reactions, it will be mainly her scene.''

There was absolute silence. Catalina flashed a quick, concerned look at her husband. He was staring rigidly past Leigh's shoulder. Clearly he was less than pleased that the focus would be on Catalina and not him.

Leigh felt her anger rising and had to fight it back. All week Kevin had been concerned with his screen time versus Catalina's. As far as Leigh was concerned, he was being thoroughly selfish and surprisingly jealous of his new wife.

Leigh was doing everything she could to build up Catalina's part, but it was still very much Kevin's movie. Surely he must realize that, she thought irritably. Jonas had certainly been right that Kevin was unexpectedly insecure. But that kind of insecurity came perilously close to unprofessionalism when it was allowed to affect what was best for the film. And by now Leigh had very little patience with it.

She had to force herself not to simply tell Kevin to grow up and stop behaving like a spoiled brat. Instead, she explained carefully, "This will be a lovely scene visually. It's a gorgeous spring day, Catalina will look breathtaking, and the water will glisten in the sunlight. Since it comes right after the scene where the two of you fight off a mountain lion, the audience will be ready for a break in the excitement.''

There was a stubbornness about Kevin's expression that Leigh was beginning to recognize as trouble. "In the script it indicates that I'm the focus of this scene, not Catalina."

"Yes." Leigh forced herself to be patient. "I'm aware of what's in the script, Kevin. But I think this scene would work better the way I've described it. True, the focus is on Catalina, but the audience will be more interested in your reaction."

"I've made a lot of movies," Kevin said pointedly. *Unlike you*, his tone clearly said. "And the ones that worked best were the ones that stuck to the script. Winging it can get you in trouble."

"I'm not winging it." Leigh's tone was sharper than she'd intended. She was getting less and less successful at hiding her irritation.

The atmosphere on the set, which had been relaxed, was growing more tense by the moment. Everyone nearby sensed a confrontation between director and star.

"Why don't we just try it and see how it works in dailies," Leigh suggested. "We'll get enough close-up shots of you to alter the scene during the editing process, if we have to."

Catalina had said very little during the entire exchange between Leigh and Kevin. Now she said in an especially tender voice that she used only with her husband, "Darling, let's just try it as Leigh suggests."

She gave him her most winsome smile—a smile, Leigh knew, that would turn men in an audience to jelly when the picture was released.

Kevin hesitated, still reluctant to give in.

Leigh nearly held her breath, waiting to see what he would do. If he pushed this confrontation to the limit and made it a test of his clout versus hers, she wasn't at all sure what would happen. Kevin Marlowe mattered a great deal more to the studio than she did. It was possible he could even get her fired. It certainly wouldn't be the first time such a thing had happened.

Looking at Catalina, not Leigh, Kevin finally said grudgingly, "All right, let's get this over with."

Leigh knew she should feel relieved. Instead she felt angry. Without saying a word to Kevin, she turned and headed toward her seat near the camera.

The scene took the entire day to shoot. Throughout it, neither Leigh nor Kevin spoke more than a few absolutely necessary words to each other. Catalina was marvelous in the scene, never once complaining about having to spend so much time in the cold mountain stream. But when the camera wasn't on her, her eyes betrayed her inner concern.

When shooting had finished for the day and Leigh was getting in her car to return to the hotel, Catalina came over to her. Kevin was in his dressing room, and by Catalina's hurried manner, Leigh sensed she wanted to speak before Kevin came out and saw her.

"Leigh, I'm sorry about today."

"You don't have anything to apologize for, Catalina."

"You know what I mean. I'm apologizing for Kevin."

"I think he should do that himself."

Catalina smiled helplessly. "Yes. But he won't. Leigh, there's already talk that I'm stealing the picture from him."

"Well, to a certain degree that's true. But you're certainly not trying to undermine him in any way. And neither am I."

"I know that. And Kevin knows it, too. But he won't admit it. There's a bitter irony here, you see. He pressured the studio to hire me, and now I'm upstaging him."

"He's still the star of this picture. It's his name that will bring in an audience, at least initially. And the two of you are terrific together. I haven't seen this kind of chemistry since Tracy and Hepburn."

"That's hardly due to any acting ability. I'm crazy about the guy, and it shows."

"What also shows is a new Kevin Marlowe. I know everyone's been saying what an auspicious debut this is for you. But after a while I think they'll also notice that Kevin's giving his best performance ever."

"Oh, I know that. I've been meaning to tell you how impressed I am with the performance you're getting out of him. Somehow you've gotten him to reveal his softer side, which is no mean feat."

"Critics will comment on that. I'm convinced that for the first time they'll stop referring to him as hunk and start talking about his acting ability."

"That would be wonderful. He tries not to show, but the truth is, it bothers him terrib critics dismiss what he does."

"Isn't that enough?"

Catalina gave a rueful smile. "Apparently not. Couldn't you stroke his ego, make him feel less threatened somehow?"

"How? By making you take a back seat to his performance? You wouldn't do that, would you?

Catalina hesitated, and for a moment Leigh thought she might actually disagree. Finally she sighed heavily and admitted, "No, I wouldn't do that. Believe it or not, Kevin wouldn't really want me to. He's a much nicer person than he appeared to be today."

Leigh didn't argue with that statement, though she didn't necessarily agree with it. She had liked Kevin well enough at first, but his charm had worn thin.

"Catalina, I'm doing my best to get along with him."

"I know you are. Believe me, I could see what it took to restrain yourself from hauling off and telling him where to go."

Leigh couldn't help responding to Catalina's wry grin. She smiled self-consciously. "Well, the truth is I have more than a little bit of a temper myself. But I'll do my best to keep it in check with Kevin."

"Good. I appreciate it. And I'll work on him when we're alone. Try to make him realize how silly he's being. Whether or not I'm a new star has nothing to do with his status as an established one."

Leigh shook her head in exasperation. "Men! I swear, in some ways they never grow up."

"No, poor dears, they don't really. Still, on occasion their boyishness is rather endearing. Well, I'd

better run. Thanks again for being so understanding.''

As Catalina raced back to the dressing room,
Leigh hoped she would be successful at mollifying
her temperamental husband. Otherwise, there would
almost certainly be a major confrontation.

AT DAILIES THAT EVENING, Kevin nodded politely to
Leigh but didn't speak. Apparently Catalina's best
efforts hadn't been too successful. But as Leigh sat
next to Zach and watched the scenes unfold, take
after take, she almost forgot about her difficulties
with Kevin. The scenes they were watching tonight
were his, and he was marvelous in them.

In one scene, in which he dressed Catalina's
wound, he was infinitely tender. That tenderness,
combined with his strong physical presence, was
captivating. If only, Leigh thought, he would continue to let himself open up in this way, he could actually be taken seriously as an actor.

Later, as they left the screening room, Jonas murmured to her under his breath. ''Incredible! I have to
admit I never got that kind of performance out of
him.''

As always, praise from Jonas made Leigh flush
with pride. ''Thanks. Now if he and I can just keep
our hands off each other's throats...''

''I heard about the problems on the set.''

''I'm sure everyone's talking. It's grade-A gossip—woman director battles with male superstar.''

"If Kevin has any sense—and I think he does, surprisingly enough—he'll realize you're the best thing that's ever happened to his career."

"Well, to change to a happier topic, your second-unit stuff looks terrific. I talked to Gary Jennings last night, and he's really impressed."

"Thanks. You know, Zach and I had a little talk today."

Leigh's eyebrows rose quizzically. "Did you now?"

"He has another project the studio's considering. They're just waiting to see how *Lodestar* turns out before giving him the go-ahead. It's an action adventure set in Africa. A nice, old-fashioned safari romance like *King Solomon's Mines*. Anyway, he asked me if I'd consider doing it."

"Oh, Jonas, how fantastic!"

Impulsively she threw her arms around him and hugged him affectionately.

"It's all due to you, Leigh."

"No way. It's all due to your ability. Period."

"I'm not gonna argue with a pretty young woman. But when this job's over, I've got the biggest bottle of the most expensive champagne you ever saw cooling in the little refrigerator in my room. We're gonna celebrate!"

Leigh laughed happily. "All right!"

Just then Zach, who'd been off talking to Kevin, came up.

"Can we talk for a minute, Leigh?"

"Of course."

"I'll leave you two," Jonas said. "See you tomorrow."

As Zach and Leigh walked toward her cottage, she said warmly, "Oh, Zach, Jonas told me that you offered him a job. I'm so glad."

"Well, I'm able to admit when I'm wrong. And I was wrong about Jonas. He's been thoroughly professional. The stuff he's given us so far is great."

"From what he told me of the project, it sounds like he'd be perfect for it."

"I think so. But the studio hasn't cleared it yet, remember. They want to make sure I can bring in *Lodestar* without any problems first."

They had reached Leigh's cottage. Smiling up at him, she asked, "Want to come in for a...nightcap?"

He smiled mischievously. "Of course."

Inside, he built a fire, then turned out the overhead light and sat next to Leigh on the sofa. He kissed her gently. It was a brief kiss, yet it awoke an instant response deep within her. Suddenly all thoughts of Jonas or the movie were out of her mind. All that mattered was the love and passion she felt for this man.

"I haven't said I love you," she murmured gently.

"I've noticed."

"I...I was afraid to, somehow."

"I think I understand."

Her eyes met his. In a voice that was low and soft, yet utterly certain, she said, "I love you, Zachary Ross Stewart."

"Oh, sweetheart, I love you, too."

Then they were in each other's arms and there was nothing but need and response to that need. Leigh gave herself to him, melting in his hands, needing him, wanting him. She felt the tremor that went through him at her touch, and gloried in her ability to arouse him that deeply.

He held her with a power and a hunger that she had no wish to resist. Tilting back her head, she watched him through half-closed eyes as he undressed her quickly, expertly, then undressed himself.

And as they lay on the sofa in front of the flickering fire, his lips searched the softness of her mouth, her throat, her full breasts. Her arms were around his back, clinging to him tightly, as a fierce joy washed over her.

I love him and he loves me. And nothing, no one, in the whole world matters more.

He looked down at her. When he spoke his voice was husky yet tender. "Do you know your hair shimmers in the firelight? And your skin glistens— it's so pale it's almost transparent."

She felt the warmth of his breath on her cheek as he bent to kiss it gently. As he continued to kiss the soft length of her body, she wondered if this were heaven. If so, it was indescribably sweet.

Her eyes were dreamy as she whispered, "Everything about you is golden—your hair, your skin." With her fingertip, she lightly traced the deep cleft in his determined chin, his firm chiseled mouth and his eyebrows, darker than his sun-bleached hair. Studying him, she thought, as she often had, that though his features lacked the symmetry to be truly handsome, he was the most beautiful thing she'd ever seen. She cupped his face with both her hands. "Even your eyes have tiny pinpoints of sunlight in them."

He gave a soft chuckle. "You've been working too hard, my sweet Leigh. You're confusing sunlight and firelight."

"And I'm embarrassing you...telling you how gorgeous you are?" Leigh laughed in delight as she drew his lips down to hers.

"You're the gorgeous one. And the softest thing I've ever touched," he whispered. "Softer than velvet, softer than angel's hair. You look so fragile, you make me want to hold back the fierce desire I feel for you for fear of hurting you."

"Don't hold back. Darling, don't hold anything back."

For the briefest moment he hesitated. Then he did as she asked. He held back nothing.

Leigh felt his mouth demand everything of hers, felt his arms enclose her tightly, felt the male strength of his golden body. Insatiable hunger and exquisite tenderness took her to a place she'd never been before, even with this man. A place where the only reality was the touch and taste and feel of him and the quickening of her own desire.

When she cried his name through ragged breaths, he let go of the last tenuous thread of restraint and shuddered against her, giving himself up completely to the transcendent joy they had created together.

At the same moment, Leigh felt wave after wave of overpowering sensation rock her to the very depths of her being. Giving way to it she soared like a bird, returning to earth on the wings of love.

Afterward, they lay together for a long while, silent, utterly happy.

TWO WEEKS PASSED in a blur of hard work. Then one evening when they'd finished viewing the dailies, Leigh invited everyone to the Indian Room. "Today is Catalina's birthday. Let's go celebrate!"

When she and Zach arrived, a three-piece combo was playing. The lounge was crowded with members from *Lodestar*'s company and as Catalina entered she was given a rousing welcome.

Leigh removed her coat, and Zach draped it over a chair at one of the small tables. When she'd gone to view the dailies, she'd worn her raincoat, buttoned and belted, over the dress she'd worn to the party at Zach's parents'. She'd felt beautiful that night in the glistening silk dress and she wanted to feel beautiful tonight—for Zach. The look he gave her assured her she'd accomplished her goal. Then he took her hand and led her to the small crowded dance floor.

Taking her in his arms, he said, "Obviously this will be my only chance to hold you for hours."

"Well," she teased, "I could say we have to get the cake. That would give us about ten minutes."

"You are beautiful in that silver dress. It feels silky," he murmured, as his hand slid sensuously down her back to her waist. "Just like your skin. Have I ever told you that you feel just like silk?" He gave her an audacious grin. "I'd never bring you back in ten minutes."

As she gazed into those blue eyes her heart turned over in joyful response. She was glad her neckline was high, otherwise she was sure the throb of her rapid pulse would show for all the world to see.

He held her close and spun around and around in perfect time to the fast music. When the tempo changed and she could catch her breath, she returned the compliment. "You don't look too shabby yourself, Mr. Stewart," she teased. "In fact, you look almost as gorgeous as Kevin."

Both Zach and Kevin were wearing gray flannel slacks and navy blue blazers. Zach wore a blue shirt, unbuttoned at the collar, and Kevin wore a white turtleneck.

"What do you mean—almost as gorgeous?" His eyes danced with pleasure as he looked down at her.

When the dance ended, they joined Catalina and Kevin at their table and now that Catalina had removed the coat she'd worn in the screening room, Leigh looked at Zach and said, "Speaking of gorgeous."

Catalina was wearing a white matte jersey sheath that molded her lush curves as if it had been poured on her. About her neck was the silver-and-turquoise necklace she and Leigh had admired just yesterday in the hotel gift shop. It was a stunning and authentic piece of jewelry, signed by the Navaho who'd crafted it. Leigh remembered the clerk quoting the price as fifteen hundred dollars.

"Catalina," she exclaimed. "You lucky thing."

"We walked into the shop before dinner and when he asked me what I wanted for my birthday, I told him."

Catalina ran her fingers over the necklace, then leaned over to lightly kiss Kevin's cheek. "I just love it. *And him.*"

Just then the doors to the lounge swung open and a waiter came through the doors carrying a huge birthday cake ablaze with twenty-six candles. Behind him followed another waiter with a serving cart on which were plates, silver, champagne and goblets. The combo struck up "Happy Birthday," and everyone in the lounge joined in the serenade.

With her heart in her eyes, Catalina looked at Kevin as she made a wish, then blew out the candles. Everyone cheered her success. Champagne flowed freely as the cake was cut and shared among all the well-wishers.

Then Catalina stood and smiled. "I don't know how to thank all of you who've helped to make this a memorable birthday," she began.

"We know," someone blurted out. "Sing for us, Catalina. I heard you in New York last summer and you were great."

That was all it took. The crowd clamored and the combo began an introduction to "Bewitched, Bothered and Bewildered."

Leigh saw Catalina quickly glance at Kevin. She wanted his approval, she supposed, but the crowd wasn't aware of anything but the momentum of the party. Someone grabbed Catalina's hand and pulled her up to the stand before the combo. The vocalist of the group handed her the mike and picked up a guitar.

From her very first note, low, throaty and sexy, Catalina silenced the crowd. She was a knockout! Everyone in the room loved her. When she tried to stop, they'd plead for one more.

Leigh glanced at Zach once when Catalina was singing "The Man I Love," expecting him to be as mesmerized as everyone else. But to her surprise, he was looking at her. In that brief exchange, she felt a connection with him that was positively sinful. She experienced a charge of passion as strong and real as if they had been making love.

To hide the blush that rose to her cheeks, she turned to see how Kevin was enjoying his bride's performance. She'd expected to see the same pride and pleasure she'd read on his face earlier. But Kevin did not look pleased. He'd sipped champagne when they'd toasted Catalina, but the drink before him now was a highball.

Leigh heard a warning bell go off in her head and she looked at Catalina, hoping she hadn't seen Kevin's expression. If he didn't stop acting the way he was, everyone—including Catalina—would pick up on it. And it would spoil Catalina's birthday.

Something a director had once said came to Leigh as she observed Catalina. He'd said an actress had to be a delicate balance of toughness and vulnerability. If she's too tough, she's worthless; if she's too vulnerable, she can be destroyed.

Kevin's jealousy could destroy not only Catalina's belief in herself as an actress, but also their marriage. Why did his ego need to be so fragile? He'd had success after success.

Standing up there before the crowd, stunningly beautiful in that white gown, the elaborate and showy necklace perfect against her ivory skin, Catalina was a woman any man should be proud of.

Look at her, Leigh wanted to say. She has a smile that can melt an ice cube from across the room. She's not only immensely talented, but she's warm and loving and fair. And she loves you, Kevin.

As she watched, he tossed down the last of his drink and signaled the bartender for a repeat. *Oh, my God*, Leigh thought. *He's jealous of her here, too.*

Leigh wondered if she should say something or do something. But what could she do? Obviously Catalina was having a wonderful time. And so was everyone else in the lounge...everyone except Kevin.

When Kevin repeated his request for another drink, the bartender shook his head and at the conclusion of Catalina's song, announced that in a national park, the last call for drinks is eleven-thirty. "Sorry, folks. The bar's closed." Then to Catalina, he added, "But that doesn't mean you have to stop singing. You're welcome to continue with your party. I just can't serve any more alcohol."

"Sure, ever'body...keep on with the party." Kevin commanded with a slightly slurred speech. "But I've had enough!!"

Leigh saw the shock on Catalina's face and knew that this was the first time she'd seen Kevin like this. Before Catalina could make her way through the crowd to her husband, he'd shoved his way to the door and disappeared.

Leigh grabbed her coat and Catalina's and tried to catch her friend before she rushed out the door after Kevin.

When Zach reached her side, Leigh handed him Catalina's coat and asked him to take it to her. "She might need some help right now. Kevin looked downright ugly."

Zach nodded and hurried away.

Later he called Leigh from his cottage. He told her that Catalina had assured him everything would be all right. He was still a little worried, though, and suggested that he and Leigh remain in their own cottages so that no one would have any trouble reaching either of them in case there was a problem.

Leigh agreed and went to bed with a worried mind. It was hours before she was able to fall asleep, and even then she slept restlessly and overslept in the morning. When a persistent and loud knocking at her door awakened her the next morning, she struggled into her robe, still half asleep to open the door to Zach.

"Kevin's gone," he announced without preamble. "Catalina called me just a few minutes ago."

CHAPTER TEN

"WHAT HAPPENED?" Leigh asked. The stunning news amazed her.

"Apparently he really blew up at Catalina back in their room. Then he hauled his driver out of bed and made him drive him somewhere. Catalina didn't realize where he was going. She thought he was just going for a drive to cool down, which he does sometimes. She waited up for him and finally fell asleep. When she woke up, it was daylight and he wasn't back. Then she checked with the driver, who'd just returned, and he told her he'd taken Kevin to Fresno to the airport."

"Oh, no."

"I checked with the airport and apparently Kevin got on an early flight to L.A." Zach's face was set in a hard, angry expression Leigh had never seen before. "He's walked out on us," he finished tersely.

"Surely he'll be right back. Once he sobers up and comes to his senses."

"Who the hell knows?" Zach took a deep breath in an effort to calm down. "I'm sorry. I shouldn't be taking out my anger on you. It's not your fault."

"Isn't it? I'm the one he was mad at."

"No. He was mad at Catalina, as well. This is nothing more than a fit of temperament, pure and simple. He's throwing his weight around and I don't like it. Seventy people are sitting around, unable to do their jobs, because Kevin decided to go off in a huff. Not to mention the thousands of dollars this is costing.''

"Does the studio know?''

"I haven't called Gary yet. I assume Kevin's going home. I'll try to reach him there. But if I can't get hold of him, or if I do and he refuses to come straight back, I'll have to let the studio know.''

"Maybe we could rearrange the shooting schedule and do some of Catalina's close-ups today.''

Zach nodded absently, his mind still on Kevin. "Maybe.'' Then, looking at Leigh, he said, "I'm sorry. You're trying to salvage something out of this disaster, and I'm just standing here thinking about strangling Kevin.''

Leigh forced a smile. "I certainly don't blame you. I'd like to give him a good swift kick in the pants myself. While you try to reach him, I'll talk to Arnie about rescheduling today's scenes. And then I'll have a talk with Catalina. Maybe she can persuade Kevin to come back before too much time is lost.''

"I don't know. She was pretty upset when I left her.''

Zach left, and Leigh had a hurried meeting with Arnie. He indicated that he'd been through this sort of problem before and could handle it without too much difficulty. Leigh knew he was glossing over the logistical problems of rearranging a minutely planned schedule at the last moment. She appreciated his reassuring calm more than she could say. Someone else might have blown up, but Arnie, professional that he was, was directing his energy toward making the best of a bad situation.

"When this is over, I'm going to buy you and your wife the best dinner in L.A.," Leigh said gratefully.

"When this is over, I'll let you," he responded with a weary smile.

A few minutes later, Leigh entered Catalina's room. Catalina gave her a mute, thoroughly despondent look, then sat down heavily in a chair by a small round table. On the table was a half-empty pot of coffee.

Sitting down opposite her, Leigh asked gently, "Is that breakfast?"

Catalina smiled, but there was no emotion in her expression. And her eyes were red-rimmed from crying. "Yes. I'm not hungry."

"I haven't eaten yet. Why don't I order bacon and eggs for both of us?"

"You're humoring me."

"No. Oh, Catalina, I'm so sorry."

"I don't understand why he did it. I knew he was getting more and more upset about the way things were going. But I never expected this."

"None of us did. Kevin's never walked out on a picture before, has he?"

"No. He prides himself on being a professional."

"What happened?"

"You saw what happened at the party. Afterward, here in our room, he just exploded. Oh, Leigh, I can hardly bear to remember the things he said."

"Was he angry at me?"

"No, it wasn't so much you as *me*. He said I'd used him to further my career, that...that I didn't really love him. And he said that I should be pleased with myself because the way *Lodestar* was going, my career was rising and his was going downhill fast."

"But that's ridiculous."

"You and I know it's ridiculous, but Kevin doesn't."

"It sounds to me like he may be going through a midlife crisis."

Catalina nodded helplessly. "He just turned forty. The other day he made a remark about all the young actors coming up who are anxious to take his place. The truth is, he's right, you know. We were at a party shortly after we were married, and we heard a studio executive say he wanted 'a young Kevin Marlowe' for a certain role. I'll never forget the expression on Kevin's face. He looked, well, devastated."

"I know. Sex symbols and youth go hand in hand. It's pathetic but true. But, Catalina, that's precisely why it's important for Kevin to finish this picture. I'm convinced it will boost his standing as an actor and not just a sex symbol."

"I agree. I tried to tell him that. But he wouldn't listen. He was beyond reason last night."

"Well, maybe he's calmed down today."

"Leigh, you don't realize how upset he was. It wasn't just a temporary thing. At first I assumed it was just the party that got to him. And all the attention I'm getting right now on the movie. But I gradually realized it's not that simple. This is a turning point in Kevin's life. He took on the responsibility of marriage, and he can see the end of his tenure as the hottest star in Hollywood. And he doesn't know what will come next."

"I see. He's got a lot to deal with right now and it just suddenly became too much for him."

Catalina nodded.

"I should have been more perceptive, more understanding," Leigh mused guiltily.

"No, don't blame yourself. It's not your fault. And it's not mine. Kevin has to deal with all these issues. No one else can do it for him. No matter how much we care about him."

"Catalina, do you think he'll come back?"

"I know that's what everyone is wondering right now. The answer is...I just don't know."

"Have you tried to reach him at home?"

"Oh, yes. I've been calling every fifteen minutes. But there's no answer. Either he's not there yet or he's not answering the phone."

"What about your servants?"

"There's only one live-in maid. And we gave her a vacation while we were going to be up here. Leigh, I want to go after him."

Leigh had been expecting this. She answered carefully, "I know you do. But that would mean shutting down production completely. As it is, we've managed to rearrange things so we can do some of your close-ups. We don't need Kevin for those shots."

"How long can you work just with me, without needing Kevin?"

"I'm afraid not very long. Since it's basically a two-character picture, and the two of you are in most of the scenes together, there's just not that much we can do without Kevin. If he doesn't return by the day after tomorrow..."

Leigh didn't finish the thought. She didn't have to. Catalina knew as well as she did what would happen. Filming would shut down entirely, at a staggering cost of $50,000 a day. And *Lodestar* would quickly go way over budget.

"Catalina, I hate to ask this, knowing how miserable you're feeling right now, but..."

"But it's time to get down to the set," Catalina finished for her. "I know. The show must go on, as they say. Don't worry. I'm not going to fall apart on you, too."

"I appreciate that. Everyone else will, as well."

"Oh, Leigh, was it only two weeks ago we were talking about how exciting this was for both of us? Our first feature. A dream come true. And now..."

Leigh didn't respond. Her own feelings were too fragile to bear close scrutiny at the moment. But as she left the room to head down to the set, she thought about Catalina's words. "A dream come true." Yes, it had been that, all right. And not just the movie. Falling in love with Zach was the real dream come true.

Now a tiny flicker of fear caught at her heart. Would that end up to be a shattered dream, too?

AT MIDMORNING, Zach came to the set. Leigh ordered a brief break, and while Catalina went off to her dressing room, alone and looking terribly unhappy, Leigh and Zach talked quietly.

"I couldn't reach him," Zach said immediately, answering Leigh's unspoken question. "I'm flying down to L.A. right away to try to talk to him in person."

Leigh knew that Zach kept his plane at Mariposa, less than an hour away. She wished she were free to drive him there. It would give them some time together, which she badly needed at the moment. All of a sudden this game had gotten very rough...with high stakes...for everyone.

"Fly carefully, won't you. Now that I've found you, I don't want anything to happen to you." She smiled, trying to make a jest of her words. Her stomach felt as if she'd swallowed a fist-sized, very hard rock.

"I've told you before, I'm a very cautious pilot. You don't need to worry. Although, sweetheart," he said, dropping his voice even lower, "I like it that you'd tell me that."

"Will you call me as soon as you can?"

"Of course. Leigh...the first thing I'll do in L.A. is try to talk to Kevin. The second thing will be to notify the studio."

She wanted to ask him not to do that, to wait at least a day or so. But she knew that was merely postponing the inevitable. Besides, in some mysterious way, news traveled fast. By this evening, Gary would probably have somehow heard about Kevin's departure, whether Zach told him or not. It would be bad enough coming from Zach. Coming from someone else, it would be awful.

Leigh worked hard for the remainder of the day. The set was unusually quiet and there was an underlying tension as people went about their work. Leigh knew what was on everyone's mind—Kevin. Yet not one person mentioned his name.

Catalina was super. While the camera was on her, she acted her heart out. But between takes, she stayed in her dressing room where her makeup artist used every trick of the trade to conceal the evidence of crying.

There was a phone in the administration trailer. Leigh kept hoping Arnie would come out of the trailer and tell her Zach was calling. But he didn't. When the sun set, they wrapped for the day and Leigh returned to the hotel—with no idea what was happening in L.A.

ZACH SAT IN HIS OFFICE at the studio, gripping the phone rigidly. The knuckles of his hand were white, and anger was etched all over his face.

"Damn it, Mel, I just want to talk to Kevin."

"I understand. But he doesn't want to talk to you. Or anyone connected with *Lodestar*."

"Mel, if I can just talk to him, maybe we can resolve this before it reaches the point of no return and we have to start talking lawsuits."

There was a heavy sigh on the other end of the line. Mel wasn't happy about his client's behavior, Zach could tell. But Kevin was his client, and Mel had to take his side.

"Look, Zach, I'm sorry this happened. When Kevin called me this morning I tried to talk him into going back. But he said there's no way in hell he'll set foot on that set again. Period."

"This means big trouble, Mel, for all of us." Zach fought to keep his voice calm and cool. It wouldn't help for him to antagonize Kevin's agent. "You do know that, don't you?"

"Yeah, I know that, kid. Believe me, I know it." In spite of himself, Mel couldn't resist adding bitterly, "*Actors!*"

"If I went to his home, would he talk to me?"

"No. He isn't answering the door, or the phone for that matter. He called me when he got into town, but at the end of the conversation he said not to bother calling back because he was unplugging the phone for a few days.''

"So that's that." Zach's voice was heavy.

"That's that. I'm sorry, kid. I really am."

"I don't have to tell you this means a lawsuit, then."

"And I don't have to tell you that we'll fight it tooth and nail. Kevin's position is that the director substantially changed the movie, lowering his status as the star."

"That's b.s., Mel, and you know it." Zach gripped the phone, wishing he could throw it all the way to Toluca Lake and knock some sense into Kevin Marlowe. The numbskull bastard, he thought.

"Maybe. But it's my client's position. If he ends up in court, that will be his defense."

There was no point in saying anything more. Zach murmured a curt goodbye and hung up.

He hesitated only for a moment before dialing Gary's office. Although it was six o'clock, he knew the executive would still be working. Studio executives regularly worked late.

A moment later, Gary came on the line.

"Zach! Are you calling from Yosemite? How is it up there?"

"I'm at the studio, Gary."

"I didn't know you were going to be here today. Are you free for dinner, by any chance? My wife's away visiting her parents and I'm fending for myself."

"Gary, I'm afraid this isn't a social call. There's a problem on the set."

There was a pregnant pause on the other end of the line. Then, in a less friendly voice, Gary responded, "What is it?"

Briefly Zach explained what had happened with Kevin.

"I don't believe it. Kevin's egotistical, sure, but he's never walked off a set before."

"Well, there's a first time for everything. Unfortunately he chose my movie to be the first he'd walk away from."

"Have you talked to him?"

"He won't talk to anyone. Told his agent what he'd done, then sealed himself up in his house."

"What about his wife, Catalina?"

"Leigh's shooting her close-ups now, to fill time while waiting for Kevin to come back. But, Gary, I don't think he's coming back."

"Can't Catalina talk to him?"

"Apparently a big part of the reason he walked had to do with a fight he had with her."

"I see."

There was a world of meaning in those two brief words.

Gary went on slowly. "The dailies have looked fabulous. This is really a shame."

"Yes, it's that, all right."

"How long can Leigh shoot around Kevin?"

"A couple of days. No more. So far we're only marginally over budget. But if Kevin isn't back by tomorrow, the figures will start going up fast."

Even over the telephone, Zach sensed Gary was reaching a quick decision. "Okay, Zach, this is what we'll do. We'll give Kevin a couple of days. I'll talk to his agent tomorrow and see what I can do. But if it doesn't look like Kevin's coming back, that's it. He's fired and we start legal action against him for breach of contract."

"Will Sutton support that?" Zach asked, referring to the head of the studio.

"Yeah. You know how cost conscious he is. He particularly hates people who break contracts."

"What about *Lodestar*?" Zach tried not to let his concern show, but he knew he failed. The fact was, this movie meant everything to him. And Gary knew that just as well as he did.

"You've been shooting for two weeks, right?"

"Right."

"You've got how many to go?"

"Four weeks to go. So far, we've been on schedule and just slightly over budget."

"What would it add to the budget to recast Kevin's part?"

Zach did some quick mental arithmetic. "I'd guess we could do it for another two or three million, not including the salary of whoever we'd hire to replace Kevin," Zach estimated.

"Do you mean that?"

"You know I do. There's no point in trying to gloss over things now."

"I had lunch with Connor Stevens a few days ago. What do you think about him for the part?"

Zach hesitated. Stevens was a relative newcomer. He'd had minor roles in three recent films that had done well. The critics had singled him out for special praise. Though he was a good deal younger than Kevin and certainly didn't have his name value, he was a good actor who just might be on the edge of stardom. All it took was the right part. And *Lodestar* could provide it.

"He and Catalina would look great together," Zach finally answered slowly.

"Anyone would look great with her. Of course, there's a lot of publicity value in Kevin and Catalina starring together. Although if their marriage is on the rocks, who knows."

"I'll call Leigh tonight and give her your suggestion. I think it's safe to say Stevens would be acceptable. Do you think he'd be interested?"

"I'm sure of it. He wants a starring role very badly. He's not expensive yet. We could probably get him for under a hundred thousand. Well, I'll let you go, Zach. Like I said, I'll try to talk to Kevin. If that doesn't work, I'll ask Sutton to give him a call. And if that doesn't work, I'll talk to Connor."

"Okay. I'll be staying in town until this resolved. I'll be in the office waiting to hear from you. And, Gary, thanks for not shutting us down."

"Are you kidding? *Lodestar*'s got too much going for it to shut down. I thought Leigh would do a good job, but even I've been surprised at the footage I've seen. How have you two been getting along together?"

Zach hesitated, then answered evasively, "Fine. Just fine. It was definitely the right decision to fire Ralph and hire Leigh."

"Good. I'm glad to hear you say that. I wondered how you two would do, considering your initial antagonism. Well, as I said, I'll let you go now. Talk to you tomorrow."

After hanging up, Zach leaned back in his black leather chair and put his feet up on his desk. He was utterly exhausted. And angrier than he could ever remember being. If he could have gotten his hands on Kevin at that moment he would have throttled him. The man was a primadonna, jeopardizing the careers of several people, not to mention the success of a twenty-million-dollar project, in a stupid fit of ego.

Zach had half expected Gary to pull the plug on the movie. It certainly wouldn't be the first time that had happened because of personnel problems. They were just lucky that Gary was so impressed with the dailies he'd seen so far.

No, Zach thought, correcting himself, it wasn't luck. It was Leigh's ability, pure and simple. She was very, very good. And because of that, *Lodestar* had a shot at surviving Kevin's ill temper.

Kevin was thoroughly unprofessional. And his treatment of Catalina was unconscionable.

Glancing at his watch, Zach saw that it was nearly seven. Leigh would have finished shooting by now and would probably be in her cottage waiting for his call. He dialed her number, and when she answered after the first ring, he began dryly, "Well, there's good news and bad news."

"Oh, God, give me the bad news first."

"Kevin won't talk to anyone. He made one call to alert his agent, and that was it. He has no intention of coming back and it doesn't look like I'll even have a chance to try to change his mind."

"Oh, Zach, he can't mean it."

"He does, love. But the good news is that Gary isn't pulling the plug on the project."

"He isn't?"

The overwhelming relief evident in her voice revealed that she'd been just as worried as he had been that the worst would happen.

"No, he isn't. And we've all got you to thank for that. He loves the dailies, thinks you're doing a super job."

"Oh, Zach, everyone is. Even Kevin, before he walked out."

"Let's not mention Kevin again. Gary said if he doesn't come back in a couple of days, he's out and the studio will initiate legal proceedings against him."

"Oh, no."

"Don't tell me you feel sorry for the guy!"

"Zach, you don't understand. He isn't causing problems on purpose. It's just a difficult time for him."

"Spare me the sob story. I can't work up one ounce of pity for the man. He's willing to put all of us out of work, knowing how much this movie means to every damn one of us."

Leigh didn't respond, and Zach went on in a calmer voice, "Gary suggested Connor Stevens to replace Kevin."

"Yes," Leigh replied in a thoughtful voice. "He's good. But he's not in Kevin's league."

"He's also not likely to walk out on us. By the way, how did it go today?"

"It was okay. Everyone tried to pretend they weren't worried about production shutting down."

"How's Catalina?"

"Professionally, she's just fine. But personally she's miserable. She wants to go back to L.A. and talk to Kevin."

"If she leaves we'll have to shut down entirely."

"I know. I told her that."

"Leigh, Kevin told his agent he doesn't intend to talk to anyone. I don't think it would do any good for Catalina to fly down here. But if she feels she has to, I won't hold it against her."

"Oh, Zach, thanks for saying that. We'll see how it goes. Maybe she'll be able to reach him by phone. She's still trying, but apparently the phone's unplugged."

"Yeah, Kevin told his agent he was going to do that."

Leigh sighed. "I don't believe it. It's so stupid."

"Yes."

"Oh, I just realized it's about time for dailies. I've got to run. Will you keep me posted on developments?"

"Sure. Leigh..."

His voice had dropped to become more intimate. Her own was softer as she responded, "Yes?"

"I miss you already."

"I miss you, too."

"Good night, love."

"Good night."

When he hung up, he leaned his head against the back of the chair and closed his eyes for a long moment. He thought of Leigh, remembering how she'd looked wearing nothing but firelight that last time they'd made love. He wished she was with him now. Going back to his house was somehow unappealing, knowing that she wouldn't be there.

At that moment, he realized just how much she'd come to mean to him.

CATALINA WORKED HARD for the next two days. But when Leigh said, "That's a take," for the last time on the second day, Catalina didn't return to her dressing room. Instead she quickly changed out of her costume, leaving her makeup on, and hurried to catch up with Leigh so that the two of them could ride down to the hotel together.

As they sat in the back seat of the station wagon, Catalina came straight to the point. "I'm flying down to L.A. tonight. There's a ten o'clock flight out of Fresno. I can just make it if I hurry."

She wasn't asking for permission, she was simply informing Leigh of her decision. But inherent in her words was a plea for understanding.

For a moment Leigh didn't speak. Then she said quietly, "I understand. Zach will, too."

"Oh, Leigh, thank you for not being angry. If you ordered me to stay, I don't know what I'd do."

"Yes, you do. You'd go to your husband, no matter what. Which is exactly what you should do."

"I'm not giving up this marriage without a fight."

"Catalina, he may not want to talk to you."

"Oh, I'm sure he doesn't. Otherwise, he'd plug the phone back in. But I'm not going to let it end this way."

She gave Leigh a long, hard look and went on, "There's just one thing I have to know. If I can persuade him to come back, will you take him back?"

"I will. But I'm afraid Zach and the studio might not. They gave Kevin two days to come back and the two days are up. They've already got someone else in mind. I didn't say anything to you before, but I think it's time you knew."

"I'm not surprised. And Kevin's certainly brought it on himself. But, Leigh, *you're* the director. What you say goes."

Leigh smiled self-deprecatingly. "Not exactly."

"Do you want Kevin to come back?"

"Yes. And I'm not just saying that because I know how much it means to you, Catalina. Kevin was doing a great job before he left. The two of you were absolutely perfect together. No one else the studio could hire at this point would be as good. I want what's best for this picture. And Kevin would be best."

"I'm so glad to hear you say that. Now all I have to do is shake some sense into that man."

"I wish you luck. I really do. Not just for the movie, but for your own sake."

Catalina responded with determination. "Luck has nothing to do with it. I'm not going to let him throw away what we've got going together."

Looking at her, Leigh hoped she was right and that it wasn't a matter of luck, but determination. If it was, Catalina's marriage—and *Lodestar*—might still have a chance.

IT WAS AFTER MIDNIGHT when Catalina let herself into her house. The lights were off, except for one in the den. She knew that must be where Kevin was, and she headed straight there. When she opened the door, she found him sitting in his favorite chair reading an old script from one of his first movies.

He looked up sharply, clearly not expecting anyone. To her relief, he didn't appear to have been drinking. He was a better actor than people had given him credit for, and he immediately steeled himself to appear nonchalant. But for an instant Catalina had seen something in his dark eyes that wrenched her heart. What she saw was fear.

Why, he's just a scared little boy, she thought. Without saying a word, she walked over to him and knelt by his chair. She took his hand and laid it against her cheek.

"I love you so much," she whispered.

The blasé expression he'd assumed crumbled in an instant.

"I've been a jerk. Why on earth do you love me still?"

"Because you need me."

He pulled her up into his lap and wrapped his arms around her. Burying his face in her neck, he said in a choked voice, "Yes, I need you. God, how I need you. For two days I stayed drunk and told myself it was all your fault. Then today I sobered up. And I realized I'm nothing without you."

"Oh, Kevin, sweetheart." She murmured words of love over and over again, at the same time raining gentle kisses over his face.

"Oh, Cat, I don't know how to make you understand what I was going through. I put everything I had into building my career. It was all I had. And I could see it ending. Maybe not this year. Or even next year. But someday. And soon."

"Kevin, look at me." She gazed deeply into his dark eyes. "Your career isn't over. And it sure isn't all you have. You've got me. You'll always have me. And..."

Taking his hand, she placed it on her stomach. "In a little over seven months you'll have our child, as well."

"Cat...are you sure?"

She grinned. "As of yesterday, yes. I've suspected it for a couple of weeks but I didn't want to say anything until it was definite."

Kevin looked so surprised, Catalina couldn't help laughing. "It's not all that amazing, you know. Women get pregnant all the time."

"It's just that I haven't given much thought to children. I haven't given much thought to anything except my career. But you know, Cat, it's really exciting."

She smiled. "Yes, I think it's kind of exciting, too. I hope you won't be one of those fathers who refuses to change a diaper."

"No way. I want to be part of my kid's life. There'll be no nannies or governesses raising him. We'll do it ourselves. If you're working, I'll take care of him."

Giving her a sheepish look, he added, "Believe it or not, I'm actually very proud of you."

For a moment Catalina was so touched she could barely speak. Then she said, "Hey, it might not be a boy, you know."

"That's okay. A girl's even better. Especially if she looks just like her mother."

"Oh, Kevin, I do love you so."

"I love you, Cat. I was a fool to come so close to losing you."

"Don't worry. I wasn't about to let that happen."

He was thoughtful for a moment. Then he said slowly, "I don't know if they'll take me back."

She knew what he meant. "Leigh wants you back."

"She does?"

"Yes."

"I'm surprised. There's no reason why she should be willing to have anything more to do with me."

"You're right, there isn't, considering how badly you treated her. But she's no fool, Kevin. She knows you're the best possible thing for *Lodestar*."

"I'm not sure Zach and the studio feel the same way."

Catalina didn't want to go into what Leigh had told her about the studio already considering a replacement for Kevin. She didn't want to shatter their fragile reconciliation. Instead she said honestly, "Well, all you can do is apologize and tell them you're ready to go back to work. Then see what they say."

"Yeah, that's true. Okay. First thing in the morning I'll call Leigh. Then I'll ask Mel to get in touch with the studio and see how things stand with them. But I want to talk to Leigh personally. You're right— I definitely owe her an apology."

"Kevin Marlowe, you're quite a guy. Now then, what do you think about the name Melanie if it's a girl?"

LEIGH WAS ALREADY UP at seven the next morning, busily trying to decide how to find something for the crew to shoot, when Kevin called. It was a short, thoroughly satisfactory conversation on both sides. He apologized, she accepted gracefully, and they agreed that Kevin would return to Yosemite that night, ready to begin work the following morning. Assuming the studio agreed.

The moment she hung up, Leigh called Zach. He had just returned from his early-morning run and was slightly out of breath when he answered the phone.

"I just talked to Kevin," she began without preamble, "and he's coming back tonight."

"It's too late."

"But..."

"I mean it, Leigh. I had a late conversation with Gary last night. He's offered the part to Stevens."

"He can't do that. It's Kevin's role."

"It *was* Kevin's role. His two days have passed. The studio isn't interested in talking to him now."

"You mean you're not."

"No, I'm not."

"Zach, he gave me his word of honor that he won't walk away again."

"Somehow I don't find that reassuring."

"Zach."

"The man can't be trusted, Leigh. Both the studio and I want him replaced. It looks like we can cut a deal with Stevens right away, and he can be ready to work in a couple of days."

"Kevin's returning tonight. He'll be ready to work first thing tomorrow morning."

"Damn it, Leigh, I don't understand your attitude. The man was awful to you."

"Yes. But that's over."

"For now. Who knows how long it would be before he'd blow up and do a disappearing act again."

"Zach, I honestly don't think that will happen. Kevin's never walked out before. There was a lot of pressure building up in him at the time, and that's the only reason it happened now. But he's resolved all that. He and Catalina are back together and he's anxious to redeem himself."

"Why on earth should you care whether or not Kevin redeems himself?"

"If he doesn't, it could be the end of his career."

"Yes. But he certainly didn't care when he left and it could have been the end of our movie. Not to mention both our careers."

"Zach, it will break him personally and professionally if he isn't allowed to return."

"Leigh, I'm not out for revenge against the man. I'm beyond anger now. I just want to get on with the movie. I can't let pity for Kevin overshadow my business sense. In this business you have to be pragmatic, not idealistic. We've lost a lot of money because of Kevin so far. Who knows how much more we'll lose if he comes back, then leaves again?"

"All right, if you want to be practical, look at it this way—Kevin's perfect in the role. You said so yourself recently."

"Stevens would be just as good."

"No, he wouldn't, and you know it."

"All right, he wouldn't. But he would at least be dependable. And right now, that's what the studio's concerned with. Leigh, even if I was willing to take Kevin back, the studio isn't. They want Stevens. Their business-affairs department has already been instructed to file suit against Kevin."

"Zach, this is insane! They can't do that."

"They're doing it. It's out of my hands now, Leigh."

"You're on their side, aren't you?

"I'm being practical and so are they. We can't let one neurotic actor ruin this for everyone else."

"You think you're being practical." Leigh didn't even try to keep the anger from her voice. "The truth is, you're going along with what the studio wants. You're not willing to fight for Kevin.''

''You're right, I'm not.''

''Well, what about me?''

''What do you mean?''

''Are you willing to fight for me? Because I intend to insist they let Kevin return.''

''Damn it, Leigh, you've got to listen to reason.''

''No, you listen. You're so worried about the studio dropping this project that you're willing to go along with anything they do, no matter who it hurts. You've lost your integrity. Well, I don't intend to lose mine.''

She slammed down the phone. And before Zach could call her back, she grabbed her jacket and purse and left the cottage. A few minutes later, her driver was taking her down to the Fresno airport to catch a flight to L.A.

CHAPTER ELEVEN

LEIGH STRODE INTO GARY JENNINGS'S OFFICE. "Is he in?" she asked the secretary.

"Yes, but Mr. Stewart's with him."

"Good," Leigh responded curtly.

And without waiting for the secretary to buzz Gary, she entered his private office.

Both Gary and Zach looked up in surprise at the sudden interruption.

"Leigh!" For a moment Zach looked intensely happy to see her. But one look at her face changed his expression.

"Leigh, what a surprise." Motioning to a chair opposite his desk, Gary went on, "Please sit down."

"What's happening on the set?" Zach asked pointedly.

"Jonas is shooting some second-unit stuff. But I shut down main production for today. There was nothing really to do, anyway."

"Well, that's all right," Gary assured her. Don't worry. You'll be back in business in a couple of days when Connor Stevens arrives. He's just waiting for us to get a deal memo to his agent."

"That's what I came down here to talk to both of you about." Gathering her courage, she forged ahead. "Gary, did Zach tell you I spoke with Kevin?"

"Yes. But it doesn't really matter at this point, does it?"

"I think it does—"

"Leigh, listen..." Zach interrupted.

"No, you listen. Both of you. What happened with Kevin was inexcusable, I agree. But it was a temporary problem that's resolved now. He's genuinely sorry for the problems he caused."

"Sorry!" Zach snapped angrily.

"Yes, *sorry*. He assures me it won't happen again."

"I'm not sure we can trust him," Gary responded tersely.

"I trust him."

"Why on earth should you?" Zach asked.

Leigh hesitated. It was a good question, and she wasn't at all sure how to answer it. Finally she said slowly, "I can't say I like Kevin a lot personally. Especially after what's happened. But he is a professional. What happened was an aberration, not at all the sort of thing he'd do under normal circumstances."

"Even so, Leigh, I think it would be safer to go with Connor. He wants this role badly and won't screw up."

"Gary, I understand that. But look at it this way—if you let Kevin come back, you'll save a lot of money by not having to reshoot his scenes. He and Catalina are very much back together now and there will be tremendous publicity value in a picture starring the two of them."

"That's true, but..."

"And Kevin's really good in this, Gary. You must have noticed that?"

"I noticed it. He's kind of surprised everyone here. But if he's unstable emotionally now, and it sure looks like he is, then we can't take any more risks with him. We're quickly reaching a point of no return on *Lodestar*. If we get any further into production and he walks out again, that's *it*. We can't afford to hire someone else and reshoot. We'd have to scrap the whole project, at a considerable financial loss."

"I know that. If I'm prepared to take that risk, knowing what it would mean to my career, can't the studio?"

"It isn't just the studio," Zach reminded her. "I don't want to have anything more to do with the man. Gary's right, he's emotionally unstable. There's no reason to trust him."

"Then let me put it this way. I'm the director. Both of you wanted me for this job. Now it's only fair that you trust me."

"Leigh..." Zach protested.

"I mean it, Zach," she insisted angrily. "I'm the one responsible for bringing in this film, yet you didn't even consult me before making the decision to replace Kevin. Maybe you can't trust Kevin. But you certainly should trust *me*. Otherwise, what on earth am I doing here?"

Both men were silent.

Leigh looked at Zach, and though she didn't say another word, he knew perfectly well what she was getting at. They'd had this argument before about Jonas. She'd put everything on the line then and been willing to lose it all rather than give in when she felt she was right.

And he knew without a doubt that she'd do the same thing right now.

As she and Zach looked at each other, the anger left her expression. Her gray eyes were desperate with a mute appeal.

Finally, he said slowly, "Leigh's right, Gary. She's the director. We should go with her judgment on this."

All the love in the world shone in Leigh's eyes as she smiled at Zach.

Gary rubbed his chin thoughtfully. "I don't know. Kevin's really been impossible."

"He'll be a lamb from now on. I'm sure of it," Leigh insisted.

"How can you be so sure?"

"Because both Catalina and I will see to it."

Still Gary hesitated. Leigh felt the seconds tick by with excruciating slowness. So much depended on his decision...Kevin's career...the future of his marriage to Catalina...and Leigh's position as a director with real authority.

Zach looked at Leigh, then turned to Gary. "She's right, you know. If Kevin does shape up, it would be best for the picture. Connor's good but he can't really take Kevin's place."

Gary came to a decision. "All right. I'll cancel the offer to Connor. He'll be upset, but I'll just have to find something else for him."

Leigh wanted to jump for joy. She flashed a huge grin at Gary. "You won't regret it. I promise."

Turning to Zach, she said in a softer tone, "Thanks."

Gary went on firmly, "Let me make one thing clear to you, Leigh. If any other problems come up because of this, you'll be responsible."

Gary was too nice to make it an outright threat. But Leigh knew perfectly well that was what it came down to. She'd gone out on a limb for Kevin. And her future as a director hung in the balance.

A few minutes later she and Zach left Gary's office. As they walked down to the parking lot, neither spoke. There was so much Leigh wanted to say, yet somehow she couldn't seem to think of the right words.

Zach walked with her to her car. Then, as they stood there, she looked up at him. "I can't tell you what your support meant to me."

"You don't have to say anything."

"It means so much to Kevin, too."

"I didn't do it for Kevin. I did it for you. For us."

She knew what he meant. If he hadn't supported her when she really needed him, their relationship couldn't possibly have survived.

Zach took her in his arms and held her for a long moment. Neither cared that it was broad daylight, the middle of the studio parking lot, and if anyone saw them it would start the kind of gossip they'd tried so hard to avoid. All that mattered was being close to each other after coming so close to losing their love.

It was a touching moment between them, but it was also bittersweet, Leigh thought sadly. Her triumph was tinged with concern. She had won, true, but at what cost? She had come so close to losing Zach. The realization that such a thing could happen simply because of the conflicts in their work was frightening.

She looked up into those blue, blue eyes and whispered helplessly, "Oh, Zach, we were right at the edge of a deep, dark chasm. For a moment I thought we would go over."

"I know, love. God, I know. We were only doing what we each thought was right."

"But what a price we would have paid for being right. I'm not at all sure it would have been worth it."

"Neither am I. That's why I gave in."

"I wonder...will you regret giving in?"

He bent his head, then gently brushed his lips across her forehead. "Not this time."

Not this time...but if there were a next time, what then?

THEY WERE BACK at the Ahwahnee that evening. Zach called a meeting of everyone in his cottage. When they were all gathered there, he announced that Kevin was returning and shooting would resume the next morning. There was an audible sigh of relief around the room, and Leigh heard someone mutter under his breath, "About time!"

As they left, Jonas stopped to talk to Leigh. "How'd you do it, kid?"

"I didn't. Catalina persuaded him to come back."

"I hope he realizes how lucky he is to have her."

"I hope so, too."

"I imagine the studio was pretty upset. They don't like it when a problem comes up and a picture goes over budget."

"No, they don't like it. But it could be worse. We didn't lose that much money. Well, I'll see you at dailies, Jonas."

When he left, Leigh turned back to Zach who was poring over some papers.

"Arnie gave me a revised budget," he explained as Leigh joined him on the sofa. "It doesn't look too bad. Assuming things go smoothly from now on."

"I think they will—"

Leigh was interrupted by a knock at the door.

Rising, Zach went to answer it. When he opened it, he found Kevin standing outside. For a moment he hesitated, then he said in a cool voice, "Come in."

Leigh was surprised to see Kevin. She hadn't expected him to show himself until he was due on the set in the morning.

He looked steadily at both Leigh and Zach. "I wanted to apologize to both of you, in person. I behaved like a damn fool and caused a lot of problems for everyone. I don't have an excuse. All I can do is say it won't happen again."

Leigh sensed what it took for Kevin to humble himself this way. And it gave her more respect for him that she'd felt up to now. But she had no idea how Zach would take Kevin's apology.

For a few tense seconds Zach merely looked at Kevin. His expression clearly indicated that as far as he was concerned, apologizing was the least Kevin could do. Watching him, Leigh prayed that he would accept the apology in the spirit with which it was given.

To her relief, he finally said, "Apology accepted. Let's put it behind us and go on from here."

"Right. Well, I'd better go. I won't be at the dailies. I've got to study my lines for tomorrow. But I'll be on the set on time."

As he started to walk out the door, he turned and said, "Thanks, Zach."

"Don't thank me, Kevin. Thank Leigh."

Kevin shot her a grateful look. "Thank you."

"That's all right," Leigh murmured.

When Kevin had gone, Zach returned to the sofa and put his arm around Leigh.

"We have to go to dailies in a few minutes," she said as her cheek rested against his shoulder.

"I know. I just want to hold you for a little while."

She wanted that, too. If it wasn't for the fact that their absence would look decidedly odd, she would have skipped the dailies and made love to Zach instead. At that moment touching him was what she wanted to do more than anything else in the world. She wanted to be as close to him as possible, to erase the lingering emotional distance that remained between them. He wanted that, as well, she knew.

But there was no time. *Lodestar* had a higher priority than lovemaking.

She sighed and Zach released her reluctantly. "Okay, love, let's go see what we've got."

Later, when they returned to Leigh's cabin, they made love with an urgency and intensity that overwhelmed both of them. Leigh knew that for both of them it was an attempt to rid themselves of the faint bitter aftertaste of their disagreement that morning.

Each did everything possible to make this as special as it always had been before. Yet as they lay in each other's arms afterward, both sensed that it wasn't quite the same somehow. Harsh reality had intruded into their fantasy world. It would take a while, perhaps a long while, to recapture the magic they'd lost.

Lying there in the dark, Leigh felt that there was still a wall between them. And she was afraid. Very afraid.

"Zach...will we be all right?" she asked.

"Yes. I promise you, Leigh, nothing will affect what we have."

But it was a promise that she knew it might be hard to keep.

SHOOTING RESUMED. Kevin was every inch the professional. Although he occasionally questioned Leigh's directions, he did not push it too far. He and Catalina were transparently happy together, and their new closeness showed in their performances. They meshed perfectly on screen, revealing a chemistry that Leigh knew would prove explosive at the box office.

The reaction was universally positive at dailies each evening. And when Leigh periodically checked in with Gary, she heard nothing but compliments. The studio was so pleased, in fact, that they were already planning on increasing the advertising budget for the movie and moving up its release date.

"You were right about Kevin," Gary said more than once.

Somehow Leigh couldn't take as much pleasure in that knowledge as she might have otherwise. Because she couldn't shake the nagging feeling that things weren't the same between her and Zach.

The evening before shooting was scheduled to finish, Leigh was in her cabin alone. Zach had gone down to L.A., there were no meetings to be held, and because of a delay in processing the film from the previous day's shooting, there were no dailies to view. For the first time since Leigh had taken on the *Lodestar* project, she had a block of free time.

She almost felt like a kid playing hooky. She could go to the bar at the Ahwahnee, where many of the company congregated each night, and relax with them over a drink. Or she could go for a nighttime jog around the well-lit hotel grounds. Or call Connie and catch up on what was happening with her. Or...

She stopped. What she really wanted to do was absolutely *nothing*. For one evening she wanted to let her mind go completely blank and her body relax. So she took a long, leisurely bath, nearly falling asleep in the warm water she'd scented with lavender bath salts. Then she slipped on an emerald green velvet caftan and ordered a slice of chocolate cake and a large glass of milk from room service.

She was just digging into the cake a few minutes later, when someone knocked at her door. Opening it, she found Catalina standing outside.

"Hi. Am I disturbing anything?"

"Nope. I was just giving in to the deep chocoholic streak in me. Come in."

They sat down and Leigh went on, "Want half?"

Catalina grinned. "No, thanks. I wouldn't dream of coming between you and that scrumptious-looking cake. Of course, the fact that I indulged in a hot fudge sundae after dinner makes it a little easier to decline. Since shooting's almost finished, I thought I could stop worrying about my figure."

"Do you mind if I eat in front of you, then?"

"Of course not. Are you sure I'm not a nuisance? It looks like you were all set to enjoy some peace and quiet."

"You're definitely not a nuisance. Actually all this peace and quiet was beginning to seem a little strange. I'm not used to it anymore."

"I know what you mean. Boy, am I looking forward to going home. Just Kevin and I for...well, a few days at least."

"Things seem to be going awfully well with you two."

Catalina nodded happily. "They are. Better than ever." Then she explained, "I know we're going to wrap tomorrow, and the day after we'll all be heading our separate ways. I wanted to talk to you one last time before that."

"I hope I'll be seeing you two again. You know, you're welcome to come into the editing room and see how *Lodestar*'s coming together."

"Thanks. That's a generous offer. We'll definitely take you up on it. But I promise we won't wear out our welcome."

Leigh had finished the cake. She set down the plate, drank the last of the milk and sighed luxuriously. "Now this is the life. I could get used to doing absolutely nothing but indulging myself."

"I seriously doubt that. You're destined for bigger and better things, Leigh."

"So are you."

Catalina looked suddenly shy. "Well, actually, there's something very special in my future I wanted to tell you about. I'm going to have a baby."

"Oh, Catalina, how wonderful! I'm so happy for you."

Impulsively Leigh leaned toward her and hugged her warmly.

"I think it's pretty wonderful, too."

"I imagine Kevin's very proud."

"I guess."

Something in Catalina's tone revealed her uncertainty.

Leigh went on carefully, "Surely he's as excited as you are."

"Well, to be honest, I'm not sure. He says he's very happy about it, and I know it's had an impact on him. It would have to, of course, since things certainly won't be the same. But sometimes I think he's a little reluctant."

"Maybe he's afraid of the responsibility."

"Maybe. Listen, Leigh, I didn't intend to get into any soul searching. I just wanted to tell you the good news."

"Does anyone else know?"

Catalina shook her head decisively. "No. And I don't want it to get out for a while. You know what will happen. Everyone will be talking about it, it'll be in all the papers. I don't want it to be a publicity thing. At least not yet."

"I understand. I won't say a word to anyone."

"You can tell Zach. I know you won't want to keep secrets from him."

Leigh was taken aback. "What...what do you mean?"

Catalina flashed her a knowing smile. "Well, since you're involved."

"You know about us?"

"Of course."

Leigh felt her heart sink. "Does everyone know?"

"Oh, no," Catalina hastened to assure her. "I'm sorry, I didn't mean to give that impression at all. Believe me, as far as I can tell no one knows. There certainly hasn't been any gossip about it."

"Then how did you know?"

"I saw the way you looked at each other sometimes. And I just knew. I may look like an empty-headed paper doll, but I'm not."

Leigh burst out laughing. "No, you're not. And to think I was convinced we'd managed to keep the greatest secret since the atom bomb was developed."

Catalina gave her a shrewd look. "I imagine it's been difficult for you—loving him and working together at the same time."

Leigh nodded.

"Well, I can certainly relate to that," Catalina went on meaningfully.

"I know. Obviously you two had your share of problems, but they seem to have worked out okay."

"They *seem* to. Of course, they seem to have worked out with you and Zach, too."

"Yes." Leigh answered enigmatically.

Catalina said abruptly, "Look at us. Prime examples of the New Woman. We have it all. But you know, *all* is actually a very big word. I wonder if it's really possible to ever have it all."

"Men never ask that question," Leigh responded thoughtfully. "They have families and careers and no one thinks twice about it."

"But the truth is they usually put most of their energy into their careers and not family life. They don't feel torn between one or the other. Women, on the other hand, are very torn."

"I know. No one asks a successful man, how did you combine your career and marriage? Successful women are always asked that. The underlying assumption is that if they pursued a career, their family must have suffered."

"And so often it does, doesn't it?" Catalina asked bluntly. "If I'm off shooting a picture, I can't be with my child. And that means letting someone else raise that child."

"Unless Kevin shares the responsibility."

"He says he'll do just that. Obviously that would be the ideal solution. But..."

Catalina hesitated, and Leigh sensed what was worrying her. It was easy for Kevin to say at this point that he would share parenting responsibilities. But when the time came, and it perhaps meant a career sacrifice on his part, would he follow through?

Catalina shook her head unhappily. "It's not fair, you know."

"No. But as someone very wise once told me, life isn't fair."

Catalina shot Leigh a rueful look. "I wonder what will happen to us? We want love and we want success at demanding careers. Yet so often the two seem to be mutually exclusive. And if we're forced to choose between the two...we wind up lacking something crucial."

"Well, I hope we won't have to choose. Maybe, with work and a lot of determination, we can combine our personal and professional lives. Anyway, isn't it lovely to think so?"

Catalina smiled ruefully. "Yes, it's lovely to think so."

Leigh went on. "You have Kevin. Soon you'll have a child. And, unless I'm very much mistaken, your career is really going to take off when this movie's released."

Catalina smiled hopefully. "I suppose so. And you're not doing too badly yourself, Leigh. In one sense you have the best of all possible worlds—working with the man you love, accomplishing something wonderful together."

Together...if there were no more conflicts between what they believed in and what they felt for each other. What a big *if* that was, Leigh thought soberly.

THE WRAP PARTY WAS HELD the next night in one of the banquet rooms of the hotel. The studio had spared no expense. Champagne flowed like...well, like champagne, Leigh thought wryly. And there was a veritable feast. Everyone was there, from Kevin and Catalina down to the grips and gaffers. All of them shared a tremendous sense of accomplishment and close feeling of comaraderie. For once, there wasn't the slightest tension among the company. They'd accomplished what they'd set out to do, and the project already had that faint smell of success.

Leigh wore a romantic cream-colored sheer cotton dress. It had a fitted bodice with a low neckline and a two-tiered full skirt that struck her midcalf. Tiny covered buttons began just above the swell of her breasts and ended at the hem. She had received many compliments on the dress and was just accepting another from Liz Bramley, when she spotted Jonas.

Standing in a corner by himself, he motioned to Leigh to join him.

"What are you doing off by yourself?" Leigh teased.

"Oh, don't worry, I'll join in the festivities in a minute. But I wanted to say something to you, without a bunch of people listening in."

"Okay, shoot."

"I don't normally give advice. Since I was never much good at taking it myself, it's kinda like the pot calling the kettle black. But there's something I feel I have to say. You can take it for what it's worth."

"Coming from you, it will be worth a lot."

"Well, here goes. You don't have to tell me whether you have final cut on this film. I know almost no director ever gets that. And that means, no matter what kind of director's cut you turn in to the studio, they can change it however they please. I've had more than my share of hassles with studios over final cuts. I like to think I was right more often than they were. But in the end, that didn't matter. 'Cause I nearly lost my career for good."

"Are you trying to tell me not to fight the studio on the final cut?"

He nodded. "Yup. You'll get a reputation for being difficult, and believe me, kid, that's the kiss of death in Hollywood."

"But, Jonas, if we don't fight for what we believe in, what's the point in even trying?"

"You can fight for what you believe in. You should, in fact. But when push comes to shove, give in gracefully. Cause you don't really have any choice."

At that moment Zach walked up. "What are you two conspiring about?"

Jonas smiled. "Nothing. Just a little fatherly talk. Well, I see some of my poker-playing teamster buddies over there. Be seeing you."

"Having fun?" Zach asked Leigh when Jonas was gone.

She put Jonas's disturbing advice out of her mind. "Oh, yes. And you?"

He nodded. "The hard part's over. Now postproduction begins. It can be a grind, but at least there's no question about what we've got to work with in the editing room."

"Are you really happy with what we've got?"

"Yes. You know I am."

"And the studio?"

Zach grinned. "I think they're already counting the gross."

"I heard you talked to Gary today. What did he think about the latest dailies?"

To Leigh's surprise, Zach hesitated. Then he answered evasively, "Oh, you know, the usual pleased response. He had some questions about the ending, but..."

"The ending? But I told him weeks ago what I planned to do."

"I know. But as you'd expect, the studio prefers unequivocally happy endings. They make for better box office."

"But this is a happy ending. They survive. They've each grown during their ordeal, and their feelings about each other have changed for the better."

"I know, Leigh. But the studio would have preferred that they walk off into the sunset together, hand in hand, after making it perfectly clear to the audience that they're going to live happily ever after, with no more problems.''

''That's unrealistic. These people were on their way to get a divorce at the beginning of the story. Their problems simply wouldn't be resolved that easily. As it is, the ending indicates that they're going to take a new look at their marriage and see if there's a chance of saving it.''

It was obvious she was getting worked up. In response, Zach said soothingly, ''Hey, don't get crazy over this. All I'm saying is that the studio prefers a straightforward, old-fashioned happy ending rather than one that leaves things kind of up in the air.''

''Do you?'' Leigh asked pointedly.

''It's better box office.''

Before Leigh could argue further, he said firmly, ''Enough. I don't want to talk shop tonight. And I sure as hell don't want to argue with you.'' Lowering his voice, he said huskily, ''What I want to do is get out of here as soon as is decently possible and have our own private celebration in my cabin.''

''Let's have it in mine,'' she said, giving him an impudent smile. ''That way, you're the one who has to get dressed and go home.''

In her cottage, Leigh laid aside her shawl and clutch. Raising herself on tiptoes, she reached her arms around Zach's neck. He wrapped his arms about her waist and effortlessly lifted her so that their faces were even. Blue eyes, their usual intensity subdued by desire, met gray eyes dreamy with love.

Zach watched the long lashes slowly descend to lie like shadows on white silk. Dropping his gaze, he saw the glossy sheen of her sensuously full lower lip. Then he, too, closed his eyes as he felt the very tip of Leigh's tongue begin a slow and deliberate tracing of his lips. Her arms tightened as she pressed closer to him, her mouth now fully against his as her tongue slipped between his lips. They'd emptied their glasses of champagne just before leaving the party and now, as he tasted the wine Leigh had enjoyed, he felt a charge of passionate desire. His entire being responded.

He ceased to be the passive receiver and began to deepen their kiss. When he felt Leigh struggle for breath, he released her lips and lifted her higher so that his mouth found that provocatively pulsing hollow at the base of her throat. There he not only tasted the sweet flavor of her skin, but he encountered her fragrance. Joy! That's what she wears. Joy!

Oh, my God, yes, he thought, this woman is sheer joy. Passionately responsive, loving...He walked to the bed and put Leigh down gently, then lay down beside her. His hands moved to unbutton the dress.

"Well," he said, as he discovered there was nothing between Leigh and her dress except a pair of sheerest panty hose.

In just minutes, she lay nude before him and he looked at her as if he'd never seen her before. "For a little thing," he teased, "you're one hell of a lot of woman."

Then his grin disappeared and he began to kiss her with rising passion. As he kissed her breasts, he caressed her shoulders, her waist and the curve of her hips. When his breathing grew ragged, Leigh gently pushed him onto his back and, kneeling beside him, began to unbutton his shirt, raining kisses across his chest and down.

When she reached his belt, she unbuckled it, slowly edging the zipper down, down, down.

He was fully aroused, and at the sight of him Leigh laid her hand on him and leaned over to place her lips on his.

"I love you, love you, love you," she whispered softly against his mouth. Her long hair fell like a soft red cloud over their faces. As she kissed him, he reached his hands up to entwine them in her hair and once again he caught the scent of her perfume.

Zach thought he was in control. But as once again he inhaled her fragrance, he discovered he could wait no longer. Turning Leigh onto her back, he lowered his hard body over hers. She gasped with pleasure and readiness as they waited at the edge of that pre-cipice of joyful encounter. As they began their soaring flight, he could feel her soft hands caressing the length of his back. Higher and higher they flew in glorious harmony until together they exploded in loving fulfillment—each crying out the other's name.

They clung tightly to each other during the descent until their fingers relaxed and their ragged breathing returned to normal. Then, Zach, still holding Leigh, rolled onto his side and tilted her face so that he could watch her eyes turn soft and dreamy again. She looked at him and smiled gently. Then the dark fringe of lashes slowly and evenly lowered to lie against her cheek. That was all it took to reignite their passion.

Later, sated with love, Leigh lay in the circle of his arm, her head upon his shoulder. With his free hand, he took hers and placed in on his chest. "Feel how my heart is beating."

"Pounding is more accurate." She smiled at him and quickly rolled over on top of him. "Am I too heavy? Will I increase your heart's pounding?"

He chuckled, and running his hands up and down her back, said, "No, you're not too heavy. Your weight won't increase my heart rate, but very likely your position will."

"Oh, Zach," he heard her say, "Aren't we lucky to have fallen in love in this beautiful place?" She slid down a bit so she could rest her cheek over his heart. For a few moments there was no sound in the room but their breathing and the roar of the Yosemite Falls. "Zach?" she murmured.

"Yes..."

"When I lie here at night and listen to the falls I think about the power in that collection of water. And, in a way, I compare it to *Lodestar*. Just think how many bits and pieces of energy, talent and work went into making it. But the audience doesn't know that. All they'll see is the final product. They'll never know how many people it took to make such a powerful film. And how grateful I am." She lifted her head and looked at him. "I asked you a question. You didn't answer."

"I'm sorry. I guess I got distracted. What was the question?"

"I asked, weren't we lucky to have fallen in love in this beautiful place?"

"This beautiful place is not where I fell in love with you," he said. "I didn't know it at the time, but I fell in love with you that first day I met you in

Gary's office, and you told me you could direct hell out of *Lodestar*.''

''When *did* you know you were in love with me?''

''When I was halfway up a mountain on a dawn run.''

CHAPTER TWELVE

LOS ANGELES SUFFERED under its usual late July heat and smog as Leigh began postproduction on *Lodestar*. Because the studio had moved up the release date from early summer to February, the pace of editing, looping and scoring had to be accelerated beyond what was normally the case.

Leigh moved into a mobile home on the studio lot next to the row of small editing cubicles. Bill Regan, the editor, supervised two teams of junior editors and assistants under Leigh's watchful eye, and they worked very long hours. Leigh downed gallons of hot coffee and stared into the Moviola, the film editor's basic tool, until her eyes were so tired they could barely focus. She was exhausted, but she didn't mind because this was a labor of love.

Early on, she invited Connie to join her in the editing room.

"I'll just watch and occasionally nod knowingly," Connie said with a grin. "There's nothing more unbearable than an old know-it-all."

"Don't be ridiculous. Why do you think I invited you here, anyway? I want free advice from one of the best editors who ever wielded a pair of scissors."

Bill Regan, who wasn't much more than a third Connie's age, looked less than enthusiastic at this statement. Catching the concern on his face, Connie said, "Don't worry, young man, I'm not after your job." Turning back to Leigh, she went on, "But I would love to see some of the footage. There are already rumors going around that you got some terrific stuff."

"I think we did. We've put together the opening scene. I think you'll find it particularly interesting because Jonas did the plane crash, and it looks wonderful."

"How is the old reprobate, anyway?"

"Just great. He may be directing Zach's next film. He will be, in fact, if the studio gives a go-ahead to the project."

Connie's face broke into a delighted smile. "I'm so glad to hear that. Jonas could be a pain in the neck. But he's a very talented man, and he deserved better treatment than he got."

"I agree. Here's the scene."

Leigh moved over so Connie could look into the Moviola. After a moment, without taking her eyes off the small screen, Connie said, "You're right, this is terrific! No one can beat Jonas for action sequences."

A few minutes later, Connie and Leigh went to the commissary for lunch. Because it was such a warm day, they chose to sit outside at a table shaded by a large striped umbrella.

Though it was a hot day, it was pleasant in the shade, and Leigh was glad she'd decided to take this lunch break with Connie. After they ordered, she said, "You know, I usually don't do this. I just have a sandwich sent in to the editing room."

"Don't overdo it," Connie cautioned. "Aside from the fact that it isn't worth the stress, it's not good for the picture. You get punchy after a while and don't work as well."

"I know, but I have no choice. The studio moved up the release date, and we only have six months to put this together."

"Mm, they must be pretty happy with what they've seen so far."

"Gary says they are. And Zach's thrilled. He won't admit it, but I think he already has visions of himself accepting his first Oscar."

Giving Leigh a shrewd look, Connie responded, "How is it going with you two?"

It was on the tip of her tongue to ask what she meant, but Leigh knew there was no point in trying to lie to Connie. She waited until the waitress had placed their iced tea on the table before answering. "We're...involved."

"Of course. I saw it coming from the very beginning. Judging by how well the shooting went, your relationship must be going well."

"Most of the time, yes."

"But..."

"But there have been disagreements. Big ones."

"There was no way you could make a movie and not have big disagreements, Leigh."

"I know. But professional differences have an awful way of spilling over into one's personal life. It has an effect. I gave in once, he gave in twice..."

"So who's counting?"

Leigh smiled wryly, "Obviously I am. And I think Zach is, too."

Connie was silent for a while before finally responding slowly, "It's ironic. Working together, especially when you're creating something, adds excitement and spice to a relationship. It brings you even closer than you would be otherwise because you're sharing the thing that's most important in your life. But at the same time, it can drive a wedge between you because you can't possibly always agree.''

"Exactly. And when you disagree, how do you decide who should win and who should lose?''

"Unfortunately there's no easy formula.''

The waitress returned with a shrimp salad for Leigh and a hamburger for Connie. For a few minutes the two women ate in silence. Then Connie said thoughtfully, ''So often we see couples working together who manage to become successful. But eventually they break up. Not because the endeavor has failed. But because their personal relationship couldn't stand the strain.''

"I know. Oh, Connie, I think about that a lot.''

"Leigh, that doesn't mean you and Zach can't last.''

"Well, that's the reality, isn't it?''

"It doesn't have to be. Some people are smart enough or determined enough not to let the love they share be destroyed. Tell me something—how do you feel about Zach?''

Leigh met Connie's frank question head-on. ''I love him, Connie. More than I ever realized it was possible to love a man. Without him...I'm not quite whole.''

"How does he feel about you?''

"He says he feels the same.''

Connie smiled warmly. ''Well, Zach Stewart didn't strike me as the sort of man to lie, either to himself or to someone else. If he said that, he meant it. I'll bet that if you two just hold on to what you feel for each other, you'll make it.''

"I hope you're right."

Connie's eyes sparkled with impudent humor. "I'll tell you something, young woman, and I don't care how obnoxious it sounds. I almost always am right!''

LEIGH WAS IN THE EDITING ROOM that evening when Zach came in. During the few days they'd been back at the studio, he hadn't come to the editing room often. Leigh knew without his having to explain that he didn't want her to feel he was constantly looking over her shoulder. Also, he was busy trying to put together his next project for the studio. Though Jonas was set to direct, the two leads still had to be cast. Because this was going to be a very expensive project, the studio had insisted that Zach line up two bankable stars. So far, he'd had difficulty finding two who were available at the same time and wanted to work together.

Now, as he came into the cubicle, his blue eyes glowed with suppressed excitement. Something, clearly, was up.

"How's it going?" he asked.

"Great. We're working on the snake scene. Want to look?''

"Sure." He bent down to look into the Moviola, and for a few minutes conversation among him and Leigh and Bill Regan concerned the pace of the scene. Finally it was agreed that it needed to move faster, and Bill set to work cutting it.

Glancing at his watch, Zach said to Leigh, "It's past seven o'clock. Come on, I'll buy you dinner. I know where to get the best steak in town.''

"But..."

"No buts. I know what late hours you've been working. You can't keep this up, especially on an empty stomach."

Looking at Zach now, Leigh knew that what she wanted was to be with him. For a while, anyway, *Lodestar* could wait.

Turning to Bill, she said, "Why don't you take off, too? Zach's right, there's a limit and we've reached it tonight."

"I'll leave shortly. My girlfriend's meeting me here at seven-thirty."

"Promise you'll take off then?"

He grinned boyishly. "I promise."

Outside the editing room, Leigh asked, "Shall we take both cars and meet at the restaurant?"

Zach shook his head. "Tonight, I'm driving." As he opened his car door for her, he said, "Get in, lean back, close your eyes and relax. Leave everything to me. After all, what's an executive producer for?"

Leigh grinned. "Very well, *mon capitaine*."

"By the way, I had some good news today."

"I thought so. What is it?"

"Carol Kennedy and Lee Turner have agreed to do *Safari*."

"Oh, Zach, that's marvelous! Does that mean the picture's a go now?"

"Not only is it a go, it's a *go* go. Carol's only free for six months, then she's contracted to start another film. So we have to get moving on the project immediately. There's no time for the studio to change its mind."

"I'm so happy for you. And I'll bet Jonas is ecstatic."

Zach grinned. "I talked to him just a few minutes ago. He's raring to go. He says he's going to make this the safari picture to end all safari pictures."

"I'll bet he will, too."

"I don't doubt it."

"I know you were worried about *Lodestar* being a one-shot deal. So how does it feel now to be a bona fide feature-film producer with a slate of productions?"

"It feels pretty darn good." He reached his right arm about Leigh's shoulder and gave her an affectionate squeeze. "But it doesn't feel half as good as you do."

Zach drove out to Santa Monica, then headed north on Pacific Coast Highway.

"Are we eating in Malibu?" Leigh asked.

"In a manner of speaking. Now don't ask questions. For once in your headstrong life, do as you're told."

"Very well," she said, giving him a wan smile. "Just don't get too used to giving orders."

Leaning against the headrest, she closed her eyes. It only seemed a moment before she opened them again. But as she looked around and saw where they were, she realized she must have fallen asleep.

"How long was I out?"

"Not long. Just about half an hour. Here we are," Zach said, turning onto a one-lane road leading from a canyon up to a plateau.

"Where is here?"

Zach pulled to a stop in front of his house. "Like I said earlier, where we can get the best steak in town. They're in my refrigerator where they've been marinating all day."

As they got out, Leigh looked around curiously. It was the first time she'd been to Zach's home. Though it was nighttime, the house was well lit by outside floodlights timed to come on automatically at dusk.

"What do you think?" Zach asked as he led her inside.

Though his tone was casual, Leigh sensed that it mattered very much to him how she responded to this place.

"It isn't what I would have expected," she answered honestly. "I always thought film producers lived in the colony in luxury and decadence."

Zach smiled. "I'm not much into decadence."

"So I see. This is…well, it's the sort of place I would want if I could afford exactly what I wanted."

His expression softened. "Do you really mean that?"

"Don't I usually say what I mean?"

"Yes. Thank God."

He took her in his arms and kissed her lightly, teasingly. "I'm very glad to hear you say that you like it. Because this is where I would like us to live once we're married."

As Zach led her into the house, Leigh was silent. She should have been prepared for the statement, yet somehow she wasn't. They hadn't talked of marriage since Zach had announced his intentions that night on location. At that time it seemed like something in the distant future. There was so much else to do first. But now…

She looked into his eyes. "I didn't know if you were still…sure."

"You mean because of the disagreement over Kevin?"

She nodded.

He led her to a sofa and they sat down together. "That had a big impact on me. On both of us, I guess. There have been times when I've sensed a distance between us, and it's bothered me."

It frightened her to hear him admit there was a problem. All at once, she felt a cold chill of apprehension sweep over her. For some time she'd tried to tell herself she was imagining the distance between them. But she wasn't.

Zach continued, "But, Leigh, that argument was because we both want *Lodestar* to make it big. I don't think it's a reflection on our relationship. And it sure as hell doesn't have anything to do with how I feel about you. I love you. And I want to marry you."

Throwing her arms around him, she buried her face against the cool, soft cotton of his pale blue shirt. "Oh, Zach, I love you, too. And I do want to marry you."

Reaching down, he tilted her chin up so that her eyes met his. "When?"

When she hesitated, he said with a touch of amusement in his voice, "Woman, you're trying my patience."

"Mm, maybe I'm playing hard to get. My mother always said it was a surefire ploy."

"Well, your mother, if I may say so, was wrong. I want to make you mine. Forever. And I want to do it as soon as possible."

No longer teasing, Leigh responded soberly, "When *Lodestar*'s released."

"That's six months away."

"I know. But...oh, Zach, you must understand that all the reasons why I wanted to keep our relationship a secret still apply."

"There's no crew to deal with now, Leigh. And the studio won't care. They know now what they've got with the movie."

"Yes. But I want *Lodestar* to be judged on its own merits instead of being surrounded by gossip about the two of us. You know what will happen. Instead of attention being paid to the film, all the talk will be about the two of us. Were we sleeping together during filming? Was that why I got the job in the first place? I went through that on *Intimacies*, and I don't want to go through it again."

It was plain that Zach didn't like what she was saying. But he couldn't argue with it. After a long, tense moment, he said firmly, "The day *Lodestar* opens, I'm buying a marriage license."

Leigh smiled warmly. "And the day after that I'll marry you." When she saw his expression soften and knew for sure that things were all right between them again, she went on, "Now about that steak you promised me..."

"First, I want to show you the rest of my home. Specifically my bedroom."

Leigh slipped her arms around his waist and snuggled close. "Lead the way," she suggested. And he did.

THE NEXT FEW MONTHS PASSED almost in a blur. Because he was busy with a hurried preproduction on *Safari*, Zach was gone quite a lot. He had to scout locations in Africa with Jonas, then spend a great deal of time there and in England, auditioning actors. When he was gone, Leigh worked around the clock, living out of the trailer on the lot. When he was in Los Angeles, she spent her nights with him at his house in Malibu.

Gary occasionally called to ask how the editing was going, but he didn't come down to the cubicle where Leigh and her team of editors labored. Like all directors, Leigh had the right to put together a rough cut of the film exactly as she chose. She would then present it to the studio. After that, it was up to them to go with her version, ask her to make changes or, if need be, take it away from her and recut it to their own liking.

Though Leigh knew it wasn't unusual for a studio to take that last, drastic step, she didn't think it would happen with her movie. She was extremely pleased with the way it was coming together in the editing room. And she thought the studio would be pleased.

Kevin and Catalina came by occasionally to check on the progress of the movie. After *Lodestar*, both had agreed to take some time off, at least until after the baby was born. Catalina was too obviously pregnant to work, and Kevin was hoping that when *Lodestar* was released it would change his image as an actor and lead to more serious roles for him. In the meantime, he didn't want to accept the same old roles he'd become known for.

Leigh enjoyed seeing them when they stopped by, especially Catalina, who was glowingly happy about her pregnancy.

"We're taking Lamaze classes together," she confided to Leigh one day when they were alone. "You should see Kevin. He puts up a good front, but I'll bet when the time comes he'll faint in the delivery room.''

Leigh chuckled. ''I wouldn't be surprised. When's the due date?''

''January tenth. Oh, Leigh, it seems so far away. I don't know if I can wait!''

''I don't think you have much choice.''

Catalina's laughter was infectious, and Leigh joined in.

Later, when Catalina left, Leigh found it hard to get back to work. She was happy for Catalina—genuinely happy. And to be truthful, she had to admit to a bit of jealousy. The longer she was with Zach, the more she wanted his child. But then she also had to admit to being a little ambivalent when it came to combining motherhood with her career. Her dream had been a long time in the making, and now that she had this first feature film *almost* under her belt, the feeling was heady.

For all Zach's support and belief in her, she knew the other side of him. The side that spelled family. That was what he came from and what he obviously admired. He wouldn't be casual about his children any more than he would be casual about his wife.

She told herself over and over that someday she would have the children she wanted. And she would continue to direct movies she could be proud of. And yet...deep inside there was a stubborn, nagging doubt. She didn't know where it came from. She only knew that no matter how hard she tried, she couldn't shake it entirely.

AT THE END OF NOVEMBER, Leigh was sitting on a dubbing stage with the composer, Maurice Rincon, scoring the picture. Rincon had written a hauntingly beautiful score, at once exciting and wistful. Leigh couldn't have been more pleased.

Before she could tell him so a telephone nearby rang. Answering it, Leigh was surprised to hear Kevin's voice. It must be very important, she knew at once, for him to interrupt her at this crucial time.

"Kevin, what is it?"

His voice was ragged. "Leigh, I'm calling from St. John's Hospital in Santa Monica. Catalina went into premature labor."

"Oh, my God. I'll be there right away."

Leigh made the normally half-hour trip from Hollywood to Santa Monica in twenty minutes. In another five minutes, she'd parked and raced into the hospital. She found Kevin alone in the waiting room of the maternity wing. Pale and distraught, he looked as if he was barely holding himself together.

She hugged him reassuringly, then asked, "What happened?"

He shook his head. "I don't know. We were out shopping for the baby. We were looking at a white christening gown and Cat was saying how lovely it was. Then suddenly she felt a sharp pain. Our doctor's office wasn't too far away. I rushed her there. He took one look at her and sent for an ambulance."

"How long has she been here?"

"Just a little over half an hour. I called you as soon as we got here. I...I didn't know what to do."

"It's all right, Kevin. I'll stay."

"Oh, Leigh, I know you were probably swamped."

"Don't be ridiculous. Have you talked to the doctor since you've been here?"

"No. I wish to hell someone would tell me something!"

"I'm sure they will as soon as they can. Meanwhile, why don't we sit down and try to relax. Want me to get you some coffee?"

"No, thanks. Leigh, I really appreciate this."

"Hey, it's okay."

Though Leigh forced herself to sound calm, there was a sick feeling in the pit of her stomach. Catalina had said the baby wasn't due until January tenth. That was more than six weeks away. If it came now, what would happen to it?

She wished desperately that Zach was there. Just his presence would make it all easier. But he was in Africa again and wouldn't be back for a week.

After what Leigh felt were the slowest forty-five minutes she'd ever experienced, Catalina's doctor came into the waiting room. Briefly, almost unemotionally, he explained that they couldn't stop Catalina's premature labor. The baby had been born.

"Your wife's just fine, Mr. Marlowe," he reassured Kevin.

"Thank, God. And the baby?"

"It's a girl. She's in an incubator now in our special preemie section. She's...doing about as well as can be expected. She weighed a little less than five pounds."

"Can I see Catalina?" Kevin asked.

"We had to put her under anesthesia and she isn't conscious yet. As soon as she is, you can speak to her. Again, let me assure you she's just fine."

"Then can I see my daughter?"

"Yes, of course. I'll show you the way."

He led Leigh and Kevin to the nursery. In a special section marked Premature Infants was a space-age array of machinery, including, the doctor carefully explained, a cardiac respiratory monitor and a transcutaneous oxygen monitor. Hooked up to the machinery was the tiniest baby Leigh had ever seen.

She was almost unbelievably tiny, lying there on her stomach on a radiant heat table, her skin purplish-red and wrinkled.

Her eyes were shut tight in sleep. But her little face already had the look of someone who had been through a great deal. A white woolen cap so small it might have fitted a cat, was perched on her head, covering most of her mat of dark, curling hair. Faintly Leigh could see her chest move as it thumped to the rhythm of the respirator she needed to help her breathe. A mad profusion of wires and tubes, electrodes and sensors sprouted from her incredibly small body.

"My daughter," Kevin whispered. "Poor little thing."

Leigh had never heard him sound that way before—his voice soft with infinite tenderness.

After a moment he pulled himself together and asked the doctor what her chances were.

"I'll be frank, Mr. Marlowe. She could have used the next six weeks to grow, to develop her respiratory system and put on weight so she'd be stronger. But she seems to be healthy, aside from being premature, of course. She's got a chance. A good one, I think. We're doing a lot nowadays with preemies. And I've called in a specialist in neonatology."

"Can I...can I touch her?"

"Yes, of course. The nurse inside there will get you a gown and mask and show you where to wash up. I've got to get back to your wife now. I'll let you know when you can see her."

The doctor left, and a couple of minutes later, Leigh, watching through the huge window, saw Kevin gently caress his newborn daughter. It was a touching sight. Kevin looked so big and strong, and his daughter looked so incredibly small and fragile. When he finally turned away, he brushed tears from his eyes.

Leigh did the same.

Later she sat alone in the waiting room while Kevin was with Catalina. When he returned, she persuaded him to leave to get something to eat with her, then she brought him back to the hospital. Catalina wasn't allowed visitors yet, aside from Kevin, so Leigh went home. But as she drove out to the beach, her thoughts were all on that tiny infant who was fighting for life.

EVERY DAY, Leigh went into the studio to work. But she left early each evening to go to the hospital and be with Kevin and Catalina. Catalina had been discharged after three days, but she and Kevin both remained at the hospital almost around the clock.

It was early December now and the maternity ward was gaily decorated. In her incubator, Melanie Leigh Marlowe lay next to a soft, golden brown teddy bear. In place of the white cap, on her head now was a red-and-white-striped cap with a tiny white pom-pom.

Friday night, while Catalina was with Melanie, Kevin and Leigh went down to the cafeteria for a cup of coffee.

"It's been the most sobering experience of my life," Kevin said quietly. "I hadn't realized just how much this baby meant to me until we nearly lost her."

"Catalina told me that it looks like she'll be fine now."

Kevin sighed heavily. "Yes, thank God. We may even be able to take her home by Christmas. I already bought her present. A doll. It's bigger than she is." He smiled shyly. "Cat told me I was being silly. It'll be a while before she can play with it. But I wanted to get her something, y'know."

Leigh smiled warmly. "I know. I got her a doll, too."

They looked at each other and laughed.

"Well, we'd better get back up there. Visiting hours are almost over, and I don't want to miss a single minute."

As they rode back up in the elevator, Leigh thought what a change had come over Kevin. She remembered how worried Catalina had been in the beginning of her pregnancy that Kevin might not take well to fatherhood. That fear had certainly been put to rest. Kevin and Catalina and little Melanie, who was growing bigger day by day, would be a very happy family indeed.

On Friday evening, as she waited in the hotel lobby with Catalina, while Kevin brought the car around, she said as much.

Catalina nodded soberly. "Yes, it's changed both of us. We know what's important and what isn't. We're a family now, and I honestly think that matters more to Kevin than his career ever did."

"I'm happy for you."

"By the way, when is Zack due back?"

"Tomorrow."

"It must be hard when he's so far away."

Leigh nodded. "It's no picnic. There are days when I want to jump on the next plane to Kenya. But I'm chained to the studio. Speaking of which, I have some news that may interest you. I talked to Gary today and he said that when you're ready to go back to work, they have a couple of projects in mind. One of them is so perfect for you that they'll hold it for a while, if need be."

"They'll have to. I'm not going back to work for several months, at least."

"Well, when you do, you'll have your choice of roles."

Catalina smiled wryly. "Remember that night up in Yosemite when we talked about the difficulty of combining career and personal life? Having it all, you said. I think I do now."

"I think you do, too."

"But you know what I learned in the process?"

"What?"

"It's all a matter of priorities. Even when you have it all, some things matter more than others. Kevin and Melanie will always matter far more to me than any career."

"Do you mean you're going to quit acting?" Leigh asked in surprise.

"Oh, no. Just put it on hold until Melanie doesn't need me so much. I can always go back to acting. But if I miss this time with her, I'll never have a second chance to make it up."

Leigh understood perfectly. It was exactly how she would have felt about her own child.

Kevin pulled up then and Leigh told them good-night. As she walked to her car, she was very thoughtful. Priorities, Catalina had said. Her first priority had always been to be a successful film director—until she met Zach.

Now he was the most important thing in her world. And her need for him frightened her because it was so much more fierce than anything she'd ever felt before.

A few minutes later, she was climbing the stairs to her apartment. Suddenly, to her surprise, the door flew open and she saw Zach standing there. With a cry of joy, she flew up the last few steps and leaped into his arms.

When they finally stopped kissing, she whispered, "I missed you."

"Good. Were you absolutely miserable?"

"Absolutely."

"So was I."

"I thought you weren't coming back until tomorrow."

"I caught an earlier plane," he said as he released her and led her inside. "I just couldn't take it anymore. Do you realize since we stopped shooting *Lodestar*, Bill Regan has seen far more of you than I have?"

"Well, we're even, because TWA has seen more of you than I have." And because she was still so excited at finding him here, she stood on tiptoe to reach her arms about his neck.

As if she were a feather, he lifted her until her lips were even with his and she began to cover his face with quick light kisses. "Oh, darling," she murmured, locking her arms about his neck. "I've been so lonesome without you."

"I know." His lips brushed against hers as he spoke. "And I've decided to do something about it." Still holding her close, he slipped one arm under her knees and walked with her to the big armchair and sat down.

Contented, Leigh curled up in his lap and sighed. "Okay. What are you going to do? Shoot *Safari* on the back lot?"

He laughed. "The studio would probably like that. It would cut the budget in half. Seriously, though, when are you turning in your rough cut?"

"It's in. Today. That's why it's so wonderful to find you here. Are you anxious to see it?"

"Yes. But for more than one reason. Once that's done, you won't have to stay in L.A."

"What are you getting at?"

"How does a honeymoon in Kenya sound?"

Leigh's breath caught in her throat. "Wonderful."

"Good. Then by the time I have to go back, we'll be married."

"Oh, how wonderful. You're here for a while."

"Three weeks," he said, tightening his arms about her. "I have to return right after Christmas." He tilted her chin with his finger and fastened those incredibly blue eyes on her. "How do you feel about being a Christmas bride?"

Leigh felt her heart lurch. How she felt about it was scared to death. She felt wonderful about being a bride, but it was the three weeks that terrified her. That was so soon.

Zach talked easily about being married at the ranch and said they could all fly up on the morning of the twenty-fourth. He said he thought it was time he met her parents, and how about tomorrow?

Dimly, through her own tumbling thoughts, she heard him, but she didn't answer. He was smiling at her, excitement dancing in his eyes. "Well, cat got your tongue? What do you say?"

What do I say? I say whatever happened to our agreement that we'd be married when Lodestar*'s released.*

Stalling, she told Zach she'd been in these clothes since early morning and asked if he'd excuse her long enough to take a quick shower and change. Then, she said, they could discuss their plans. She really couldn't tell if he was oblivious to her surprise or not. She'd met this steam-rolling side of Zach before.

"You're excused, if you come back in your Yosemite outfit—know the one I mean?" he teased.

She knew the one he meant—the extravagantly beautiful burgundy silk nightgown and matching velvet robe.

She gave him a quick kiss as she slid out of his lap and suggested he make a pot of coffee for them. "There's chocolate pie in the kitchen," she told him. "Connie made one yesterday and shared it."

As she showered, Leigh tried to sort out her feelings. The stinging needles of warm water massaged her tired shoulders. She felt hot then cold, excited and happy, then terrified. It was clear that Zach would always take risks to get what he wanted. And she'd already taken some bigger risks than she was accustomed to. However, in this case, the risk they would both take could have dire consequences on their professional as well as personal lives. Perhaps

Zach was willing to take that risk, but Leigh still wasn't sure she was.

But as she dried off with a thick towel, she thought again of the man she'd fallen in love with and found it more and more difficult to make a logical choice.

Well, she decided, she couldn't hide all evening. They had things to talk about and decisions to make. She brushed her hair and touched her lips with gloss and her lashes with mascara. Then she picked up her bottle of Joy and applied a touch behind each ear and in the hollow of her throat. She dropped the silk-and-lace gown over her head and stepped into a pair of slippers.

As she slipped on the velvet robe, she felt sensuous and beautiful—remembering the many love-filled nights in Yosemite when he'd told her she was.

As they sat at the kitchen table drinking coffee and eating Connie's pie, Zach reached for her free hand. "You're unusually quiet. Did I terrify you with my proposal? I meant to make you swoon with delight."

Leigh hesitated, then said, "It is just that there are a lot of things to consider."

"Haven't we considered all the important things? Such as that I love you and you love me."

"I haven't even had time to tell you Melanie Leigh Marlowe is doing great. She'll be home before Christmas."

"I'm glad." His expression softened as he rubbed his thumb across the back of her hand. "It pleases me that you're so taken with that little one. When I'm lonesome for you, you know the picture of you that pops most often into my head?"

"Opening the door to you in my sexy night-gown?" she quipped.

"No." His voice turned serious. "It's the one of you helping that little boy fly the kite on the beach. I love kids and look forward to having some of my own. It's a bonus for me that you like them, too."

Leigh's smile was tentative. She tried to cover it by offering Zach more pie, more coffee. As she walked past him to get the coffeepot, he pulled her down onto his lap.

"It's not like you to be so quiet," he said, cupping her face between his hands and forcing her to look at him. "What's wrong, love?"

"It's happening so fast." As soon as she said the words, she realized they sounded stupid. She was crazily in love with this man. She knew it and so did he.

"Fast!" he repeated. "We've been attracted to each other from the day we met. That was in April. This is December. That's not fast. We're not kids. If we don't know now what we want, we won't ever know."

When Leigh tried to rise, he tightened his arms about her. "No. Don't run away from this. If there's a problem, let's talk about it."

"Well," she began, her voice very soft, "we said we'd be married after *Lodestar* was released. I guess I just wanted the one finished before I took on the next big commitment in my life."

"Maybe I'm being selfish, but I miss you so. And your work on *Lodestar*'s completed. It just seems the right time for us to marry and you to come back to Africa with me." He smiled at her and kissed the tip of her nose. "So tell me, what's the problem?"

When she didn't answer, he asked, "Is it the wedding? You want a big wedding?"

"Oh, no. I'd like Kevin and Catalina and Connie and Stan—if it's possible—but no, it isn't the wedding."

"Have you changed your mind? About me?" His blue eyes darkened and the puzzlement in them pierced her heart.

How did she tell him? How did she say she wanted it all. Career and marriage—him and children. And success with all of it.

She thought of Catalina who'd just begun a career and had already changed her mind about what was important to her. And Connie—Connie who'd loved someone she couldn't have and so she'd poured herself into her work.

Leigh had meant to be firmly established in her career as a director before she fell in love. She'd been so careful. And then she'd met this man who just by holding her against his heart caused her own to beat like some wild bird held captive.

Wrapping her arms about his neck, she looked straight into his eyes. "No, my darling. I haven't changed mind mind about you. I love you, Zach. I'll marry you and go back to Africa with you. *If...*"

"If what? Ask me, I'm easy...I'll promise anything." He grinned wickedly at her. "Make love to you every day and twice on Sunday?"

"Be serious. There'll have to be compromises on both our parts. I do want to keep working...so when we have children—"

Suddenly Zach brought his mouth to hers and silenced her questions with a deep kiss. When he released her, he said, "We've been over all that. We can work out everything we need to. To have a good marriage, Leigh, there must be trust. Remember the morning we were running and saw the rock climbers on El Capitan?"

She nodded.

"We talked about how they had to trust each other—linked only by a rope. Trust isn't something you use only in a special situation like rock climbing. Trust has to always be there. It has to be there every day." He looked long and hard at her. "Do you believe that I love you?"

She nodded.

"Then trust me."

It was decision time, Leigh knew. Time to choose, time to make the commitment. In his words, time to cut the deal. With her fingers lightly tracing the contours of his face, she looked deep into his eyes. Zack would be there when she needed him—he was that kind of man. And she'd try very hard to understand his needs so he'd always be glad he'd chosen her.

Leigh took her hands from Zach's face and said, "I do—I will trust you. Although I don't promise you your household will be bland and peaceful, I do promise you it will be filled with love." Then she offered him her right hand. "Deal?" she whispered.

He clasped her small hand in his and brought his mouth to hers. His voice was husky with love as he repeated, "Deal," before kissing her deeply.

When at last he raised his lips from hers, Leigh laid her head against his shoulder. "I'm exhausted," she said. "Do you think you have enough strength left to carry me to bed?"

With Leigh in his arms, he rose and flipped off the kitchen light switch as he walked down the hall toward her bedroom. In front of the *Gone with the Wind* poster, he stopped and with a grin, said,

"Goodnight Rhett and Scarlett...wherever you are." Then, looking down at Leigh, he said, "I hope, my love, that when you wake up in the morning you are wearing that same satisified smile that Scarlett wore the morning after Rhett carried her up the stairs."

"I have so far." Then grinning up at him, she added, "Trust me."

CHAPTER THIRTEEN

ON DECEMBER 8, Leigh, Zach, Gary and a half dozen other studio executives gathered in a screening room to see Leigh's rough cut of *Lodestar*. Leigh was only mildly nervous. She felt tremendous confidence that the movie was good—certainly as good as she could make it. At a little under ninety minutes in length, the running time was perfect. She'd pared it down so that there wasn't a single extraneous scene, and the pace was never slow. She couldn't help worrying a little about the studio executives' response, but basically she was very confident. If she knew anything at all about movies—and she felt she did—*Lodestar* was a good one.

She'd seen the rough cut in its entirety, but no one else had, including Zach. Now as they sat down in the plush seats of the executive screening room, Zach flashed her a reassuring smile. "I can't wait to see this."

She returned his smile. "I can't wait for you to see it."

Gary arrived and sat down next to Leigh. "You've no idea what a pleasure it is to get ready to watch a film that I already know is pretty good. It sure beats watching one that's been a problem from the beginning of production."

"Well, I hope you still feel that way when it's over," Leigh replied modestly.

"I'm sure I will."

Seeing that everyone was there, Zach pushed the intercom button on the console next to his chair and told the projectionist he could start the film. In a moment the lights had dimmed and the first credits began to roll. As Leigh saw the words, "A Zachary Stewart Production...A Leigh Adams Film," she felt a rush of pride that she knew must be akin to what a mother experienced after giving birth. She'd nurtured this film, given it life, shaped it and with the help of a lot of people made it what it was. At that moment as the first scene unfolded, the pride and excitement she felt made every single hard day's work, every problem, every disagreement with Zach and others worth it.

In the darkness, she reached out to take Zach's hand and clasp it in hers. "We did it," she whispered to him, "together."

In the darkness she sensed rather than saw his smile in response.

Though she was intimately familiar with every single frame of the movie, having viewed them over and over again, she wasn't bored watching the movie now. Seeing it with people who hadn't seen the whole film before made it all fresh and exciting.

Throughout the ninety minutes of the film, no one said a word. Leigh sensed that the small group of men were responding favorably to the movie. There was certainly no bored rustling around in seats. Everyone's attention was focused on the screen.

Leigh felt her confidence soar. *Lodestar* was going to be well received.

When it ended and the lights came on, there were murmurs of congratulations from everyone in the room.

"Just great, Leigh," Gary said enthusiastically. "You and Zach make quite a team. Now I've got to leave right away to get to a dinner meeting, but why don't we meet in my office tomorrow afternoon? Say three o'clock?"

"Fine," Leigh agreed.

"Can you make it, Zach?"

Zach nodded. "I don't leave again for Africa for a couple of weeks."

"Good," Gary responded. "See you both then. I think we've got a winner here."

Out in the parking lot, Leigh threw her arms around Zach and hugged him tightly. "Oh, it's wonderful to be a success!"

He laughed indulgently. "It's gone to your head already. Before I know it you'll be too important to return my calls."

"Oh, I'll never forget the little people who made me what I am today," Leigh quipped.

They laughed together. Then, looking down at her, Zach said more seriously, "It's fantastic, sweetheart. It really is. You made it everything I hoped it would be."

"*We* made it, Zach. You and I. Together."

"Yes. *Together.* And it's only the beginning. You'll get a lot of offers once this is released. But I'd like it very much if we could find another project to do together."

"I'd like that, too." Smiling up at him, she said, "How about dinner at some restaurant on the beach?

Lobster with drawn butter...maybe a little mud pie for dessert?''

''Sounds terrific. And afterward we'll go back to my place for...coffee.''

''Right. *Coffee.*''

Her gray eyes were lit by silver sparkles that were half amusement, half excitement.

AT THREE O'CLOCK the next afternoon, Leigh and Zach sat in Gary's office. ''I meant what I said yesterday. The movie's just great. Everyone thought so.''

''Thanks,'' Leigh responded with a broad smile.

''There's just one thing,'' Gary went on. ''About the ending...''

''Yes?''

''Well, I've discussed this with Zach and I'm sure he mentioned it to you. We thought a more straightforward ending would be more...''

He searched for a word and Leigh finished for him, ''Commercial?''

''Well, yes. It's been our experience that audiences like to have all the pieces put neatly together at the end of a story.''

''I believe they also like to see an ending that's credible. And that's what *Lodestar* has.''

Gary flashed a quick look at Zach. Leigh felt a sudden chill. Her exuberance disappeared instantly. If Gary and Zach teamed up against her...

''What do you think, Zach?'' Gary asked.

''I like Leigh's ending. I think *Lodestar* is absolutely perfect artistically as it stands now.''

''Artistically, perhaps, but let's be realistic. It isn't enough to put out a good product. You have to be able to sell it. If no one goes to see a movie, it doesn't matter much how good it is."

"I don't agree with that at all," Leigh replied tartly. She wanted to add that she thought his choice of the word "product" was pathetic, but she forced herself not to do so.

"Well, you're certainly entitled to your opinion," Gary said, "but the fact is you're not financially responsible. We are. If the movie loses money, we pay the price, you don't."

"I do in the sense that it affects my career."

"Yes, but that's not quite the same thing."

"Look, Gary," Zach interjected, "why are you so convinced that audiences won't go with Leigh's ending?"

"It's not just my personal opinion, Zach. All of us agree. It's a subtle, serious ending, one that leaves the future of the protagonists up in the air. We want something simpler—more commercial, to use your word."

"I think the ending we have now is very touching," Leigh insisted. "I'm convinced audiences will respond to it."

"You may be convinced of that, but we aren't. And the financial stakes are simply too high to risk finding out if you're right."

"Then what do you suggest?" Zach asked bluntly.

"We talked it over this morning and pretty much agree that the final scene should be the one just before the current ending."

"You mean where Joe and Mary Beth get to the edge of the small town and realize they've made it?"

Gary nodded. "Exactly. That shot where they look at each other and Joe says, 'We're going to be all right.'"

"But," Leigh replied sharply, "he simply meant that they were going to live, he wasn't referring to their marriage."

"I know that. But if we use that as the ending, the audience will assume their marriage is back on the track and everything's going to be fine."

"But the whole point of the movie was that they had serious problems that couldn't be wished away. The way it ends now, we know they're going to make another attempt to work on those problems and there's a chance—a good one—that they'll resolve them. But even if they don't they'll be okay because they've both grown stronger as a result of their ordeal."

"I understand all that, Leigh," Gary responded in a tone that was less patient than before. "But as I said, we don't think an audience will accept that."

"Don't you think you may be underestimating the audience?"

"I think I know a little more about audiences than you do. I've overseen a lot of movies. This is only your second."

Leigh felt absolutely furious. She was being patronized and she didn't like it one bit. More important, what Gary was suggesting wasn't a minor change. It went to the very heart of what *Lodestar* was all about. She hadn't worked so hard for all these months to let her film be turned into less than it could be.

"I won't make that change," she said flatly.

For a moment there was a strained silence in the room. Then Gary said in a voice that brooked no discussion, "I'll speak plainly. We want the ending changed. If you won't do it, we'll do it ourselves. We're not asking you, Leigh, we're telling you."

Stunned, she instinctively turned to Zach. She didn't actually say anything. She didn't have to. He knew what she wanted.

"Gary, is there any room for discussion about this?" Zach asked.

"No. I'm sorry. I'd hoped you would see it our way."

"Take it or leave it. That's it?"

"That's it. But, Zach, we're convinced this will make for a more successful film. And that's really what we all want, isn't it? It won't do either you or Leigh any good if your first feature is a bomb."

Leigh said dryly, "I was under the impression you liked the movie."

"I do. It's very, very good. But that doesn't necessarily mean it will make it at the box office. We all know that."

Zach was silent.

Leigh felt a sinking sensation. If Zach wasn't willing to fight for this, she had no chance at all.

Rising slowly, she said, "I've given you my cut. I honestly think it's the best way to go, and I won't alter it. I'm willing to make minor changes, but this...this isn't right."

"Leigh, do you realize what you're saying?"

She nodded silently.

"Very well. We'll take care of it ourselves."

Turning on her heel, she strode from the room.

Zach caught up with her outside the building. "You have a hell of a way with dramatic exits."

"There didn't seem to be much point in sticking around."

"You could have been a little less rude about it."

"So could Gary."

Zach stopped her and spun her around to face him. "Listen to me. I know you're mad as hell, but try to be unemotional about this. I've had my share of battles with the studio. I know when to push and when not to. Believe me, this is a no-win situation."

"You could have argued with him!"

"I realize that's what you wanted me to do. And if it would have done any good at all, I would have. But I know a brick wall when I come up against one, Leigh. Gary wasn't just giving us his personal opinion today. He was speaking for the studio and the powers-that-be above him. They want a different ending. And they're going to get it whether we like it or not. Arguing with them will get us nowhere."

"I don't think you even wanted to argue with him."

"What the hell does that mean?"

"You agree with him, don't you?"

"I agree that the ending he's suggesting is probably more commercial. It's safer..."

"Just like Ralph Hastings was safer?" Leigh shot back angrily.

Zach flushed and Leigh realized she'd been unfair. That was hitting below the belt.

He didn't say a word. Instead, he took her arm and led her to his office. Ignoring his secretary's cheery greeting, he and Leigh went into his private office. There they stood facing each other.

"You're so worried about this being a financial success that you don't really care about the artistic integrity of the film," Leigh said accusingly. "What if *Lodestar* doesn't make a fortune. It will be a fine film."

"That's unfair. I'm no schlock merchant. But if the film's a financial failure it won't matter how good it is. Both of us will have a hard time getting jobs again."

"You're already working on *Safari*..."

"Which can still be canceled. And even if they don't cancel the shoot they can take away my authority, even bar me from the production. My name would be on it, but that wouldn't mean a thing. This sort of thing has happened before, Leigh, to other producers, too many times to count."

"Zach, I don't think *Lodestar*'s going to fail. I'm convinced I'm right and the studio is wrong. The ending we have now is so powerful, surely audiences will respond. They'll be so affected by it that they'll accept it."

"And if you're wrong?"

Leigh hesitated. This, she knew, got to the heart of the matter. Only recently Zach had talked to her about trust and had asked her to trust him. Now he wasn't trusting her.

"I can't argue with you," she whispered helplessly. "Either you believe in me or you don't. Either we're on the same side or we're not."

Suddenly the anger left Zach's expression. His eyes, which had grown hard and unyielding, softened. "Leigh, my love, don't do this. Don't let this come between us."

"It already has, hasn't it?"

As she turned to leave, he crossed the few feet that separated them and took her into his arms. "Sweetheart, please, this doesn't have to happen."

"Maybe it does. From the very beginning I was afraid it would come to this. It nearly did with Kevin. We had a reprieve then, but this time there is no reprieve. Oh, Zach, we want it all, you and I. Maybe we want too much."

"Don't say that. Leigh, last night we were so close."

"Last night we thought we could have each other and *Lodestar*, too. Today it looks as if we'll have to choose. I'm afraid it's all too clear what we've each chosen."

"Damn it, Leigh, I won't let this happen."

"Will you fight the studio with me?"

"I told you—that's a battle we couldn't possibly win."

"But we could at least *try*."

"And in the process lose everything we've both worked so hard to achieve."

"Under these terms, it isn't worth having."

"You'd throw away your whole career, your future, on a point of principle?"

She nodded.

Then, in one last desperate attempt to make him understand, she explained, "Don't you see, Zach, there's a line you can't cross. You have to say, so far and no further. I meant what I said to Gary, I'll make changes in the movie. I'm not being pigheaded or egotistical. But I'm right about the ending and they're wrong. If I change it, what does that make me?"

"It makes you a pragmatist who's a hell of a lot more likely to have a career in this town."

"In that case, I can do without having a career in this town." She gave him a look of infinite compassion and understanding. "But you can't, can you?"

"Leigh..."

She put her fingertips to his lips. "No, don't say anything, darling. It's only words and we're passed the point where they mean anything."

Standing on tiptoe, she kissed him sweetly, gently. Her voice broke as she finished, "I'm not angry now. Honestly. We each have to do what we have to do. But, oh, I *do* love you."

Forcing herself to step out of his arms, she turned and hurried from the room.

THE NEXT EVENING she went to the studio to clear her things out of her office. She waited until she was sure everyone, especially Zach, was gone. On her desk she found a note from Bill Regan, saying he had a surprise for her in the editing room. Clearly he hadn't been informed yet of the latest turn of events.

The editing room was empty and silent as Leigh walked in. On the Moviola was a note from Bill explaining that he'd put together some outtakes from the movie that he thought she would find amusing. Leigh doubted very much that she'd find anything amusing tonight, but she turned on the Moviola, anyway.

Scene after scene passed before her eyes. Herself standing on the set talking to Kevin and Catalina...Kevin mugging for the camera while Catalina laughed appreciatively at his antics...Zach clowning around...

Suddenly Leigh felt tears sting her eyes. She didn't want to watch any more but she couldn't take her eyes off the tiny screen.

Kevin and Catalina blowing their lines, then joking about it...Zach standing in the background, watching, smiling, talking to Leigh between takes...the special looks that passed between them...

A tear coursed down Leigh's cheek and fell onto the crisp white collar of her blouse. Another followed. Then another. She could no longer see the screen through the blur of tears. But it didn't matter for she was seeing it all in her mind now, remembering each tender moment when love was new and anything was possible.

It had all been so magical. But magic, as Luke had taught her, was an illusion. Lovely, but not real.

"Oh, Zach," she whispered. "What have we lost?"

IT HAD BEEN A WEEK since Zach had seen Leigh. Now, as he sat in a meeting with Jonas, he found himself thinking of her instead of the shooting schedule they were supposed to be discussing. Not a waking hour passed that he hadn't thought about calling her. More than once he'd actually picked up the receiver, only to put it down again. What was there to say? They'd said it all. Unless one of them was willing to give in, there was no point in talking. It would only make the hurt that much worse.

God, how it hurt. Worse than he'd imagined possible. Worse than his divorce.

"Zach!"

Startled, Zach looked at Jonas. "What?"

"You haven't heard a word I've said for at least ten minutes, have you?"

Zach sighed. "I'm afraid not. Sorry. Where were we?"

Jonas gave him a shrewd, appraising look. "Want to talk about what's wrong?"

"I don't think so. Thanks, anyway."

"I'm not much good at taking advice, but I'm great at giving it."

Zach forced a smile. "Unfortunately it isn't a case of deciding what to do. The problem is trying to figure out how to live with the unavoidable."

"That's always a problem, all right. Well, let me know if you change your mind and want to talk. It won't go any further."

"I know, Jonas. Thanks. Let's get back to this. Where were we?"

"The wounded-elephant scene."

"Oh, yeah. How about this..."

For an hour Zach discussed the schedule with Jonas. When the meeting finally broke up and Zach went home, he felt absolutely desolate. His house was full of memories of Leigh, and his bed was cold and lonely.

Impulsively he decided that he would fly up to his parents' ranch the next day. It was only a week till Christmas and he'd planned on flying up for the holiday, anyway. Instead of waiting, he would go now, because he badly needed to see his family. Needed to get away from here, from the overpowering memories. And the loneliness that never seemed to go away...

The next afternoon, he sat on the riverbank, idly twirling a stick in the water. Hearing footsteps, he turned and saw his father approaching.

"Want some company, son?"

"Sure. Pull up a rock and join me."

They sat together in silence for some minutes, watching the river flow by. Then Zach's father asked quietly, "Want to tell me why you came up here?"

"I told you. Just to visit."

"That's not the truth, and you and I both know it. I wasn't going to say anything. I figured you had your reasons and maybe I shouldn't interfere. But your mother said if I didn't talk to you, then she would. So here I am."

Zach smiled, but there was no humor in the smile. "Were you two always this perceptive and I just didn't realize it?"

"Oh, you'd be amazed at the things we knew and you didn't think we knew," he answered softly. "So what is it now? Something's bothering you."

"Remember Leigh?"

"How could I forget? How is she?"

"I don't know. I haven't seen her for a while."

"I see."

Looking at his father, Zach went on, "I...asked her to marry me."

"Your mother said you would. And she's usually right. What happened? Did she turn you down?"

"No. It's a little more complicated than that."

As concisely as he could, he explained the situation to his father, who listened intently without interrupting.

When Zach was finished, his father responded carefully, "What you're saying is that you disagree about the movie?"

"In a way. Actually I think she's right about her ending being the right one artistically. It's true to the characters. But the studio's convinced it wouldn't be a success. Financially, at least."

"But Leigh's fighting them?"

"Yeah. She stuck to her guns, all right."

"Doesn't surprise me. She struck me as someone with strong beliefs. I admire that. You don't run across it as much nowadays as you used to."

"Those beliefs could cause problems with her career. And even if she could persuade the studio to go with her ending, the movie might well be a critical success but a box-office failure."

"Would that be so terrible?"

Zach looked at his father in surprise. "If the movie flops, then so do I. I thought failure was unacceptable for a Stewart."

His father shot him an appraising glance. "Did you? I guess that all depends on what you mean by failure. Not trying is certainly failure. But as long as you do your best and can be honestly proud of what you've done, I don't call that failure."

"Even if everyone else does?"

His father grinned. "Now one thing Stewarts have never been too concerned about is what anyone else thinks. As long as we know we're doing the right thing, that's all that matters."

"It could be the end of my career as a feature-film producer."

"I understand."

"Are you telling me it's all right if I fail...even if I lose everything?"

John Stewart smiled. "It isn't the end of the world. You just pick yourself up and start all over again. Stewarts are good at that."

So is Leigh, Zach thought. She was willing to risk everything for what she believed in. And if she lost it all, then she'd just try again.

Looking at his father, Zach asked shyly, "I suppose I'm too old to be hugging you?"

"You'll never be too old for that, son."

When Zach pulled away from his father's affectionate bear hug, he rose and headed back toward the house.

"Where ya going?" his father shouted after him.

"Back to L.A. To take care of unfinished business."

CHAPTER FOURTEEN

EACH DAY, Leigh had expected Zach to call. When he didn't, she told herself it was pointless for him to call, anyway. It was over between them. Period.

And yet...every time the phone rang, she ran to answer it. And when it wasn't Zach's voice on the other end of the line, she breathed a heartfelt sigh of disappointment.

As she lifted the receiver of the ringing telephone, she vowed not to let her disappointment get the best of her.

"Leigh, it's Gary Jennings."

Leigh stared at the telephone in surprise. Of all the people she'd expected to call her, Gary was the last.

"Gary...hello."

"I hope we're still on speaking terms."

"Of course. I didn't take what happened personally. You made a business decision. I just didn't agree with it."

"I'm glad you feel that way about it. That was how it was. Definitely nothing personal. But I didn't call to go into that. I wanted to let you know there's going to be a sneak preview of *Lodestar* at Mann's Chinese Theater tomorrow night at eight o'clock."

"Really? I hadn't heard anything about it."

"It's somewhat of a last-minute thing. To test the movie before we have the formal premiere and open it in general release. It gives us a chance to get an idea of what a representative audience thinks. If they don't like it, we can make changes. If they do, then we know we're on to something."

"I see."

"Leigh, I'd like it very much if you'd come."

She hesitated. She appreciated Gary's call, but she hadn't changed her mind about what they'd done to her movie.

"Gary, I don't mean to sound as if I bear a grudge, because I don't, honestly. But I'd prefer not to come."

"Leigh, I spoke to Zach. He explained that you two had a falling-out. He suggested I tell you that he won't be there tomorrow. Does that change your mind?"

She hesitated. The thought of seeing Zach again had certainly been part of her refusal. She couldn't bear to see him while the wound was still fresh. But even so...

"Gary, I don't think..."

"Leigh. Please. I really want to know what you think about the movie."

She realized that Gary was trying to be nice and the least she could do was respond accordingly. "Okay. I'll be there."

"I'll meet you there. We can sit together. It'll be interesting to see how the audience responds."

"Yes." Actually she couldn't work up much real enthusiasm. The audience would be responding to a film that was less than her true vision of it. It would hurt, seeing it in its altered form. It would hurt a lot. Almost, but not quite, as much as it hurt to think about Zach.

The next evening at ten minutes to eight, Leigh arrived at the theater. She'd dressed casually, in gray wool slacks and a matching sweater and poncho. The weather was unusually cold for an L.A. December.

Gary was sitting just inside the lobby. "Leigh, good to see you. How've you been the past couple of weeks?"

"Fine." It was such a standard response, she had no trouble saying it. Even though it was far from the truth.

"Let's go inside. The theater's nearly full."

They sat at the rear of the large theater, where they could have a good view of the audience. "It's remarkable what a sense of the success or failure of a movie you get from being in a theater this way," Gary went on amiably. "I was in Houston recently at a sneak preview of another film, and when it was over, no one said a word. Nothing. The audience was absolutely silent as it filed out. Unfortunately it looks like that picture's in trouble."

Just then the house lights dimmed. Various announcements came on the screen, then *Lodestar* began. Despite herself, Leigh felt tremendous pride to see it on the huge screen. It was infinitely better than viewing it on the small screen at the studio. The maginificent mountain vistas in the movie cried out for this size screen.

The film was breathtaking, she thought. She sensed the audience responding to it immediately. When Kevin appeared, there was a low murmur throughout the room. Then when Catalina appeared there was another stir of interest. As Leigh had expected, she grabbed the audience right away.

As the movie unfolded, the audience reacted just as Leigh had hoped they would. They laughed at the occasional moments of humor, gasped at the adventure and suspense and were quiet, their eyes riveted on the screen, during the tender moments.

Leigh sensed that the audience was with her every step of the way, and it thrilled her to realize she'd been right about the story. It had that universal quality that touched people deeply at the same time that it entertained them.

And yet...the excitement she should have felt simply wasn't there. And she knew perfectly well why. Because Zach wasn't there, sharing it with her.

Suddenly her eyes were so filled she was afraid the tears would spill over. She supposed that Gary would think she was just moved by the movie. What broke her heart was that she was right about the movie...but Zach had been right that they were meant to belong to each other.

Where had their magic gone?

Luke could have told her. She had stopped believing. And as Luke had told her so long ago, you had to believe in magic in order to make it happen. She simply hadn't believed in Zach enough, trusted him enough. In her pain and anger over *Lodestar*, she'd lost sight of what really mattered—their love for each other.

Her bed was much too big without him, her life was empty and joyless. It didn't matter who was right and who was wrong. All that mattered was that she wanted him, needed him, and she'd driven him away.

I'll call him, she decided. *The minute I leave here. I'll say whatever I must, do whatever I must to get him back.*

She just prayed it wasn't too late.

Absently she glanced back at the screen. It was the final scene where Joe and Mary Beth reached safety. Leigh steeled herself not to feel disappointment. It wasn't her ending, true, but there was nothing she could do about it.

To her stunned surprise, the movie didn't end there. It went on, with her original ending intact. Five minutes later, when "The End" flashed on the screen and the lights came back up, the audience burst into enthusiastic applause. But Leigh was almost oblivious to this sure sign of a hit as she turned to Gary.

"I thought you were going to change it?"

"We were. Listen to that, Leigh! They love it!"

As people rose around them and the crowd slowly moved out of the theater, they overheard snatches of conversation.

"That was a good movie!"

"Kevin Marlowe's so sexy."

"I didn't know he could act."

"And that girl. What's her name? She was really something."

Leigh and Gary walked out together, listening to the comments. Not one person reacted negatively.

Leigh was confused and thrilled at the same time.

"Gary, I don't understand."

He grinned at her. Relief was apparent in his voice. "I do. It's a hit. Believe me, you don't get this kind of response every day."

"But the ending...what happened, why did you change your mind?"

"Come on over here in this corner, away from the crowd, and I'll explain it all to you."

When they reached a relatively quiet corner, Gary began, "First, I want to say that we always liked your version. We just didn't think it was commercial. We were afraid audiences would be let down by the less-than-perfect ending. That's why we decided to change it."

"But you didn't change it."

"No. We were going to, but Zach talked me into trying this sneak preview of your version. I'll be honest, Leigh. If the audience hadn't responded well, we'd have gone ahead and changed the ending. Now, well, it looks like you were right. And I'm glad. After all, what we all want is a successful film. And it looks like *Lodestar* will be that."

"Zach talked you into doing this?"

Gary nodded. "Yeah. He kept on at me until I gave in. Said if I didn't at least try this, he'd take his future projects to another studio. Frankly, Leigh, he put himself on the line for you. I was pretty irritated with him at first, but now I'm glad he was so insistent. Listen, I've got to run. I have to phone in a report on how this went tonight. This is one report I'm looking forward to making. I'll call you next week. We'll have lunch."

Leigh nodded, barely taking in Gary's parting words. All she could think of was Zach...he'd put himself on the line for her...for *her*.

As she walked outside, most of the crowd had dispersed. She was extremely thoughtful as she turned to walk down to the parking lot. Suddenly she had the sensation that she wasn't alone. Looking up, she saw Zach standing a few feet away, watching her quietly.

It didn't matter that she hadn't seen him for more than a week, or that they had argued bitterly the last time they'd been together. All that mattered was that he was here.

She threw herself into his arms and gave herself up to his deep kiss, oblivious to the fact that he'd been holding a long box and had dropped it as he embraced her.

When she finally pulled away, she looked up at him and whispered, "Thank you."

"You don't have anything to thank me for."

"I do. Gary told me what you did for me."

"In a way it was as much for myself as for you."

"I'm glad the preview went well. But, oh, Zach, nothing, not even *Lodestar*, really matters without you. I've had several long lonely nights to think it over. I've learned something about priorities. And my first priority is *you*."

"My love."

"I would have come to you if you hadn't come to me tonight. I was determined that somehow we would work things out. I know I have to learn to compromise. I can't have everything my own way."

"Ah, so from now on you're going to be the soul of congeniality?" he teased, brushing the tip of her nose with his lips.

"Well..." she hedged mischievously.

They both laughed and Zack bent down to retrieve the box. "For you," he said, handing the long florist's box to her.

Untying the ribbon, Leigh lifted off the lid and folded back the green tissue paper. Inside lay a dozen long-stemmed white roses. Looking up at Zach with tears swimming in her eyes, she gave a crooked little smile and quipped, "Another truce?"

"Nope," he said, blinking away a bit of moisture from his own eyes. "Surrender."

"Well, it isn't high noon, but I did promise to kiss you in front of Mann's Chinese Theater." And holding her box of roses in the crook of her arm, she reached up with her other hand and drew Zach's face down to meet hers in a sweet and bonding kiss.

As they walked to the parking lot, Zack said soberly, "We'll always have differences of opinion."

"Yes. Personally I find those differences stimulating."

Running a finger lightly down her spine, Zach agreed, "Yes, very stimulating."

She looked up at him, with a twinkle in her gray eyes. "What happens now?"

"Now—we get married and figure out how to raise kids and make movies at the same time."

"Are you sure?"

"Yes."

She grinned in delight. "What a night! Now I have everything I ever wanted," she murmured.

"Do you know what happens when you get everything you ever wanted?"

She shook her head.

He whispered huskily, "You live happily ever after."

"Just like in the movies," Leigh responded, before he pulled her into another kiss.

Discover the new and unique

Harlequin Gothic and Regency Romance Specials!

Gothic Romance	Regency Romance
DOUBLE MASQUERADE Dulcie Hollyock	TO CATCH AN EARL Rosina Pyatt
LEGACY OF RAVEN'S RISE Helen B. Hicks	TRAITOR'S HEIR Jasmine Cresswell
THE FOURTH LETTER Alison Quinn	MAN ABOUT TOWN Toni Marsh Bruyere

A new and exciting world of romance reading

Harlequin Gothic and Regency Romance Specials!

Available in September wherever paperback books are sold, or through Harlequin Reader Service:

Harlequin Reader Service
In the U.S.
P.O. Box 52040
Phoenix, AZ 85072-9988

In Canada
P.O. Box 2800, Postal Station A
5170 Yonge Street
Willowdale, Ontario M2N 6J3

CR-C-1

*You're invited to accept
4 books and a
surprise gift Free!*

Acceptance Card

Mail to: **Harlequin Reader Service®**

In the U.S.
2504 West Southern Ave.
Tempe, AZ 85282

In Canada
P.O. Box 2800, Postal Station A
5170 Yonge Street
Willowdale, Ontario M2N 6J3

YES! Please send me 4 free Harlequin Superromance® novels and my free surprise gift. Then send me 4 brand new novels every month as they come off the presses. Bill me at the low price of $2.50 each—a 10% saving off the retail price. There are no shipping, handling or other hidden costs. There is no minimum number of books I must purchase. I can always return a shipment and cancel at any time. Even if I never buy another book from Harlequin, the 4 free novels and the surprise gift are mine to keep forever.

134 BPS-BPGE

Name _____ (PLEASE PRINT)

Address _____ Apt. No. _____

City _____ State/Prov. _____ Zip/Postal Code _____

This offer is limited to one order per household and not valid to present subscribers. Price is subject to change.   ACSR-SUB-1

What readers say about
HARLEQUIN SUPERROMANCE™

"Bravo! Your SUPERROMANCE [is]...super!"
R.V.,* Montgomery, Illinois

"I am impatiently awaiting
the next SUPERROMANCE."
J.D., Sandusky, Ohio

"Delightful...great."
C.B., Fort Wayne, Indiana

"Terrific love stories. Just
keep them coming!"
M.G., Toronto, Ontario

H·A·R·L·E·Q·U·I·N
FIRST·CLASS
Sweepstakes

OFFICIAL RULES

1. NO PURCHASE NECESSARY. To enter, complete the official entry/order form. Be sure to indicate whether or not you wish to take advantage of our subscription offer.

2. Entry blanks have been preselected for the prizes offered. Your response will be checked to see if you are a winner. In the event that these preselected responses are not claimed, a random drawing will be held from all entries received to award not less than $150,000 in prizes. This is in addition to any free, surprise or mystery gifts which might be offered. Versions of this sweepstakes with different prizes will appear in Preview Service Mailings by Harlequin Books and their affiliates. Winners selected will receive the prize offered in their sweepstakes brochure.

3. This promotion is being conducted under the supervision of Marden-Kane, an independent judging organization. By entering the sweepstakes, each entrant accepts and agrees to be bound by these rules and the decisions of the judges, which shall be final and binding. Odds of winning in the random drawing are dependent upon the total number of entries received. Taxes, if any, are the sole responsibility of the prize winners. Prizes are nontransferable. All entries must be received by August 31, 1986.

4. The following prizes will be awarded:

   (1) Grand Prize: Rolls-Royce™ or $100,000 Cash!
   (Rolls-Royce being offered by permission of Rolls-Royce Motors Inc.)

   (1) Second Prize: A trip for two to Paris for 7 days/6 nights. Trip includes air transportation on the Concorde, hotel accommodations...PLUS...$5,000 spending money!

   (1) Third Prize: A luxurious Mink Coat!

5. This offer is open to residents of the U.S. and Canada, 18 years or older, except employees of Harlequin Books, its affiliates, subsidiaries, Marden-Kane and all other agencies and persons connected with conducting this sweepstakes. All Federal, State and local laws apply. Void in the province of Quebec and wherever prohibited or restricted by law. Winners will be notified by mail and may be required to execute an affidavit of eligibility and release, which must be returned within 14 days after notification. Canadian winners will be required to answer a skill-testing question. Winners consent to the use of their name, photograph and/or likeness for advertising and publicity purposes in conjunction with this and similar promotions without additional compensation. One prize per family or household.

6. For a list of our most current prize winners, send a stamped, self-addressed envelope to: WINNERS LIST, c/o Marden-Kane, P.O. Box 10404, Long Island City, New York 11101